WAIT SOFTLY BROTHER

Also by Kathryn Kuitenbrouwer

All the Broken Things
The Nettle Spinner
Perfecting
Way Up

WAIT SOFTLY BROTHER

A NOVEL

KATHRYN KUITENBROUWER

A Buckrider Book

Al Purdy, "The Dead Poet," *Beyond Remembering: The Collected Poems of Al Purdy*, ed. Sam Solecki (Harbour Publishing, 2000). Reprinted with permission of the publisher.

Published by Buckrider Books
an imprint of Wolsak and Wynn Publishers
280 James Street North
Hamilton, ON L8R2L3
www.wolsakandwynn.ca

Editor for Buckrider Books: Paul Vermeersch | Editor: Aeman Ansari
Copy editor: Andrew Wilmot
Cover design: David Drummond
Cover image: Jonathan Smith / Shutterstock
Interior design: Jennifer Rawlinson
Author photograph: Tracey A Clarke
Typeset in Minion and Autoradiographic
Printed by Brant Service Press Ltd., Brantford, Canada

Printed on certified 100% post-consumer Rolland Enviro Paper.

10 9 8 7 6 5 4 3 2 1

The publisher gratefully acknowledges the support of the Ontario Arts Council, the Canada Council for the Arts and the Government of Canada.

Library and Archives Canada Cataloguing in Publication

Title: Wait softly brother : a novel / Kathryn Kuitenbrouwer.
Names: Kuitenbrouwer, Kathryn, 1965- author.
Identifiers: Canadiana 20230226469 | ISBN 9781989496664 (softcover)
Classification: LCC PS8571.U4 W34 2023 | DDC C813/.6—dc23

For my brother

THE DEAD POET

by Al Purdy

I was altered in the placenta
by the dead brother before me
who built a place in the womb
knowing I was coming:
he wrote words on the walls of flesh
painting a woman inside a woman
whispering a faint lullaby
that sings in my blind heart still

The others were lumberjacks
backwoods wrestlers and farmers
their women were meek and mild
nothing of them survives
but an image inside an image
of a cookstove and the kettle boiling
– how else explain myself to myself
where does the song come from?

Now on my wanderings:
at the Alhambra's lyric dazzle
where the Moors built stone poems
a wan white face peering out
– and the shadow in Plato's cave
remembers the small dead one
– at Samarkand in pale blue light
the words came slowly from him
– I recall the music of blood
on the Street of the Silversmiths

Sleep softly spirit of earth
as the days and nights join hands
when everything becomes one thing
wait softly brother
but do not expect it to happen
that great whoop announcing resurrection
expect only a small whisper
of birds nesting and green things growing
and a brief saying of them
and know where the words came from

Perhaps if I make myself write I shall find out what is wrong with me.

— Dodie Smith, *I Capture the Castle*

DAY ONE

I PULL OFF IN TRENTON and text my therapist because I am sad and I need to hear her voice. Mandy is actually my best friend, but, you know, same difference. There are two Harrier jump jets hovering overhead. The military base is close by and I could have gone straight to Mum and Dad's, so why do I stop here? The jets are quiet, stealthy, but I can feel anxiety rising, like I'm being watched. I send Mandy that emoji with the skull and crossbones and then the broken heart one. It's pathetic. I'm pathetic. And when she calls, I answer with the Bluetooth and tell her there's been a death in the family and I'm heading to my parents for a while.

"Who died?"

"Me," I say. "I died."

She laughs nervously. Then goes quiet. Then asks, "Are you okay?"

I say, "You think about leaving your marriage, you fantasize about it, try it on in your mind, but when you actually go ahead and do it, it's not at all like you thought. You couldn't really fathom the injury it causes to yourself and then you think maybe no pain, no gain. Then it turns out that it hurts other people, too, and the narcissism that led to you leaving, that self-protective ego thing – or so you told yourself when you did it – is actually serving no one. Or maybe it is serving some unconscious need."

She really is an analyst. So I know to add that last.

And she bites the bait. "So, you're on a healing journey."

Of course, I hate that kind of sentimentality. I picture the font it comes in and it nauseates me. I take a long, slow breath. I stare at the road, at the rain as it starts up again, listening to her voice soften. "Kathryn?" she says. "Are you there?"

"Yes," I whisper. I'm wondering if it is bad form to yell at her. I don't because, even though I need to yell, she doesn't deserve it. It's me I need to yell at. So I say that "it feels like more of a terrible wound. I keep thinking about the mystic Margery Kempe and all of her weeping and wailing."

"Tell me what happened. Go slow." She's such a good person. I'm so lucky.

I say, "It started yesterday. I went out to the back patio to drink my tea. The first day warm enough to do so this spring. And, Mandy, there was a dead cardinal out there. The wind picked up its feathers and ruffled them prettily." And I'm sobbing.

"Poor thing," she says, about the bird or about me I am not sure.

"Such a sorry sight to see it robbed of flight. I suppose it hit a window." Our house is replete with windows, looks out over the lake. It's worth millions. Enough for all manner of freedoms, you'd think. "I put it in a shoebox and tossed it in the garbage can."

"And that did it."

"Yeah, it was the start of a very ugly argument. One of those arguments that dredges up the shit of generations. One there's no coming back from. It started with me saying I was struggling with my manuscript. That I needed to know more about Wulf, and he said, 'Your brother is never coming back no matter how much ink you spill,' and I blew a fucking gasket."

This morning in the doorway, it's me and Matthew and the boys – Magnus, Ross and Harry. They are just old enough, teenagers all three of them, to repress why I might be leaving and so abruptly. It's not them, I tell them. Which only leaves one person to blame. They turn and stare at their father, who shows us his palms as if their bloodlessness is evidence of innocence. He says, "What? I didn't do anything." At which I scoff because this is precisely the problem. These arguments go round and round. Twenty years of frustration, fights that give in to incremental change, that end in lackadaisical, predictable backsliding. Fights that result in him continuing to do nothing, to not be there, to annex himself from us under the guise of work.

"I hope you'll be happy now," he says to me the night before I leave.

"It's not happiness I'm after," I say.

He says he thought we would be one of those marriages that survived because we lead such separate lives.

It's like I'm a wayward character in a story I suddenly refuse. For the first two acts, I liked the drama, the rising action, while also waiting for the main players to lock into their respective arcs, to dare to engage, to risk change. But somewhere along the plot it's clear that it's me who is changing, me who has outgrown this story, me who finally walks.

"You've changed." His tone is accusatory.

"Yes! Yes, I have." For that is what I thought characters were supposed to do. That is how narrative works and how could I not? How could I refuse the call to change?

I say, "It's never been happiness I wanted. Not really. I wanted a marriage." I wanted the fairy tale is what I mean.

Be careful what you want.

"Are you sure?" he says. By which he means there will be no going back. By which he means I can't turn the clocks back on this decision once I make it. Because, whatever happiness or unhappiness might mean to him, he will never reflect, never puzzle, never confront the piece of this story that belongs to him. He's churlish standing in the doorway to the house like there's something there he won't ever let me have back. But the thing I wanted, that's been a husk for years. He's a minor character in this. The sort that doesn't change at all. And the character he won't change from is one I can no longer abide. You know the part of the Hollywood blockbuster where the hero blasts through fire and escapes? That's me. Only the fire is a suburban home with a lonely housewife.

O, simpering cliché!

And when I am done telling Mandy all this, and apologizing for trotting out the same old, same old, she says, "I support you." And for this I am grateful. I watch the aircraft accelerate and disappear. And then she says, "A novel about Wulf?"

"Well, autofiction."

"What's that? Like memoir but not true? Kathryn, Wulf never lived."

"I know. I know." That in itself feels sad enough to occupy a story.

I get off the phone and drive on, up the 401, buzzing to the Batawa exit, an entire town built around a shoe factory. Then I head north, up through Frankford, across the Trent-Severn Waterway, and farther north, snaking through Stirling to that godforsaken plot. It's still raining. The culvert under the laneway is conducting a tumult of water and there are pools and vernal ponds dotting the front field. The old cattle pond has burst at its seams. A couple of ducks airlift as I pull up. I'm driving backwards in time, back to the home where I grew up, where Mum and Dad still live, in a land so rocky even sheep can barely be sustained – a place where the oceans receded after the last ice age, leaving a landscape prone to bog and cedar copse, sweet air, mosquitoes and a history of depression. The land the Scots claimed because it reminded them of the home they'd left, not stopping to consider how their expansion might affect those currently occupying it. The stone croft house where I was raised was built five generations ago. A solid edifice to misery and my family's devotion to it.

The front door swells shut in the spring and no one ever uses it anyway – too fancy for the likes of us. So, I'm at the old side door, the one through the kitchen. I should have called first.

"What's going on?" Mum says. Dad's head pokes out behind her.

"Invite her in, at least," he says.

"Of course." Mum shifts aside.

It's all I can do to sputter out that we've argued again, Matthew and I, with the boys all throwing in their two cents, making it worse.

"I couldn't stand it anymore," I say.

Her eyes are bright with this information, as if leaving is a possibility she has never considered, as if I have opened up a portal into some grand venture. Then the brightness collapses into an accusatory twinge, her cheeks alive with fear. "So, you just left?" Mum says. A whole lifetime unfolds in an eyeblink. "It can't be all that bad."

"Mum," I say, "it's been years of not-all-that-bad."

"And let me guess, you want to stay here."

I nod, chastened, barely in the door, water now heaving out of the sky and glacier-cold tears, plenty of them, runnelling down my face. I'm calving some horrendous disaster. I can't decide whether my anguish is about the story I can't manufacture about Wulf or the one I can't contain about my marriage. I keep thinking maybe I have picked my marriage apart in pursuing Wulf. It is true that if you start to scratch at the threads of any narrative, you discover it is just another enchantment. You discover there is no such thing as realism. All of it just made up. All of life, all of everything.

I'm sobbing by now, bent over on the couch. No one ever talks about how hard it is to start a story over again.

"Oh, honey," says Mum, and Dad goes to put the kettle on since words fail him in the primordial way they seem to fail all men.

Mum tucks the Woolrich blanket around me, and Dad hands me a proper cup of tea. They stand there in a kind of tableau, assessing me, waiting for whatever comes next. Dad eventually says, "You poor bairn," and Mum snickers. The Gaelic always sets her off, since it is not him but rather his own father speaking through him. He cocks his eyebrow at me with some expectation that I will give them reasons, calm their anxiety.

"I don't really want to talk about it," I say. And then I dare to say the thing I have been thinking about. I'm trying to make the big deal it is seem like no big deal, to minimize my desire. "I'm writing about Wulf."

They fold their arms across their chests and nod, mouths arcing to the devil or hell, I do not know which. "There's nothing to say," Mum says. Dad just looks stern because, of course, she is right. "Maybe you should call Matthew and apologize. Twenty-five years is a long history to leave."

"He took a mistress," I say. Which is strictly speaking true, but it was some years ago and is only a loose thread in the larger yarn. Something I am not above using, though, since it is shorthand for "not my fault, really." They soften a little but not enough to get me all that far.

"Poor bairn," says Mum. She is sarcastic of course. There is nothing she has not already seen in her long life. She's thinking, 'What's a mistress, in the long view?' Mum's eyes flit to Dad with the scrutiny of one who has stayed and conquered, and something, some energy of that or some secret past, concusses the room.

"You made a promise to Matthew," says Dad.

Mum nods.

The edifice of marriage – those who've committed to it, who protect it to death do they part. To be buried side by side, I think, as the ultimate goal of life, the measure of a successful union. Dad clears his throat and says, "I'd like to call Matthew; I feel sorry for him." He starts to shuffle toward the stairs, to make a private call.

"Sorry for *him*?"

He stops and stares me down. "Yes, sorry for him. Who will cook for those boys?"

"So, I'm a charwoman, then?"

"Don't be stupid." He ambles down the hallway to the kitchen, where the old landline resides. They keep it for when storms take out cell service, which is more and more often these days.

"I wish you'd sit down," I call after him. He turns and looks at me while I plead: "Tell me the story of Wulf." I know it hundreds of times over, long inscribed as it is. It's old family lore, but we like a silly old tale to keep us tethered to one another. I give him the puppy eyes, make myself irresistible. "Please," I say. "Tell it to me again."

And he returns and lowers himself into the La-Z-Boy, switches the heating pad on and settles in. He has not taken his eyes off me the whole time, like prey gauging a cat's pounce.

"It was a time of great sorrow in the family. We were just the two of us, before you and your sisters came. And your grandmother so aloof. The McIvers do not really do any sort of emotion."

"Except me."

"Yes, you are exceptional in that regard."

"What did he look like?"

"Ugly. Like every baby. A wet little nothing."

"He came and he went, I always said," adds Mum. She is rocking a little. "I do wish you wouldn't dwell so."

"Mum went into shock. Her organs were failing and the doctor, and this was unusual at the time, called me into the delivery room."

"I was dying." Mum says it like an accusation, as if I might have been the culprit in her demise.

"Let Dad tell it."

"The doctors said that one or the other could be saved but not both. Of course, I chose your mother."

"Do you ever regret it?"

They laugh.

"Well, you'd not be here," Dad says. He clears his throat. "The priest came and did his priestly thing. I named him Wulf as your mother and I had previously discussed, after the poem. He was buried before your mother had recuperated enough to know he was gone." Mum looks at Dad, mutters something about the old story being just that, a story. I say I know that but just the same. It's lore and that is its own sort of home, is it not? She tilts her head in reluctant agreement, the clenching along her jaw a path so well-trod, she's got grooves there.

I think of the time before houses and people. I think of the ancient ocean spread out over the land. I think of all manner of sea beasts that cavorted here, right beneath where I now sit. Whales – narwhal, beluga – and other sea creatures. Shark. Walrus even, some say. Seal. And then, though I know it is whimsical, I think of the basement filled to the brim with salt water, the lap of tide, a concrete lung filling and emptying. This is nonsense, of course. The sea was long gone before the stones were piled to make this farmhouse. Before it was built into a knoll facing south to veil against the weather, my great-grandfather chiselling and setting the lime mortar between these stalwart boulders.

"Where do you think the dead go when they go?" I say now. I think I might be bringing Mum to the edge of tears, for she knows I am thinking of wee Wulf. And I am not ashamed to say that I do not care. I would be happy to see some feeling. But no.

"They haunt us," she says. And to keep it together, she sniffs and says that if I want to stay, I will be put to work. "Speaking of ghosts, we are clearing out the pig shed."

They've been hoarding for years, accreting to the hoard that five past generations of McIvers have stacked in this space. The sediment of not-letting-go, mould and mouse excreta.

"That sounds fair," I say.

"You'll find all sorts of stories in there, that's for sure."

"I only really want one," I say, a retort they ignore.

They say, "Well," and glance to one another, then rise in unison. They are creatures of habit and it is time for their afternoon constitutional. I watch them through a north-facing window as they meander in their wellingtons. I love them, I think, their old bodies moving in sync. It would have been nice to stay married for all time like them. I wanted that. I stand there overlong, recalling the supple skin along Matthew's clavicle, how I used to snuffle and bite him there. What is the difference between a ghost and a memory, I wonder, and where does adoration go when it goes? I think it stays to haunt us, too.

My parents are long on their walk. I give up waiting for them. The tea in my mug is cold, the milk puckered on its surface, so I settle on the couch for a nap. I shudder away thoughts of Matthew and the boys, the flutter of my jacket as I threw it in the car, the way the suitcase I hastily packed clipped my leg to bleeding as I heaved it into the trunk. They're like photographs seen from the distance of ages. I can't take any of it in. I hear my phone ringing and make myself impervious to its jangle. It stops and begins and stops and begins again, as I drift in and out of sleep. Its persistence foretells. I reach for it eventually and swipe it open.

"Hi," Matthew says. "How are you?"

"Tired," I say. "Really fucking tired." I say goodbye before he gets anything more out. He calls back and I put the device on silent, mutter at my phone to shut the fuck up, and then there is, for some long minutes, quiet.

I wake up with Mum and Dad peering at me. Dad is waving a soup ladle.

"Is she awake?" says Mum.

"Dead to the world."

I try to keep my eyes from fluttering. "Awake," says Mum. "You can't fool the fool."

I shake my head, mutter, "Not awake. Dreaming."

"The soup will grow cold," says Dad.

I heave myself up from the couch, grab a Kleenex and empty my nose. The dinner table itself is something from Denmark circa 1970. The chairs match, upholstered in black Naugahyde. There is fresh-baked bread, sliced and warm, and an immaculate pat of salted butter on the table. Each plate is willow patterned and flanked by the requisite silver, heavy and ancient, hauled over the ocean with a class expectation that never materialized. Great-grandmum's dowry. The napkins are folded into little snails and nestled up to the wineglasses. There are salad bowls and a mended tureen at the centre of all this. My father serves, and then they wait for my hands to clench in prayer.

"May we thank God for this bounty, and thank Him for the safekeeping of family," says Dad, raising an eyebrow in my direction.

"For richer, for poorer," I mutter. "Until death do us part."

"Now, Kathryn," says Mum. And once I've eaten, she leans in and gives me that look, one that would chill even the devil to the bone. "You'll want to go to your room, now. It'll be an early day of sorting tomorrow."

DAY TWO

THE PIG SHED BOXES CONTAIN multitudes. A photograph of Mum, twenty years younger than I am right now, newly married and just before she became pregnant with Wulf. I hold it up and she grabs it from my hands. "In the Poconos," she says, "they had these honeymoon packages. Heart-shaped beds, everyone there newly married. It was a place of blissful beginnings."

"We have the same body," I say. "Those are just my legs."

"Well, I certainly do not have that body anymore."

"No," I say. "Nor do I, I suppose. But what a babe you were."

"I was a catch," she says, squinting at it.

"And so happy." I peer into the frame, willing it to give me more, to offer up its story. I have never seen my mother smile so openly as in this picture. "Maybe we can put the best pictures aside and make an album, and get rid of the rest."

But no, she will not get rid of photographs. There is something particular about them, some magic to them that makes them impossible to burn or bury. "We will archive them," she says. By midmorning we have worked our way through one and a half small shoeboxes. The material in the pig shed seems suddenly insurmountable. We will never succeed in cleaning it up. "Wasn't it one of Hercules's labours to divert a river to clean out a barn?"

"Tantalus."

"No, Mum, he was the guy with the rock."

"That was Sisyphus, I think."

"At any rate, maybe the question to ask is 'Will you miss it?' Or maybe, 'Will someone else enjoy it more than you?'"

"How can you know what you will miss before you miss it? Just when it's too late?"

And I can feel the dig, so I stop and glare at her for a bit. She's impervious to my moods, though. She has been barricading herself from them for as long as I can recall. I am her creation, so whenever I misbehave, she just carries on until I adjust to whatever she expects. That way, I get to maintain my role as transgressor instead of occupying the one I would much prefer – that of being myself.

"What exactly are you working on these days?" she finally asks, by way of oiling the crank in our conversation.

"Autofiction," I say.

Mum's eyebrows flare. "Whatever that is."

"It's a sort of memoir."

"And how do you expect to write a memoir? Given your memory, I mean."

Mum and Dad used to say that if my head weren't screwed on to my body, I'd forget where I left it. "There will likely be lacunae," I say. "That is kind of the point."

She nods.

"Since it's about Wulf," I say, and I can see her freeze again.

"We keep telling you. There's no story there." She huffs a bit and then shrieks a quiet "That's my story," which is factual. Wulf is her stillbirth, her old wound, her story. "I do wish you'd stop all this nonsense."

"The nonsense of the writing or the nonsense of leaving Matthew?"

"It's all the same, isn't it?"

This is a curve I hadn't expected. The thought that she sees clearly how one thing unleashes the next. How thoughts cascade into actions. How vulnerable we are to our traumas, as we write. One is the other; it's all tangled together.

"You won't solve yourself by picking at this," she says.

I dare, then. "It's just this, Mum. I was telling this friend of mine, she's a sort of therapist, about Wulf, about your stillbirth, and she said it's common for mothers to be depressed afterwards, especially when they don't have support."

"I never had time to be depressed. You came right afterwards."

"That is my point. It occurs to me that you might have had a lot of un-worked-through grief and, who knows, self-blame." I don't mention that some of this unworked-through grief has become her legacy to me. Instead, I pull out another box, crack the tape with my Opinel knife. It's a box of porcelain women experiencing pastel motherhood, drinking tea and wearing long swirling gowns in meadows. It's a box of idealism that the Royal Doulton brand invented to keep women nostalgic and thoughtless. "Charity pile, right?" I say.

"These are going in my bedroom," she says. "Why do you hate women so?"

What I hear is: Why do you hate *me* so?

"I love you, Mum. I love women, too," I say. "I just wish they wouldn't buy into this."

"Buy into having pretty things?"

"Yes. No. That's not it."

"What is it, then?"

"Mum, what if all women did what I'm doing?"

"Left their families?"

"Left mediocrity, left unhappy situations, sought joy."

"I'm not unhappy. Why do you get to proclaim that we're all unhappy? May-be there are a lot of happy women in happy situations. Besides, what would the men do?"

I laugh of course. Because: What *would* the men do? And as I laugh, my eyes catch hold again of the photograph of my mum at twenty-one, her smile opening up the universe. I pick it up and smile back at her. "Do you remember who you were?" I say.

"It's a long time ago," she says. It's true. She's an old lady now, thick with age but still attractive.

"I wonder if these happy memories sustain us in unhealthy ways."

"There you go again. It's not because you're unhappy that the rest of us have to be, too."

"I'm not even sure I care about happiness," I say.

And then I hear Dad pushing a wheelbarrow into the pig shed.

"I care about freedom," I say. "I care about my body rediscovering joy."

And Dad, because he would do almost anything to avoid conflict, says, "Load her up!" And because we would do anything to avoid dragging him into this, we comply.

For days, I haul bags of photographs and document boxes from the pig shed, and we pore through them deciding what to file, what to throw away, what to keep. Everything I think I might be able to use, I set aside to digitize, promising Mum that I won't damage anything, and that once I am done, I will archive everything in plastic bins, safe from mould and from the rains, which have, incidentally, not abated.

Toward the end of the week, at breakfast, Mum ceremoniously hands me a manila envelope.

"It's for your memoir," she says. "Some correspondence mailed to your great-grandfather. You might as well have it. It's about his father, Russell Boyt, who would have been your great-great-grandfather. Though there was little great about him by all accounts. I was thinking this will help you with the Civil War bits of your book. He fought, you know. They say he was cuckoo – even before the war."

"First of all, Mum, we don't say 'cuckoo' anymore, and second of all, you're kidding, right?"

"Nothing is *really* known about him," she says, like she hasn't heard me. "Well, a little is known."

"I'm not writing a family history. I'm writing an extended fictional essay about my dead brother."

She purses her lips in that dangerous way she has. I have crossed a line. She says, "You never know. You might need it," and starts to walk away.

I look down at the envelope in my hands. I pull the letter out. It's on blue airmail paper. There's another envelope inside the first. The gist of the note on the blue paper is that the enclosed much older envelope was found in an archive of dead letters at a post office being dismantled in Richmond, Virginia, in 1969. The archivist is certain we are the proper recipients of this letter. "Wait," I say. "Was I there the day this came in the mail?"

"Oh, no, you'd have been at school."

Private Russell Boyt is the name on the front of the envelope, and he is, in fact, my great-great-grandfather.

"He was more or less disowned by the family," Mum says. "Insane. He was institutionalized after the war."

I gently pull the older letter from its envelope. It's foxed and yellowed, brittle, a scrawl of dainty grey quill-pen cursive:

> Dear Pvte Boyt. I do not know why you did what you did and I suppose you must have reasons of your own. For my part I wish I never was tangled in your business and you never got tangled in mine. And yet if you send me back my rightful property I think I can carry on some. Otherwise wee Charles requires new breeches and a decent flaxen shirt. Please do send money and news when you can.
> Sincerely, Cristiana Muldon.

"My God," I say. "Have you read this? Who was she?"

"I think she was a mistress."

I hand the letter to Mum. "I'm really not planning to write anything particularly historical," I say. I do not want this. This is the last thing I want.

She pushes my arm away. "Throw it out if you don't want it."

Bait.

I am stupid. I bring the letter up to my room. Sit on the bed and read it over. It smells of some kind of perfume – rose, maybe, and dust and a hint of barnyard, which might be its years of sitting in the pig shed. I know Mum gave me the letter to distract me from my fixation on Wulf. But I won't be waylaid.

I tell myself this, but who am I kidding? The thing has its hooks in me already. They say that everything you write, just like everything you dream, is a replica of you, or your unconscious self. They say you can't write a character who is not, in some true way, an aspect of yourself. If this is true, then all fiction is autobiography. All writing is self. Maybe I can find my way to Wulf this way. Maybe it's the only way to him. I set the letter on my dresser and sit down to write. I try to become Russell Boyt, my mentally ill ancestor.

1864

VIRGINIA. HOW STUPID OF ME to come here. A city boy. I was recruited to this war in Toronto, at the university. A war with such atrocities piling up – we saw the images in the newspapers – that most thinking men refused to go. And so the US government created a tantalizing loophole. If you were a man of means, you could simply hire a substitute. They even called it substitution. And so we came – from all over the world – to fight for the cause of the freedom of all men in the stead of rich men who would rather get richer than die ignobly in a filthy farmer's field. I know better now.

But in 1864, I was naïve enough to think that the war might be my ticket out of the middling hell my father was concocting for me: a white picket fence, a suitable wife, a life of desperation – or so, at the time, I imagined it. It seemed like a horrible prospect until I threw it away. Then, on the train to my new life, regrets came quickly. Money was one issue. Pay was inconsistently meted out and the initial three hundred dollars was spent a thousand times in my mind before it was even to hand. An adventure, I'd thought. Mother had used the term fool, and Father would not even look at me by the end. He did not believe in the equality of all men. He had stocks in cotton.

The industrialist who hired me to fight in his place was named Ebenezer Wilkes. He came to Toronto to fetch me. It was a twenty-hour journey by trains to Washington, and we made it together. During that time, Eb outlined precisely how he anticipated I would deploy certain military skills he himself did not have (nor did I, but he did not know this). He had lofty ideas of our identities merging, something I resisted not least because I doubted the existence of any pre-existing identity in me. Father believed me to be a milquetoast.

Eb and I disembarked in Washington. Eb wanted to show me the industry his father founded. His father (God rest his soul), as a young man, had lost his left leg below the knee to a thresher and by necessity and discomfort had become a limb-maker – an innovator of body parts first for himself and then for other broken men. His father contested the position of first American limb-maker against a Mister Palmer but had been quiet about it. He was a man who hardly talked if he could avoid it, sending instructions to the factory floor on little scraps of paper. Achingly shy, he had been known to duck under the office door window if he saw someone coming.

I thought how Eb must be the very opposite of his shy father in temperament. Then he said, "I know what you're thinking. My mother – and rest her soul, too – used to say I came out babbling. And that I never did or never will stop." I relaxed then, wondering how on earth such meekness and joviality could co-exist. My own father shrank into a nasty wee raging homunculus and nestled in my chest cavity.

In the factory, Eb grabbed me by the shoulder, gestured to the eaves from which hung countless articulated legs and some mechanical arms and hands. There was a prototype hand stuck to a piece of elm on a workbench. Eb made me try the lever that got the opposable thumb working – the entire hand was a tight coiled spring.

"Imagine you had an operating hand like that," said Eb. I shuddered. I had a vivid imagination and did not want to exercise it on this. I was far too sensitive to fight in a war. My father referred to my personality as unstable. Some of the other limbs had gears and were a marvel to see if I didn't think too long and hard on why a person might want one.

Eb said, "The technology is astonishing."

I wonder now if it was then that my body took on the ways of prosthesis, that I shifted from the fleshly anatomy of a human subject to something mechanical, a kind of machine-fellow. The legs hung like sides of curing lamb. Eb reached up to caress one. "When the war is won, you'll come and work for us," I recall him saying.

The pong of joint grease and metal fighting corrosion, resin and maple wood shaving wafted through me.

"There is always a mutilation to resection, and our work is never done. Even a half-trained anatomist would be useful to us." He called me his twin soldier then.

I smiled and thanked him. I thought how I would rather finish my medical training and salve minor wounds and marry back in Toronto, but it was too late for such thinking. On the train, I mentally tallied that I would need exactly seven hundred Canadian dollars for the final duration of my schooling, and I would rather kill myself than borrow money from Father.

It's true that I had the steadiest hand of any of the interns in my year, but that didn't amount to much as I also had the flutteriest head. The sight of blood and the flurry of any sort of emotion worried me. *Lumbricals. Hypothenar.* Did the roots of trees worry their trunks so?

"It's a good set-up," I said to Eb by way of stopping the recursive thoughts.

Eb smiled. His gums shone pink and edged each pearly tooth like bunting. His face lit up at the smallest provocation. "Fight like a tiger in my place, will you?"

I smiled back at Eb's teeth. "Sure, I will."

And now, months into this substitution, I was in the thick of a very bad story. My comrades and I had taken to riffling through the uniforms of the dead. I first read Henry Muldon's letter after peeling it out of his pocket. A private named Bellair goaded me to do it. I began to make up the man's story right away. In my imagination, I pictured him tugging at the left cuff of his uniform. It was dark out, and he was using the murky candlelight to look at himself in the window bought with the bounty he'd received.

Now he was dead and rotting on a farmer's field in Virginia. A substitute soldier of a Colored Brigade. In death we are not all equal – I'm ashamed to admit that I recall thinking as such. The uniform jacket he wore was woollen, already too hot for the end of May and, to my mind, probably the finest thing he'd ever had on his body. I was ever making up lives for people I met. It was a harmless way to be in the world, or so I then thought.

With this letter, he had packed three other items into the interior pocket of his uniform jacket: (1) a 24K gold locket, engraved with flowering vines; (2) a bundle of lined paper sliced carefully from the household accounting book, one of only two books likely kept at the house; and (3) a fountain pen and pottery inkwell filled with ink and stoppered with a bit of cork. We all kept such letter kits in these times. We wanted our bodies to speak for us if they were found. Those of us who knew how to write, that is. Whether we were sentimental was debatable; we faced death and boredom, and both prospects allowed for a slippage in manliness.

I imagined Henry taking himself in at the mica windowpane, a renegade hair looping out of his eyebrow. He was already mentally composing his first letter home: *Dearest Cristiana, the men here are made of courage. I do my best to mimic them in the hope I attain something like what they seem naturally to have. The war is nearly won, and many lie dead. I thank God* – and here he faltered a little, having brought himself near to crying. What was he doing? He slammed his fist into his pocket and felt the first tearing of the fabric's seams (like mine, it was a cheap replica of a standard military-issue uniform, we substitute soldiers not deemed worthy of the real thing) and also a wad of single-dollar bills I forgot to mention, seven of them, the first monthly payout he had received as compensation for this substitution upon which he was embarking.

All of this I stole from his bloodied corpse.

My parents thought me mad. And if I was not then mad, I would soon become so. This war was one to which I was ill-suited. I was at odds with the rules set out in it.

When Henry actually got a chance to write a first note, it was the morning after his first "battle" – more a skirmish in fact, but it was enough to make things real. I imagine he took out his writing kit, propped himself up – his uniform already smeared and frayed with experience – on the most symbolic tree he could find, a spindly burr oak that knobbed acutely into his trapezius, and wrote: *Dear Soldier, if you should find me dead, please carry this letter to Cristiana Muldon, my beloved. Dear Cristiana, you are strong and now you must be stronger still. Know I fought with you in my heart, and with our child in my every waking thought. Let it not trouble you that I shall not wake again. The cause is a just one and for our future, too.* It went on like this for some time, Henry imagining a future that did not hold him, luxuriating in the ache that travelled down his shoulder.

It was this very epistle that I brought to the Muldon cabin.

What Christiana Muldon must have thought of me – a young, pasty-white substitute soldier from Upper Canada – is unclear. She might very well have hated me. I would not blame her. It was shortly after the First Battle of Petersburg, June 9, 1864. I had taken French leave out of guilt, exacerbated by Bellair, who had scavenged Henry Muldon's body with me, but had had a change of heart when he realized how close Muldon's widow resided. We drew straws as to who would take the risk to go. Unsurprisingly, I lost.

She was a scowling beauty at the door to their cabin.

"It was strange to see a whole troop of coloured men in uniform raging forward," I admitted to Cristiana. "I had never before touched a coloured person." I recall I was worried she might ask for what few items I had taken, and I did not fancy giving them up. I could not have said why.

When the widow invited me in, I could see she was scared. Her fright triggered bad feelings all throughout me. I was ill-suited to my own body. I admit that I liked her right away, the bold way she had, and I knew my attraction was not a good thing. I knew this would lead down the wrong path. I was a stupid boy then, and I am a stupid man now. Nothing much has changed.

I skirted a wooden crate full of cur puppies to get inside – what looked like bulldog and beagle and bloodhound intermingled. They mewled up at me. I could feel the eyes of any number of neighbour folk peeping from nearby porches and windows. It made me antsy to be scrutinized, but then everything made me feel like that in those days.

"Don't mind the mess," she said, though the cabin was beyond reproach. Her

little baby, Charles, slept like a perfect saint. He was tucked in a blanket, and I could not see him.

I was then twenty-two years old, soft-spoken and unshaven. I told her I was substituting for the son of a wealthy inventor who had hired me up north, sorely misjudging my fitness.

"He fell nobly," I said, because I thought that was the right way to go about breaking the news to her. Cristiana gestured for me to tell her no more.

She said that she did not have the stomach for grim detail. She did not want her husband's body-slosh and woundings in her mind.

"I have wee Charles to consider," she said.

I leant toward her and confided in low tones how I had buried him. I handed her a swatch of Henry's uniform, and I began to cry.

I unfolded the letter and pointed. The letter read: *You will know something something hid something something to never forget me.* The pertinent information was an inky berm. "My salty tears," I explained, and I looked directly into Cristiana's eyes for the first time. "I cry easily these days. I am a messy soldier in that regard." Did she note a wavering along my mouth? She must have thought me a poor act. I wondered whether she knew that I had kept Henry's gold locket and his writing kit. If she did, she must have thought me despicable.

In fact, I was desperate.

She scanned her nail along the melted sentence. "This one line. It seems it was of some import. What did it say?"

Of course I knew. It was the whereabouts of some treasure her husband had buried. But I hung my head and claimed ignorance. Now I can say with utmost assurance that some things are better left in the ground. But have I mentioned that I was young and very stupid? I thought at the time that if there was even the smallest chance that that treasure could buy my freedom, it was worth keeping the information to myself. Along my sinews when first I read it, even as the rust settled in, a plan was forming. I could rid myself of this plague y war and my dependence on my father. If only I had the means. It was like a wish being fulfilled – this dead man with his mysterious letter, his strange locket, which I had now around my neck and tucked secretly into my uniform.

And then, as if she could read my thoughts, she said, "He certainly had a locket on his person."

My brow furrowed unwittingly before I caught myself. "My unit expects me back within the day," I said.

"Oh?" she said.

I doffed my cap. "My sincerest condolences, Missus Muldon." I handed her a crumpled dollar bill. It was Muldon's meted pay, or one-tenth of it, for I had also stolen that. Which she must have known for she replied, "Well, you devil!" in such a way it surely made my eyes pop.

"I found it on his person," I muttered.

Cristiana pressed the bit of uniform to her nose. "It smells of lanolin and dirt. I cannot detect his odour."

She did not cry at that moment, though I thought she might. I got walking and only heard her shriek when I was a quarter mile away, just past the settlement outskirts. I was not heartless, I guess, for that shriek awoke in me some feelings. I turned back toward her shack, a small pulse of agony moving through me for what I had done. I had not felt quite myself for weeks and weeks.

DAY SIX

I LOVE THE MALLEABILITY OF the novel as a form. I love how it can be put into service for all manner of means, how language can be playful in this way. It's always been a thing with me, this driving toward the edge of what is believable. I have always been curious about the limits of faith. The book about Wulf is another such project. My plan is to narrate a life for him, to animate him, to create a person out of a ghost. And to be fair to my parents, I do not really understand what drives this need. But I have been doing this long enough to know that the only way to figure that out is to do it. For writing is a special kind of doing. A kind of embodied arrival.

And here I am writing Boyt's story when I really just want my brother back, even if having him back means only words on paper. Honestly, I didn't want to engage in Mum's Civil War archive. I did try to resist, but it's an earth magnet of a story. Tantalizing. Russell Boyt as a vocal experiment. The poor widow. And the rest I can just make up.

And when we make up, I suppose we get somewhere, don't we, the imagination being the playground of the unconscious. Freud got this much right. The creative act is where we find ourselves. But the trick is in the analysis. And most of us, myself included, don't really want to muck about in that. Sure, it doesn't escape me that Boyt keeps leaving just as I have done. I also can't deny that the concept of civil war is pertinent to my marriage – a terrain in dispute by its very citizens. But I would rather not dwell in the objective reality of my life. Let fiction do the work of healing. Let me play my way out of my misery. Let me write.

Mum says I wasn't there when this dead letter arrived at the croft house, but I distinctly remember Russell Boyt's letter coming in the post. I was four or so. We had only just moved back to this family homestead, and my parents had just begun reclaiming corners of it in which to fit our lives. Lives are stories or stories tucked into other stories. My parents know this. That is what families do, don't they? They set out a fiction that poses as a truth and the members of the family, they perform their roles.

And much to Mum's chagrin I have discarded mine. I am adrift from their story. Flailing about for a new one. And I am happy enough to tether myself to Boyt's. It will keep me together while the world ends, as it seems to be, the rain having pummelled us in the night. The walls of my bedroom are sodden; the wet has breached the mortar, leaving a yellow-and-brown stain there on the whitewashed parging.

That day the letter came, it was dry and sunny. Mum and I had taken lunch and napped, each activity programmed – the way she controlled things – timed, meted out against some dark energy she would or could not acknowledge. And after sleep, we took our afternoon walk. In all weather, we walked into the cedar bush in the middle of the farm. I was small, skinny at four. Fairyland, we called it, because no matter where we left the path, when we returned, it would seem to be the same place. Mum liked magic. She dwelled in some interstitial space. She never really seemed to be all the way present. Dreamy. Depressed, I think now. She must have been after what she had endured: a nine-month pregnancy, a dead baby, no time or space to mourn. But I did not know this about depression then, I only knew to tread carefully. To be quiet. To not disturb her brooding body.

We threaded off the path into the bush and everything changed. It was as if we were embarking on some risky transgression, out of time and place. Mum would say, "Shh" and "Hush," if I dared interrupt her moony quiet. And so, I left her behind and dug deeper into that place, down a short incline, the topography spongy and near barren, only the pink-black mulch of cedar foliage, and whatever moss and mushroom survived it.

It was much bleaker in here than on the path – an ancient seabed, fossils urging up here and there like strange spring blossoms. The air inside this forest bower was damp, aromatic. The trunks of the trees made nice chairs – that ruddy vertical bark, the way the cedars joined together at the base. I let her walk on and nestled into one. She never fussed about me, never worried I would be lost. She loved my independence. A mosquito probed the skin of my arm. I watched her fill up and fly off. I tracked an ant up the bark next to me. I could feel my body humming. The ant was pulling the tiniest quartz stone. I leaned back: *Where are you going with that stone?* The ant turned, flailed its antennae. It was like it was speaking to me, suggesting that I climb. So, I latched onto branches near the stem and pulled myself up higher and higher. It was easy. Even when we got older, my sisters never climbed at all. I reached the top of the tree, and the sway was lovely.

"Kathryn?" Mum called after some time had passed. I had forgotten about her down there.

"I'm here." I said this to the cloud.

"Where?"

"I can't see you, but I can hear you," I said, which was a fib because I was not even looking for her. "I'm here, up at the very top."

I heard cracking twigs, the sigh of cedar leaves underfoot. She must be pushing into fairyland.

"Say something so I can find you," she said. "It's time to get back to the house. *Coronation Street* is on."

"Something," I sang out.

"Cheeky monkey."

And then I looked down. I saw her cherry tam, her owl glasses, her soft brown hair, bangs tight to her scalp. I saw it all at once. She looked up and I could see that she'd seen me, too.

"Can you see Carlisle?" she called. We'd been reading King Arthur.

"I can see a cloud, and I can see the laneway and the gate and the mailbox. Well, not the mailbox. I can see the flag."

"Is it up?"

"Yep." As I said this, I saw something, a white blur across the road from the mailbox. Something on the move that looked like laundry snapping dry in a sharp breeze. "My brother!" I said and pointed.

And she said, "Nonsense."

I knew about my brother by then. I knew he was a ghost, and so I looked for him everywhere. I wasn't afraid of such things. They seemed, at four years of age, to be real.

"Shall we go see what the postman brought?"

It was harder getting down. Sap on my clothes and a little tear in my T-shirt. "We can dress you up, but we can't take you out." She said this to me almost every day, but right now I was not dressed up. I was wearing shorts and a T-shirt and a red fur vest trimmed with black binding, my cap pistols and my holster and my Billy boots. My socks had fallen down and were bunched at the toes of my boots. I had a hat on – a floppy, black-and-white sun hat that kept my thoughts in. Mum and I ducked under cedar boughs. We disturbed the wet stillness and came out onto the path. I looked for Wulf, but he was already gone into the ether or wherever the spirits went. We had walked far from where we started, but we had ended up in the same place.

"See?" Mum said. "Fairyland."

"Have you ever seen the fairies?"

"Haven't you?"

Fairies were tricky. "Fairies don't like to be seen is the thing," I said.

In the mail was a big letter. We brought it back to the house. Mum slid a knife under the tape that sealed it, pried open its little copper clasp and peered in.

 She frowned when she tilted the envelope. A letter on very thin paper slipped out and then a second older envelope, already ancient. The second envelope had many stamps on it. We touched each stamp and named the pictures on them. Lincoln. Washington.

She pointed out the ink stains. "This has a very old date. It's curious."

"How old? King Arthur old?"

"Maybe not as old as that." She traced her fingers over the stamps. "But this has been trying to find us for a very long time. Someone mailed it before you were born, before I was born, even before Nana was born. They used to call these stamps or cancellations 'killers.'"

The word stabbed at me. "Killers?"

"Because they 'kill' the stamp, so that people don't reuse them. Post office clerks made them by cutting patterns into bottle corks." Mum was staring out the window toward the front of the property, so I stood up and looked out at the back. There was a pony far back there that a city woman boarded, and I could see it yanking at grass. I pulled my pistols from their holsters and made soft *pow pow* noises.

"Don't point those guns at Mackie. Never point a gun at a living thing."

I aimed at a rock instead.

How did she know? Dad claimed she had eyes in the back of her head. She didn't really, I had checked. I turned then to see her reading the letter.

Dead things. Living things. Killers. The flap of cloth at the end of the lane. "Are there such things as ghosts, Mum?"

"In a manner of speaking."

"What does 'in a manner of speaking' mean?"

"It means that there are ghosts but not really."

Mothers were strange. "So there are ghosts."

"They are like dreams. Important but not real. You can't touch them."

"I saw him. I'm sure of it."

"Nonsense." She believed in fairies and ghosts but not Wulf. She did not countenance mentions of Wulf. He was dead, she said, and not ever coming back. But I had seen him.

That flare of white cloth, then nothing. I saw it and now write it into being. I sometimes wonder if she somehow wrote me into being as a writer. Made it possible to see words as real and reality as unreal. Placed me in this territory between nothing and something where I could make things out of the alphabet. Words can feel like water if they work well, plunging like wavelets over each other. This is who I am when I am at my best, a watery conduit for language.

This letter with its killer stamps, this waft of my brother. Maybe they are the same story. The thing is, I have been writing about my brother ever since I started writing. He pops up in my early work – a dead boy, a prodigal son, a baby, an abortion – and I never see it until I'm far into the process, this dead brother iterating himself through me, a crisis I didn't know I had. He seems to emerge in my real life, too, as a brother who dies and as sons, three of them, like a fairy tale.

And so I have decided to write about it, to explore the parameters of brothers, of maleness, hoping to – I don't know – purge it, come to terms, work through. It is a vague wish, treating my stillborn brother like a hunk of clay I can form into something. Enliven him – as if words can do the alchemy of bringing him back to life. Mum is sure that you can't know someone you have never met, but I wonder: Doesn't the lack form him somehow? Don't words do things? And in the dearth of actual material on Wulf, I am faced with the Civil War archive. And because I am me (obsessive), I dive in deeper, in some vain hope that by writing this, I will locate that. But life is not a fairy tale, is it?

1864

I HAD UNCLASPED THE LOCKET taken from Henry Muldon's neck. The night before I'd spent time in my tent inspecting it, then fastened the thing to a long leather string because it felt talismanic, and I needed all the help I could get. I was lying on my cot. It was very early morning and I was absent-mindedly trying to gain purchase on the locket latch with my filthy, chipped thumbnail.

The locket itself was heart shaped and of a heavy gold – not a cheap trinket – and on its front, engraved into the metal, was a scrolling pattern that mimicked vines; I did not recognize the flowers and did not feel inclined to waste time deciphering what they might be. For all I knew they were some imagined Edenic blossom only located along the waysides of the goldsmith's cortex. I wished suddenly that I had stayed home to complete my medical training back at the University of Toronto and vowed, as I passed my thumbnail under the edge of the locket's lid, to return to my training before my twenty-fifth birthday – if I lived, I thought wryly.

I had no idea how I might afford this promise for I had no intention in asking my father for funding. He was a monster, and I had surely burned that bridge for my own sake. But in one thing he had been correct: I should never have left Toronto or school. I missed anatomy courses mostly, found I craved the Latin.

After a time, the locket gave way with an elegant dull sough and I was suddenly staring into the face of a most beautiful woman, her hair all piled up on her head. "Oh, my," I whispered as I peered closer. I shut the locket, breathed deep twice and reopened it so that I could masturbate while gazing upon her plump bottom lip and the slight sadness in her eyes. I had not defiled myself in months. I am ashamed now to recount this, but at the time, I thought how this one time would surely not be considered excessive. And there would be some certain relief. I hoped no one would overhear how monumental and banal my emission had been.

When I was spent and tidied, I lay back stupidly on my mouldy cot and turned the locket over. There was a faded inscription that I could not read. The scrolled initials read "J.P."

And now, I stood awkward and shaky at the widow's threshold, fingering that locket at my chest, the crateful of puppy eyes trained up at me. I had heard her shriek and felt a certain magnetism. I wondered, What had this woman's dead substitute husband to do with the peach-skinned goddess in the locket, her hair piled upon her head to show how elongated, how equine her perfect neck was? I wanted to leave, but I had knocked and it was too late. Standing there at the widow's door-well, I felt myself dissociate, break right in two – a not altogether unpleasant feeling.

"Hullo," she said when she pulled the door open. The baby was awake and chirring at her hip. Two years old or thereabouts. I heard a grinding in the background and wondered was it real or was it more of the same? Was it coming from me?

I held out the gold locket.

Cristiana's lips pouted. I was again afraid of her and immediately angry because of that fear. The baby drooled, a burble of snot from its right nostril, its hair a messy golden blond halo. He was whiter than her, whiter than Henry, and I at first wondered if he was her baby or some foundling she had rescued. There were many orphans in those days. But no. The boy looked like her and like the dead man around his lips. I loved babies of any sort and this one was outstanding for his beauty.

Cristiana took the locket but did not thank me as I had wished she would. She looked at me with unmitigated disgust and went back inside the house to set the baby down in its cradle. The child immediately began to protest. Cristiana stood holding the locket and staring at me. I thought how she clearly hated me. Well, what I had done was hateful, so it was only fair. I stood very still; I had already proven a terrible soldier with this temperament. I froze in battle. I self-loathed. And worse, I had some indelible aggrandizement ideation. I thought that everyone ought to love me, perhaps because I despised myself so wholly.

"Come in," she said, "why don't you?"

And so I took an exaggerated step through the open doorway and stood again statue-still. There was a glimmer of laughter on her lips. Was she laughing at me? She slipped a knife under the lid of the locket and popped it open. The tuft of hair fell to the floor. She gasped and picked it up. Then she looked into the case and back up at me, her mouth dancing with accusation. "You've stolen the image," she said. She leant out the front door, to see who might be looking, and then, seeing only children skipping down the dirt road, she shut the door and turned to me. "I would do near anything to get back that image," she said.

I knew she was desperate, but I was, too. A better man would have handed over her rightful belongings. After all, her husband lay rotting, and she had fewer prospects than most anyone. But somehow this, in that moment, felt opportune. I just wanted contact. I wanted what I had never had, not from my parents nor any other person. Is that unforgivable?

The grinding sound persisted. It ate at me, a sort of frantic backdrop to my already-poor reasoning. This scene was happening differently than I had imagined it, and this annoyed me. That everlasting whine of mechanicals. I wished I knew where it came from. I tilted my face toward the window but it wasn't anywhere outside. It seemed to emanate from within my eardrum. Is this what losing one's mind sounded like? I hadn't imagined madness would have a sound.

"So you do have it," she said.

She said it like that, and I had no defence. The lie I had concocted was flat and bald and clear. I felt as if she had seen me defiling myself. This caused me to blush. I cocked my head but it only made the noise amplify. "Image?" I said.

Cristiana stared me down in such a way that I began to know the anger in her eyeballs. I tried to look at her lips, but they hated me, too. I could see how she was struggling to make her eyes neutral. I should have just reached into my uniform jacket and riffled through my wallet for the tinted daguerreotype, but I was too lonely and in love with it, and with myself, to give it back. So I turned nasty and said, "What's Henry Muldon doing with a white lady's picture in a locket, anyway?" and fully gave myself away.

The baby wailed, choking on its own frustration, and then wailed some more.

Cristiana snarled. "What do you know about it?" She fetched the squalling baby and then pulled her shirt aside and stuck it there to her tit.

Her shoes made a nice sound on the wooden floor, a counterpoint to the squeal of mechanicals in my head; she walked around letting the kid suck at her. It was more than a toddler, I now realized, maybe three or four, but small, malnourished or sickly – I did not know which. I had never seen anything like it. She caught me staring and shoved a pinky between the baby's lips and her breast and popped him off. The whole scene was so unnerving.

It seemed to me a taunt. I had to swallow. "You ought to feed that bairn cow's milk."

"With what money will I buy cow's milk?"

Baby Charles screwed up his face and bawled. Drips of blue-white milk emerged like tears from all over her taut nipple. I swallowed again – I had been salivating continuously. Cristiana laughed mercilessly from a deep part of her gut and let the baby back on her tit. "He'll eat me whole, this child," she said, not looking at me. The baby did seem voracious; she was all skin and bone.

She perched on a farm chair and told me to sit down. "I'll make coffee when Charles is done," she said. I don't know why I did not stop things there. It was as if I was caught in this universal grinding machine, in a web of badness I did not put in place.

"That's kind of you," I said. Is it wrong to say that this felt destined? But maybe destiny is another way of saying how much I benefited from the way things were.

She said, "In the future, things will be different."

"Yes, I am fighting for that future."

"Are you?" The settlement in which she lived was all Black folks, verdant where it wasn't dusty and earth trodden. I could hear neighbours talking and I could hear the clanging of some enterprise in the distance. By this I considered that she was so far from the brutality of the war that she did not really reckon its import. Either that, or she did not have faith in the progressive outcome we soldiers had been contracted to believe in.

I tried again to recount to her the battle in which Henry had fallen by way of proving to her my dedication to this better future. But something uncanny stopped me. She – her meaning – was changing right before my eyes. I had thought her hateful, but now, as I looked at her, I saw she was not. I began to wonder how this could happen, how my mind could change impressions just like that. It would have been better – safer – to keep such things in more control. But my head wouldn't ever keep a thing straight. One minute I am bent on leaving and the next one I find I have returned. I sell myself into a caper and find myself killing people, and it's all pretty easy. I fall away from reality and find myself floating in some strange dream, only I am awake. And all the while this dirge-like noise infiltrates me. I know this is not normal. I've gone strange.

One minute she was just a person, one I would never see again, and the next she was someone for whom I felt this strange blossoming in my heart. If my mother had been watching, she would have rolled her eyes and said, "Of course you would fall in love with a forbidden woman. You never could do anything right." She was correct twice. One, I was falling in love; and two, it was impossible, for she was a free Black woman caught in that story and I was caught in my own.

Wee Charles's eyelids thinned with baby sleep. Cristiana pulled him off her and buttoned herself up. She swaddled the boy in a sheet and laid him on his side in the cradle again. Then she stoked the woodstove's firebox and set a kettle to boil. I liked the sound of her shoes on the floorboards. It bent the grinding sound away from me. She calmed me. I was assessing all this as she set about making coffee.

"I need the daguerreotype, Private Boyt."

"Russell is fine," I said. "Call me Russell."

She stood too close now, to where I sat in the sawback chair. The locket dangled between us, its chain looped around her thumb. It was closed tight, one inch and a half wide. A hundred dollars of metal, maybe more. I did not really know about the worth of things.

"The daguerreotype means a lot to us," Cristiana said. I knew she would not give up until I had given her the image, but I was stupid with the game of it. There was something in it for me, and I was hungry for that something. It's repulsive to think how I must have seemed to her. I was not a good man. I tell you, I was a cog in this terrible story.

She smelled of sweat, milk, urine, cast iron and something flowery I couldn't identify. It occurred to me to go, but I couldn't seem to get myself to do that. Her smell was beguiling.

"I wish I could help you," I said. "I really do wish I could."

Cristiana let her face fall a little to the side. She gave me a sour look because of course I could have helped her. "You ravaged my dead husband's uniform," she said. "You read his letter, and you do know where that portrait is."

"What would a Negro man want with –"

And then her indignation caught fire. "That photograph means a great deal to me and to the baby. It means the price of an old golden locket, certainly."

"I guess that locket is worth a bit. You could sell it."

"You don't understand."

I blinked. I wondered if she could see how strange I was, my organs ossified and gear grinding like clockwork to keep me going. I suddenly saw in my mind's eye my father, furious and yelling in the dining room. The contact of knucklebone on jaw, his grating voice telling me I was no proper son, that I ought to man up, boyo, and then my body twisting against the fists of his torrid release. It happened often that he beat me, and I would be tender and bruised the next morning, my mother accused of coddling me. Had this ossification begun there, I wondered, or in the blood as it passed from father to son back through time? Maybe I could find some solace here with Cristiana. Her voice made me homesick for some reason.

She bent down to stare me straight in the face. I tasted her breath, felt the locket slide back and forth along the inside of my thigh. Her eyes were orbs scanning me. She could see right into me, like my skin was a window. This harried me all through. I thought about the landscape I'd walked through to get here – hedges and forests and ravaged fields, a nation of trees and corpses. The image of the beautiful woman in the locket was seared into my mind, anyway, right? I had no need of it. So why did I not give it to her? Why was I so mingy? I think the dynamic made me feel more powerful than I was. It gave me a sense of control, of being if not loved at least wanted. I justified keeping it by reasoning that it was nice to have something lovely tucked away when I was fighting – it would give me courage, make me feel lucky.

I did not want Cristiana to look down at my lap. All my thoughts had shifted down there, to the stiff helplessness of it.

"Cristiana," I said. "Missus Muldon?"

She smiled sadly at me and nodded.

I fumbled at my jacket pocket, the wool already brittle and frayed after one lousy battle; what would it be like if I saw the war out? I'd be bedraggled. My wallet was supple calfskin, a gift from my mother to celebrate passing my entrance exams. The image was nestled between the bills I had stolen from Henry Muldon's pocket. I told myself it wasn't strictly stealing since the man was dead. I held the picture and tried to take in the whole of the woman's face for future reference. The woman in the photograph was beautiful.

"Who is she?" I asked.

"Charles Muldon's paternal grandmother," said Cristiana.

She seemed to believe that I would give it back now, but I was not so sure. She had not moved away. She leant down. Everything about her swirled through my senses. I tried to sort the lineage, realized I was scowling.

"Your child?" I said. "But the woman in the image is white." It made me wonder if maybe this love I felt might be more possible than I had previously thought. "Is that allowed?"

"No," she said. Cristiana was staring directly at the bulge in my trousers. There were strings binding me and her, and I couldn't do a thing. She was playing me. "What did it feel like, anyway?" she said, anger bracketing her question. I was confused.

I thought she might have meant the battle, the surge and pop of it, the way it went from game to real and then back to game, and how the detritus of it might have been someone you half liked the day before. I had fought in four battles and I did not always know whether I was awake or dreaming. But she didn't mean that.

"What did it feel like to touch your first Negro? What did my Henry feel like to you?" She spat this at me.

Like touching cold stone, I wanted to admit but didn't. So instead, I steeled myself against the look she gave me. I crossed my hands over my erection. She could look at me all she liked. I had sinned imagining myself with Henry Muldon's lily-white mother – she was probably as old as my own mother, if she still lived, but I would admit to not caring – it was a fantasy. A pathetic and shameful one, but who can help such things? Besides, my thoughts were

35

scattering and I could not seem to hold them. To distract myself, I put the photograph back in my wallet.

I was thinking, How could Muldon have this mother? It had not really occurred to me before that such a thing could happen, and the transgression of that thought was overwhelming. Gears grinding.

"I asked you something, Private Boyt."

I felt like crying. It had been a long, neurotic day. I shifted to put my wallet back in my pocket and came awfully close to Cristiana in doing so. The movement rustled up more of her smell. I was trapped inside it. I felt she was manipulating me. She hadn't stopped peering at me; she was a mesmerist entrancing me to give this thing back. Her face was very round, her neck strong and exactly right on her. What she must think of me. I told myself that I didn't care, but I knew this was an untruth. I was a person who cared what everyone thought of me. I was a person who craved everyone's adoration and who never felt right with the world unless I had it.

She waited for me to answer her question.

"It felt sad." I pushed back in the chair, felt the locket slip down along my trousers and heard it clang when it hit the floor. Automatically, I dropped my arm between my legs to pick it up, and when I had it in my hand and was again sitting up, she took my hand and placed the locket around my filthy neck and kissed me. Her tongue and teeth seemed to know me.

Then she stopped and said, "Can I have the photograph now? You can sell the locket. It is worth something."

"No, ma'am," I whispered. I could not move. My whole body felt so corroded, inside and out, that nothing would work. I did not know where I was or why.

She looked at me as if I were a madman.

"I need to keep the picture is all," I said to her. "I think it might lend me some protection."

I watched the slide of her cheek, the curl of her ear, the tight hair under her kerchief. And when I looked up, the boy was leaning over the edge of the cradle, sucking his thumb, watching. I felt simultaneously sick and glorious, my whole body filled with want and the near-expression of that want. This business, I thought, will only lead down the pathway to hell. Everything had gone so still, like a dream, the kind where your legs stiffen and you can't move when you awaken. To fill the room's quiet, I said, "Who is J.P.?"

Cristiana frowned. "Charles's grandmother, Jessamine Peabody, formerly Muldon. She hungered for Henry's father. She was only a girl at the time but rich enough to do as she pleased."

I could not breathe well. "This doesn't end well," I said, thinking this here, in this shack, in this country, but she misunderstood.

"It did not. Henry's father was lynched when the relationship was discovered," she said. "The baby she had six months later was spared, nursed by a faithful servant. And Jessamine was married off to a Gordon Peabody, fifty years her senior, plantation gentry. Jessamine bought Henry's freedom after her father and her husband died. The ending might have been adequate, I suppose, if my poor Henry hadn't also just died."

I pulled the image out of my wallet again just as the baby pulled his thumb to unstopper his mouth and went into full-out wailing. Cristiana laughed while looking at me, and got up to go put the baby back down, patted it until it shut up. When she had calmed the boy, she turned back to me and said, "Give me that image now. I need it, and Charles is its rightful owner. It may be that Jessamine lives still. She is Charles's only hope." Any bartering, even if it meant her own death I now realized, would be worth the price for that image.

"It's Charles's heritage, scant proof but something to bring to Jessamine if things get right when the war is over," she said. I did not know much about how such things might work. But I began to see how little power she knew herself to have and how she must deploy whatever she could. I sometimes wonder what the world would be like if these games did not need playing. I sometimes try to imagine a future in which we cared for one another. But humans are a scourge, it seems, and I was such a one.

I did not want to relinquish that picture at all. "Thank you for your hospitality," I said. I wanted this entanglement, though now I am sorely regretful I did. I wish I had never met her or Charles, for things have gone very badly since. She had kissed me, but it was to get something from me. She was making a fool of me, as my mother would say. As anyone would say, but I wouldn't know this until much later, long after this day. She was incandescent with anger, devoted to it. She *was* anger.

"There is the matter of the letter's contents, too," she said, "which I believe you have destroyed for your own benefit." She told me much later that she wanted to cry but could not, that she had not cried in her whole lifetime. "Maybe you need some time to think about it." She pulled the door open, and immediately the puppies began yipping. She had a hand on her hip, and watched me as I watched the pups. "Our business is hardly over."

"I guess not." I reached into the whelping crate and hauled one of the curs out by its scruff, said hallo to it, then tucked it into my collarbone. It melted flat, smelled of talc and pee. I loved dogs of any sort.

"You can have it," Cristiana said. "Keep the locket, too, and your tiresome shame and all the rest of it."

I could feel the locket pressing on my rib cage, under the dog's belly. I had heard of soldiering dogs – why not my own? I did not yet feel the curse of ow-ing, did not expect to, either. "I doubt we will ever meet again," I said. Another untruth, her fury like a fog around me. I was this mess of need and hurt and water-stiffened bolts. "There, mangled deaths are such particular sorrows, they catch in my throat."

Cristiana stared at me. She looked abandoned. "You'll be back," she said, but her feet toed in anxiously as if she did not quite believe her own proclamation.

This had been a long dark day. The hard softness of her lips when she had kissed me. What did it matter? "I will likely die tomorrow," I said.

"Give it up, then," she insisted, "please." Panic edged her talk. She meant that line I'd obscured in the letter, about the location of whatever Henry Muldon had buried.

"I don't owe one damn thing," I said, trying out some quavering bravado. I started walking away with the pup tucked into the crease of my neck. Then I turned back and called, "I did weep reading your man's letter." I promised myself that if I lived, I would return for that corpse's treasure. And the farther away I walked, I found I could not slough her – she was eros twirling around me. I convinced myself that this might be what love comprised even as I knew it was foolish and unrequited. I was sick, believe me.

When I arrived back in camp, I set up under a willow and unpacked Henry Muldon's writing kit. *Dear Cristiana,* I wrote, *thank you for the cup of coffee. Your husband's treasure is six feet down betwixt the southeast corner of the cabin and the hickory your uncle planted upon your marriage, he wrote that you must follow the instructions therein. I am sorry not to have told you sooner. Sincerely,*

Pte R M Boyt. I was by then quite sure that I might love Cristiana. Love was a strange, damp feeling, I decided, if this was love. It has taken me all this lifetime to see that this was not love at all. It was rather war and loneliness and my own sickly mind. Or maybe it was the only sort of love that can be conjured under these circumstances.

DAY SEVEN

WHERE DOES ALL THIS BUSINESS about love come from? I'm kind of appalled at what comes out of me sometimes. Not so much "how dare this privileged asshole get away with this" as "why does my subconscious manufacture a character who is this desperate and awful?" I'm clearly more needy than I want to think. And all this transaction, as if love can be defined through economic terms. What am I working through? Well, I am working through a lifetime of reading happily-ever-after fairy tales, as well as marriage plots from nineteenth-century novels and every rom-com ever, is what. The kind of story we women have long been fed. And that for a long time I fell for. Here is this Russell Boyt, a figment of my imagination, a wealthy twat who thinks he can blame his behaviour on the war or on madness, and I know this guy. But if I can write this character, I must also be this guy or how else can I conjure him? Or have I just been victim to him in some paradigmatic way?

The whole thing has enraged me. With the burden of my own creation, I storm downstairs to where Mum and Dad are tuned into the news, all of which is about weather and possible evacuations. "You really brought a spot of weather with you," Dad says, peering up at me.

"Fuck off," I mutter, and turn into the kitchen.

"What have I done to deserve that, now?"

"The patriarchy," I yell from the sink. "That's what."

"I didn't do that."

"Well, you haven't done a thing to stop it, so that's just as bad."

"He's eighty-five," Mum says.

"Yes, he's had eighty-five years, and what has he done for us?" I come back into the doorway and shake a carrot at him. "Remember that time you asked me why I never dated guys from university?"

"And you accused me of sending you there for your MRS?"

"Exactly." Sure, he paid all that tuition like a modern-day dowry in hope of me finding a suitable husband.

"I do remember."

"Well?"

"Well?"

"Well?"

A standoff. Just what I want. "It was incredibly sexist."

"Yes, but you must admit that if you had listened to me you mightn't be in this muddle."

"I'm not in a muddle. I'm very happy," I say, which is when I begin to cry again.

"Oh, for heaven's sake. Go to your room."

I stand there nibbling at the carrot, tears streaming down my face. Eventually they turn back to the news, which is showing a rescue mission in Almonte where a newly built bridge has washed out, leaving people stranded on the highway. I let the tears run. No sense in fighting it as it'll only make it worse.

They seem surprised to find me there ten minutes later when Dad gets up to turn off the television. Their console is circa 1984 and requires pliers to turn it off, the knob having long gone missing.

"I used to see him from time to time," I say.

"Who?" says Mum.

"My brother."

"You had a very vivid imagination."

"I still do."

"It's channelled better now."

"I suppose."

"How is the Civil War novel going?"

"It's autofiction," I say dully. I am tired of explaining the difference. "All the flooding is reminding me of the foundation hole."

"Oh gosh yes," says Dad. "Wasn't that something?"

"Yes," I say. "It really was. I must have been about three."

And then I recall all this, that we were staying in the croft house, preparing to build a new dwelling on the property. We were crammed into the main floor because the upstairs had burned in the '30s and no one had since repaired it. My two sisters and I were crammed into bunk beds set up in the living room. I remember Dad peering into the mirror on the bathroom door to check his shaving job and get his tie just right for work in the city. He latched the door quietly when he left, but in a few minutes, he was back inside, scratching his head in wonderment.

"I remember you saying, 'I guess we won't be building the house in that spot because the foundation hole is full to the top with water.' And I said, 'What's the matter with this house?'"

My dad would have been twenty-three years old then, barely a man, roughly the age I have imagined Russell Boyt to be in the thick of a war he barely understood. They had that foundation hole dug in 1970, at the very same time that the Vietnam War raged. I would not have known this at the time, but while our proposed house site filled with water, the National Guardsman killed four anti-war protesters at Kent State. I wonder now if humans are such divided creatures – cut off from themselves in such a way that they are in poor sync even with their own species – that civil wars are inevitable. Mum had this saying that so-and-so was too smart for their own good. Is there another creature who would die for their beliefs? We cleave so heartily to our stories.

Back then, my dad said, "This house is too old to fix. And too small for us."

"And I won't live in a haunted house," Mum chimed in.

"I recall sliding over the edge of the bed and hanging there, bat-style. My jammies were yellow and dirty at the knees," I say.

"You were always one for being dirty," Mum recalls. She is smiling at me, but there is a wariness to her. She wants to keep the narrative contained. She wants this memory recalled just so, her way.

"We all went out," I say. "The night before, by bedtime, the excavators had left, and the hole was massive, ready for our house. 'That's a lot of rain,' I said, looking out at the pond that had sprung up in the foundation hole. 'Nope,' Dad said. 'It's groundwater.' I asked if I could swim in it, and Mum said, 'No. The sides might cave in, and besides, how would you get out?' Maggie asked, 'What's groundwater?' And you, Dad, you told us about underground streams and how you had heard there was a lot of water around here, but you'd never imagined so much. I inched closer toward the pool. It smelled mossy. And Mum clutched my hand so hard. I watched a sparkle coursing under the water, something bright heading west."

Mum looks a bit frantic at the direction the conversation is going. She interrupts to say, "And – yes, that's right, Kathryn – I took you girls inside where it was safe."

But that is not what I recall. It is coming back to me. "I saw my brother, I saw him swimming, his sweet little face. I pointed and said, 'Look. I see him. It's Wulf.' And Mum said, 'Don't be silly,' and muttered something about it being the sun glancing on the surface –"

"No –"

"– and that is when you softened your hold on me, let go my hand, and I slipped feet-first into the cold swell."

"It did not happen like that," says Mum. She gets that stern look. Stubborn. Mum.

"It was bone-cold, Mum. A sudden shock. It was as if I had never before known the contour of my own body. But more than that. Something deeper ignited in that split second when I crashed through the surface tension. And you and Dad were yelling at me to swim and come back, and then I saw you running, I supposed, to the phone in the farmhouse, to call emergency services, and Dad throwing something – a rope?"

"That – none of it – ever happened. But if it did, and I am not saying it did, you would have been fine. You were always a good swimmer owing to –" Dad is saying.

"– owing to the wee webs between your first two fingers."

A birth defect. Something hereditary.

"I did swim that day," I say. "I can't have made that up."

"It's more a misremembering, I expect," says Mum. "There was the old quarry on Highway 14."

I nod because there will be no agreement here. She is intransigent. She will not have the story out. I look at the first two fingers on my right hand, pull them apart like peace signs and wave. "It's true. I could always swim."

"Yes, you were a wonder in the water," says Dad. He is trying to smooth things over.

"Like a sea creature," I say.

And Mum cringes.

They say there is a feeling of abiding peace that comes with freezing to death. A euphoria. When I was finally pulled out of that makeshift temporary pond, Mum was nowhere to be found. Just as she's walked away now.

My mum is gaslighting me. I do not know why, but I know this feeling. I also know this: after this incident with the foundation, everything changed. They

abandoned any plan to build a new house. They set about replacing windows in the croft house. They tuckpointed and they roofed. It became a lifelong enterprise, and inside this artifact, now 180 years old, amid ghosts both ancient and fresh, they made some kind of a life – for themselves and for me and my sisters.

I go to my room. I stare out at the drizzling rain and I try to catch the tail of this recollection. One minute it is my baby sister, Frances, who plunges in to grab me, but, in another moment, my father pulls off his jacket, swings it out and hauls me in. In another, I swim the width of the foundation back and forth, refusing to come out. I wonder suddenly whether Mum let my hand go on purpose. She is not the sort of person to take a risk, but she knew I was and she knew I'd revel in swimming. There was a before and after of selfness in this incident, as if the cold formed something of me, brought me into something. A line of knowledge. That I could swim even before I had learned to swim. I look carefully at my hands, the little flaps of skin that connect my fingers. I got bullied a lot for them in my youth – all manner of slurs – but I've grown to love them. Why does she not want me to remember?

DAY EIGHT

MORE RAIN. IT HAS NOT let up for the week I've been back. I come downstairs and watch Dad from the stoop as he tucks into the woods on the east side of the property, where the artesian spring–fed pond has urged its waters wider and wider over the years, swamped over with the crud of plants and small creatures. His orange slicker gleams against the verdant cedars and then he is gone for more than half an hour. When he returns to the house, he is clutching rocks that he lets spill out onto the kitchen table in front of me. I am bleary with sodden dream and a regret that won't be pinned down.

"Trilobite," he says, pointing.

"Nice."

"And this one. Trace fossil." A trace fossil is the contrail of a ground creature that's been immortalized in stone. "The path of some meandering fool who died finding her way."

"Is that supposed to be a jibe?"

"Golly, no." Then he starts in about the end times, gesturing at the news – half the county underwater, neighbours boating out of their homes to safety, no sandbagging ample enough against the deluge. Wonders whether the flood is as prophesied. Tells me the waters are rising, the well is fuller than it ever was. I mention again about the old foundation, how I watched a sparkle coursing under the water, something bright. Dad looks strangely at me as I ask him of my falling in after seeing Wulf.

"There was never a boy in the water."

"Did the flooding sway your decision not to build?"

"I don't imagine it factored. There was just too much water and I didn't have the money to monkey around with another mistake like that. I had it filled in after a week."

"A week? I thought a day."

"Maybe it was a day. I don't recall."

"Why do you not want to talk about this?"

Mum walks in and says it's because I'm foolish and then asks what I fancy for breakfast.

"I want porridge, but there's no need for you to go to the trouble. I can make my own."

"Nonsense, the stove is fired up and there's a pot simmering from ours."

Dad lines the fossils up, then reconfigures them in a swirl. "How old do you reckon they are?" And then "Maybe your boys might like them. You can take them home with you when you go."

"Dad."

The idea of going home – back to the city – repulses me. It sends a kind of cellular horror all through me. Maybe I have broken this thing called home. "I can't," I say.

"Can't what?"

"Forget it." It feels like work getting up, like a load of muck is weighing my legs down, like my heart is its own kind of fossil, a thing dying to find its way. "I don't want to talk about it."

"Forgive me for asking." His sarcasm a way to lighten things.

"I'll start in the basement today."

Their eyes harden a bit as I head there. My misery requires fungus to undo it, I think. Even as I pull the door, the musty odour soothes me. I require lichen, moss, the sort of plants that can live forever on the mere recollection of water. The walls of the basement exude forest, and I can see small holes bored by mice and moles. The dismal smell I want is everywhere. I should go for a swim in the old pond. It's far too cold out to do this, but I contemplate how invigorating it might be. There is a kind of pull along my skin. It's strange to harbour these yearnings. Perhaps, like Dad has accused me of, I have brought the weather. As if my decision to leave a place of deep discomfort – this micro-shift in the universe – is a kind of suction for all the rain in all the world's clouds.

I've barely had time for my eyes to adjust to the dim light when I am summoned again.

"Kathryn!" Mum calls. "Your porridge grows cold."

And while I am eating, as if to appease me, Mum hands me an envelope with a folded-up obit wrapped around a photograph of my great-grandmother with a baby. On the back of the photograph, a note in my mum's writing: *Boyt's son, Nigel, with his wife, Molly, and Nan (Bea)*. She also plunks down five buttons, two of which are sewn to what seem to be small swatches of boiled wool cloth. They are metal, military.

"The buttons," she says, "are thought to have been Russell Boyt's. I found all of this in the pig shed this morning while you were sleeping. I'd forgotten I had it. Forgotten where it was, anyway."

"Her eyes are odd," I say. "Like little onyx marbles."

"That would be the seal in her. She had webbed hands like you."

That old story, I think, and roll my eyes. The family mythology is obviously apocryphal, that my great-grandmother McIver was stolen from the Scottish coast and sequestered away in the rubble of the Canadian Shield amid the erratics and glacial till. A poor Gaelic seal, so far from home that she could never escape again. A selkie. A seal-woman.

Seal-folk is the other name for amphibians who can pull their sealskin off and cavort like people. But when they dare to do so, they make themselves vulnerable, for without their skin they cannot return to their homes in the water. The old stories tend to revolve around a smitten fisherman stealing the skin of a beautiful selkie woman and hiding it away, marrying her, making her a mother. And this selkie woman is torn between her responsibility on earth, to her babies and her man, and her yearning for that fluid, more-than-human self, that water-tending one. And that's because selkies mean freedom, they mean being in your own skin, they mean open seas, not this landlocked hardscrabble place.

It's always one of the children who finds the skin and brings it to the hostage selkie. It's her own halfling kid who hands her back that freedom. And that is how they lose her, for once she has the skin, she rushes home to the sea, never to return. That is how the stories go.

"Just stories is all," I say, as if I am one to talk.

"Yes," says Mum. "Family nonsense."

"Folktales."

"My nan used to say her mum sang a strange song sometimes, late at night."

"What song?"

"I couldn't tell you. But Nan said it was not Gaelic to her ear. She always said it sounded like a song that might have sprung from the watery depths. But you know how Nan was, so superstitious, so romantic."

I bring the swatch of uniform and the buttons up to my nose to catch his scent. Dust. Lanolin. Does insanity have an odour? I wonder if it's true that madness lies dormant in a person's stomach flora, awaiting the proper conditions to blossom. "Mum." We settle on patched Muskoka chairs on the front stoop, blackflies out but not yet biting. "I feel like I wrote this into being. It's as if I magicked these objects by writing them."

"What?" she says.

"Sorry." Because how can I expect her to understand how writing makes things happen? I say instead, "Forget it," and "But did you see the obituary at the bottom of the page?"

"Charles Muldon? Oh, he wasn't anyone to us. I showed it in case you might be able to figure it out on that ancestry thingie of yours, or on your Google. Your dad and I think he might have been a friend of Boyt's. You know, someone he fought alongside, or someone in the hospital. Listen," she says. "I've been thinking, and I've decided I don't have a lot of faith in this project of yours. The *sort-of* memoir thing. It seems to be too upsetting to you."

I ignore this, keep to the topic, and say, "I think that Charles was the mistress's son."

"How odd," she says.

"I imagine him to be light skinned. Cristiana was Black."

"How do you know?"

"I found a photograph of someone named Eliza Goss. I can't quite figure out their relationship. But they were certainly related."

And then out of the blue she says, "I got an email from Matthew this morning."

49

"What?"

"He says to say hi."

That sounds right. I leave my marriage and my husband musters a thin greeting through his mother-in-law. I feel a bristle of animal fury rising on my skin. "I miss Wulf" is how it comes up, a subtextual parry to her interference in my life, to the bullshit mess of this. But I mean it, too. I do miss him, in this uncanny way, as if he were the missing thing – the home – that would complete me. As if I'm a selkie and he is the very skin that would have given me an intact self. It's also as if I can locate solace only in the imagined, in my never-brother, the one I endlessly try to conjure. My repetitive compulsion.

"You never knew him," she says. "None of us knew him."

"They say no one is knowable." I'm certainly feeling this about myself. This person who knows they need to leave their family but that nevertheless feels shattered by having done so. "No one is knowable, but, for some reason, I seem only to be able to write this brother into existence. Even as I write this Civil War story, I am writing him – a boy who goes to war never to return."

"You're being headstrong."

"I'm headstrong? Me? What about you?" I tell her that it is as if her quiet and willful grief somehow created Wulf, even in his death. Maybe it's people's memories that make ghosts, I say. Or maybe she was the ghost I always felt in my midst. I tell her that her depression affected me, that it had a heft, that it acted like silt infiltrating me, her sadness a bog in which I grew up. And that I miss him in the way one misses a clear day, misses hope, misses a thing that can never be, an object that can never be held. Yeah, I really let her have it.

I'm lying. I do not dare say any of this.

What I say is "I can't sit still anymore. Do you want to go for a walk?" By which I mean 'Let us walk this away.'

And as we trudge the old cowpath on the east side of the house, through prickly ash and beach pea, I say, "There was something strange Dad said at breakfast."

"Oh?"

"He said that the foundation hole was filled with water for a week. I thought it was just a day. I thought they came right away to fill it in."

"It was a week or more."

"It must have been a worry to you with us so young."

"I suppose it must have been." She won't look at me, keeps her eyes downcast, brushes the stalks of last year's wildflowers as she walks by. "I barely recall those early days," she adds, and looks up long enough for me to catch some trace of sorrow, salt water pooling along her eyelashes.

"Is everything okay?" I ask.

"Tired," she says. "Bad sleep last night. Sorry." She presses her face into her cotton blouse sleeve. "I'm okay."

1864

IT HAD TAKEN ME MOST of a day to bring that damned letter to Muldon's widow and to return to camp, a task that should have taken far less time. A task I could easily have given to any old sutler. I worried about being missed, but, in the end, there was a coney roast in full swing and no one had noticed me missing. My compatriots had been out hunting.

Bellair held out a plate of meat and bread to me. "Hungry?"

"Thanks," I said. I was famished.

My own weakness cranked up and down my skin. I ate the rabbit meat too fast. My dastardly innards felt like ungreased cast-iron fittings. I slowed down with the bread, watching the other men, their weird fluid movements and joking ways. I did like Bellair, my new friend, the way he wore his cap like an amulet crammed down upon his scalp even as he slept. He was looking out from under it at me. "You sure took your time with that fella's widow," he said.

I saw he was curious about the widow but did not answer, tried to stop my lip from twitching. I recalled Cristiana's kiss. She had just wanted something from me was all, and I had been ungentlemanly. Still, it had thrilled me.

A person could be court-martialled for walking away. I had clearly crossed some line. And I could be in dire trouble for consorting with an ex-slave. It wasn't like the war made any of this good. Then I had another horrid thought:

What if Ebenezer Wilkes – the man for whom I substituted, the limb-maker – caught wind of my dalliance, and felt himself misrepresented? The danger of what had just transpired scurried through me, a hot dancing along my nerves. Since I knew the names of even the tiniest of these nerves – these hot tributaries – I began to chant them to calm myself: *musculocutaneous, ulnar, radial*. God is in the details, was that how the expression went? I doubted that more and more.

I suddenly realized I was gnawing on my fingernails, but I couldn't stop. I looked over at the fellows enjoying each other's company; some men had begun harmonizing. Memories plagued me, caught me in stupid loops. I was wondering whether my and Eb's identities had merged in our substitution. *Were we twins?* I felt a convulsion down my body – a tic – and tried to suppress it. Perhaps Eb had really entered me, knew my thoughts even. I knew it would not do to be in love with Cristiana. No polite society would condone this sort of mingling. Yet I could not get her smell out of my head.

I got up and wandered toward the men. Coney grease travelled down my wrists, which I licked. "Tell me how you cooked this rabbit, will you?" I knew I looked lost, my body unconfident and awkward standing there. I wanted to cry, solely for the release. But no one would tolerate a crying soldier.

Bellair said they had rolled it in mud and tossed it in the embers of the fire. "How do they cook rabbit where you come from?" he said, as if to cheer me by asking questions of home. He must have seen how forlorn I was. I was dejected, it is true.

"In copper cookery on a proper hob." As I said this, I recalled a particular thrashing from my father when I was still quite young. It was so severe that I could not walk properly for some days. I did not like to recollect this. "They stew it with parsnips and onions and sage, and serve it on fine bone china, but it doesn't taste so good as this." That last family dinner. The china was so resonant in my mind, and what he had done to me so amplified that I began to laugh maniacally.

The first hit from my father had come as a surprise, but the subsequent ones I simply tolerated, smiling faintly at my mother's impotent horror. I wanted to tell her I did not feel a thing; instead I murmured to my father that he was dead to me. The next day, my parents and the servants and even I acted as if nothing had happened.

"My kin would not deign to eat out of doors in inclement weather," I whispered to Bellair.

"Are you all right?" Bellair said.

I suddenly realized I *was* crying, and I wiped my arm along my eyes and streaming nose. "It seems a long time ago, indeed." It was clear from his face that he had no idea what I might mean. But he was kind. He moved over a little, to shield me from view of the other men.

I would have liked to leave this place then. The week before, another substitute soldier had deserted the army and been caught curled naked and fetal in the woods. They court-martialled and jailed him. Rumour went around that this man had enlisted six times at different recruitment offices and deserted five, collected five substitution bounties over a number of months. In that time, the man raised over a thousand dollars, more than enough to put a body through medical training in Toronto. I had gone to where the man festered in his jail behind the bivouac and slipped him a piece of hardtack when no one watched.

"You run from battle when all is confusion," the man said.

"I never asked you," I said, and laughed a nervous laugh. I was afraid of spies. They were said to be everywhere. But I did want the information, and he could see that. The man had a gnarled scar running down along his ear to below his collar.

"Any scoundrel can read you, boy."

My nerves jangled like crazy. I felt in that moment Eb's presence like an engine or a creeping illness moving through me. "To hell with you."

"I'm on my way there right now," the man said.

That night, rolling over and over in my bunk, I prayed for sleep, but none came. It rained and was clammy in the tent and the men snored. The pup was curled under my cot, asleep. As usual, Bellair slept like a prince. I dwelled on the locket portrait – Jessamine, that neck, her hair piled up – and then on Cristiana, who had somehow blossomed into feelings I couldn't contain. My penis stiffened up. I endured this until it subsided. The medical profession believed that excessive masturbation caused nervous disorders. But what was excessive? I would try to curb my desire. I would not give into the madness that was overtaking me. Eventually I slept.

The bugle sounded at 4:00 a.m. and the drummer rolled out an adrenal pummel.

The next days were drills and canteen filling, and talk and song and march. By way of forgetting, I told myself that Cristiana Muldon was nobody and that what had happened had not happened. This stratagem did not work. I felt sick with the space put between us, and the way the realness of my time with her began to dissipate into mere story. I missed her, it is strange to say, and the more I thought of her, the farther we trudged away. I thought that I would never see her again. I named the pup Little Tiger and let it scramble my thoughts. That was what a dog was for.

By mid-month, the volley turned serious and we were all in. I wondered how long I could keep to the margins, and if there were any margins anymore in this heated hell-battle. There were rebel soldiers everywhere, loading and shooting where they weren't scattered dead and dismembered. It's strange how memory operates. I have wholly forgotten much of the war, but there are certain days that persist in my mind. Perhaps they were the more horrific ones. Those dying whose moaning revolted me most. Oh God, I was so ill-suited to this type of work. This one day, early in my war time, I slid against the muck of one of my own company and landed on my side facing some horror that had once been Voigt, the strapping private who had shot and cooked the rabbit dinner weeks before. I got up quickly and found I could not move. And so, I stared out at the melee as if I were a figure in an oil painting of war and not in a real one.

Bellair had been fighting alongside me, smirking against the blistering nowness of it, muttering to "push on push on," as much to himself as to me, it seemed. By this time, we'd done many guard duties together, being at the unfortunate end of the alphabet, and in all that time I'd never anticipated what a brute he would be in real action. Don't die, I thought, of Bellair and of myself, my heart clocking me like a boxer inside my rib cage, hitting, hitting as if a speed bag. I had to crap.

Bellair found me on the field and urged me on, but he did not have to crap. He wasn't dying, as I was, of cramping. Then Bellair said, "Mind to your left."

A wounded reb was sighting an Enfield directly at me. Close enough to kill, was all I had time to think as Bellair lunged, bayonetting him clean down the sternum. The man died smiling.

"Push on!" Bellair was shouting now, from the sheer thrill of it.

I got up then, some power in me again. Shells were flying. The noise of it was something terrible. If I stuck close to Bellair, I could almost catch the spirit of it. My bayonet dripped with another rebel soldier's blood – I'd taken a piece of him, too. How grotesque to be a soldier in this civil war. The dead soldier looked almost serene.

"Let's go!"

"I can't," I said, and lurched to sitting beside the dead man. The battle sounds fell away, then. There was nothing. This was okay after all. Before me, fanned out in a beautiful pattern – arranged just for me – was a tangle of bodies, dead or still groaning horses and unidentified bits and pieces. It came to my mind that humans were just so much meat. I wished myself back in that cabin with Cristiana and the baby, Charles. Bellair plunked himself down beside me in that very moment.

I said, "I think I am in love with Henry Muldon's widow." It came out flat and plain. How odd to say such a thing. As if I thought I could change the scene by changing the subject.

"Is she not a darky?" said Bellair.

I turned to him and felt this fury in me rising. "Cristiana is beautiful. Take your insult back."

Bellair stared at me. "That'll get you some trouble," he said. He clearly thought me pitiable. And then he joked, "Love comes fast in wartime, don't it?" We sat a beat longer before he whispered into my ear, "Push on, soldier." We'd been fighting back to back, moving forward incrementally. That was the point, wasn't it, to gain ground in this awful place? Bellair got up and left me alone then. I gazed upon the viscera of a victim to my left. There would be maggots soon enough, but for now it was alarming – glistening entrails, pink and creature-like up against the rough fabric of the uniform. I could make no sense of it in the pretty landscape. Why was I here? Soil kicked up near me and there was Bellair, his straggle moustache curling into his mouth, sweat and dirt bathing his face.

"Boyt," he said. "You've got to move, boy."

I was afraid. Not the regular sort that made me sometimes say stupid things or hold back but full body terror. "I have the trots," I said.

"No," Bellair said and crouched beside me. "You do not."

I leaned back into the rebel corpse. I gestured at the acres of death, the landscape dotted with crumpled blue and grey uniforms, the splash of red – both cloth and fluid. "How do you do this?" And then I squinted and drew a spiral from out in, from one dead thing to the next. We both knew we would be digging in the morning, if we lived.

Bellair's eyes softened. He placed his palm on my chest. When he touched me, I felt the locket of Henry Muldon, the heart shape of it emboss my skin. "You have to just stop caring," he said. "Is there not some iota of hatred in you? Nurture it and let it thrive."

I shook through my whole self. I wouldn't cry again, I told myself, but even so I could feel my chest convulsing against this admonition. The booming demand of Father, then, saying, "Boy!" to me that last dinner before I left. His great, haired fist slamming down on the oaken table. "You make me thoroughly sick!" he bellowed and then quietly resumed chewing his roast and salting his potatoes while making gentle conversation with Mother. My father's disgust was self-pity, which seemed worse. I would not have dared to hit him.

I looked back up at Bellair's expectant face, my mouth surely contorted against all that was gathering in me. What an enormous resource of anger one needed to hold the tears back. The regimental band sounded faintly to the north, a rallying patriot's song, a fife. I tried to let it feed this hatred that Bellair had only had to hint at for it to appear – some beguilement it was.

I got up, leaned into some future death.

"That's it, lad," said Bellair, slapping my shoulder. "Let us push on."

The line was already dozens of yards away, pulsing forward. From the distance, I watched men kill and fall and fall killing, a theatre complete with music. There were children and women watching from across the river, taking tea. There was a photographer preparing his equipment to document the aftermath.

"No cowards here," Bellair said and smiled at me.

I imagined the hard nugget of newfound rage I was supposed to be, to fight like a tiger. The image was handy, I supposed, but also full of menace. I plunged forward with Bellair, feeding my malice from the revolt I felt as we skirted the countless dead.

How angry were the dead? I wondered senselessly. Around me, the wounded whispered and muttered, "Save me, leave me, push on, push on," a ghost babble saturating me. My rage was now so acute I wanted to inflict it from my own hands just to get it off me – right off me, goddammit. The dying men's evil thoughts were whispering right into my skull.

"There there, Sir Boyt," said Bellair, laughing as I sent a bullet straight through a massive enemy farmer. "Boyt's back in the land of the living!" And Bellair was right. I finished the pimpled boy with a thrust and twist of my bayonet.

In camp that night, exhausted, some remorse came to me, a viscous shroud of it. "How devilish a thing courage is," I confided to Bellair.

Bellair looked at me queerly.

"The impression of my father's loathing for me is enough to see me kill a dozen or more. Yet my father and his hatred live on."

"That is crazed thinking, Boyt."

I looked up from under my cap. "Maybe I am crazed then," I said and left it there. I would like to know if a man could make himself mad by seeing through a falseness. I witnessed in myself a yawning chasm between thought and action. It was a great mouth waiting to swallow me up. I could feel its abrasive, mechanical tongue licking me at my edges. I was part of this war. Not in it but *of* it.

"You just need sleep," said Bellair.

"Okay," I said. But still, I could feel the bad thing churning toward me.

DAY EIGHT

HOW STRANGE THE BASEMENT LOOKS at night, dim bulbs flaring, soft water cascading down the stone foundation. I give thought to my great-grandfather Nigel heaving these stones, his heart straining with the effort, with the future, as he pulled up each stone one by one, finding whatever flat side might best civilize nature into this structure, keep the chaos at bay with straight lines and mortar. I lean on a wall, letting the water wick into my nightdress. Lime and hay and sand, the grit of it scraping my arms. I don't care; I like the sudden sensation of feeling something. I want to arouse shame for having left my marriage or nostalgia for my boys, but there is nothing. Well. There is something. There is a jumbled yearning to step out of this skin and into another. The boys will come back to me. It will take time, but they find happiness in their way.

I am clearly not myself. I have not been myself for years. Matthew's admission of an affair took me by surprise, and there was a chasm in which hope flourished in that admission. I thought perhaps an openness – a truthfulness – might be nurtured. He answered my questions, but when I had too many, when my queries went on for weeks, the chasm shut and he refused to go there. Marital transgression is boring, I suppose. Cliché. This affair happened before our marriage, though, and for some reason it shook me to think that the whole edifice had been built atop a secret. That I did not have all the information. That

I had not been given the benefit of honesty ahead of saying my "I do."

I tried for five years to cover over this new knowledge. But in the end it flayed me. In the end I was left skinless. I was not myself, as I mentioned. And it is my opinion that you can only be not-yourself for so long before it becomes untenable. I did not leave to hurt anyone. I left for me – because anger had almost eaten me. I left so that I could find my way back, in order to be me for my children, and for myself. And now I can't sleep. I can't quite say why I have come down here in the night. The house is quiet and I awoke from an odd dream – I must have been more disturbed by that photograph of my great-grandmother than I thought. A seal swam around me in my dream. She had haunting eyes. She came to me while I was swimming front crawl in a black lake of some sort. She nudged me as a dog might. Her eyes were shiny black marbles, just like my great-grandmother's.

The violence in the last Civil War section alarmed even me. Maybe it elicited this dream. What fury lies buried in me and how easily it is excavated. I want to think that the battle scene is just an act of representation – that I want to accurately depict how men are formed by this flawed patriarchy. But I have to admit, the fury is mine. Or at least it emerges through my hands. And in order to get away from both it and my keyboard, I have headed down into the deep of the house – how fitting.

I'm wide awake now. I crouch to sit on a stool. I should be cold but I'm not. The boxes I have gone through are stacked beside me, while the rest of the family hoard is everywhere else. There is almost no room down here. It is a hazard, heaps of objects cascading out of boxes. The sump pump is running to keep water out of the house – a losing battle, for it has begun to collect under a mess of chairs and crates.

Those eyes in that dream. The seal seemed stricken with some need she could not express. The water lapped at us. I start going through the box closest to me as quietly as possible. I want to get my mind off that dream and the battle scene, and exhaust myself enough that I might fall asleep again. I both love and hate the way a dream, like writing, can bring stuff up from the subconscious. I haven't wanted to think about Matthew and that secret of his. What good will dredging that up do me? But there is no going past a problem, only through. My dreams and my writing fingers know this. They are the body's wisdom speaking.

But what a drag insomnia is. I'm so bleary headed, so *exhausted*. As I shift broken china and photos so water damaged it would be a miracle to discern their subjects, I think how like a dream this basement is, too. It's a memory repository, its cardboard boxes sinking into one another, the must of ages pluming up as I scrabble through them. Five generations of familial objects tossed willy-nilly. In front of me is an old travelling chest hidden under a stamp collection, a yogurt maker, a foxed file folder holding who knows what and the mouldering textbooks of my baby sister's entire undergraduate biochemistry degree. Teetering on top of this heap is the old mildew-spattered Remington portable.

I pull it down and try out the QWERTY. It's stiff but working. I did a bit of sleuthing about this typewriter the other day, when I first noticed it, and discovered a fun fact: Remington invented the typewriter when their gun sales dwindled after the war. I like to imagine all those war-torn soldiers, beleaguered and permanently damaged, laying their weapons down and plucking out their tortured plots – the stories of their lives.

Write what you know. Was that Remington's branding?

I've been thinking of reconditioning this beast, amused by the idea of writing a Civil War novel on it. I wonder if Stephen Crane wrote *The Red Badge of Courage* on a Remington. He did not fight in the war, of course; he had not even been born yet.

I put the typewriter on the stairs to bring up, then move more junk. There's suddenly a funky smell of leather in the room. I try to track it, but it seems to be everywhere. I look up, into shelves built up the walls and into supporting posts. Little white spiders cling to an ancient tangle of cobweb. The spiders look like stick figure drawings. I can see through them in the dim light. My nose is so busy tracking that I don't hear Mum until she is partway down the stairs.

"You needn't sneak," she says.

"I'm not sneaking," I say. "I couldn't sleep. I had a weird dream about my great-grandmother." Why does she make me feel guilty even as I have no reason to? "I just came down to sort through more stuff. Do you smell something off?"

"Basement smell."

"More like dead animal or pelt."

"No," she says. "I don't smell anything like that." And there is that clenched jaw again, that guarded face.

"I was in the water," I say.

"Not this again."

"In my dream, I mean. I was in the water and she was a seal. You know when a dream feels prophetic?"

"I don't dream," she says.

"You don't remember your dreams," I correct her.

She sniffs and repeats that she doesn't dream. Maybe the world can be split into those who do and those who do not dream. Maybe the dreamers are just a bunch of fools who can't escape their petty trauma. After all, as Mum would assert, it is in the past, where it can't hurt me.

"She was poking me," I say. "As if she had something to tell me."

"Well, I'm not a therapist, but I do know one thing. Some things in the past are better left there. Let them rot. From compost comes food and flowers."

"Now there's a quotable quote," I say. "I love it, Mum." And I wish I could take her advice, but there is some part of me that is so seduced by what has already transpired that I cannot let it go. I am devoted to it. So much so that when she turns to leave, I ask if she remembers the doll. "It was porcelain. I keep expecting it to turn up in all this debris."

She faces me. She's an old lady now, my mum, but she looks like a child, her face a network of wrinkles. "What doll?" she says.

"I must have been four or five," I say. "Remember how you wouldn't let us back in the house in winter unless our mittens were wet? I went to the back door and knocked until you came to the door. I put my hands out to show you."

"I needed a little time alone," Mum says.

"I didn't understand that at the time," I say. "But now I've my own children, I totally get it. I lock myself in the bathroom to read sometimes."

"You should go home," she says.

"For crying out loud. The mittens were on a string, so I wouldn't lose them. I had on snow pants and a fur coat made from Nana's old winter bear coat. You'd quilted a golden satin lining into it, do you remember? Like the bear in 'Snow-White and Rose-Red,' you told me."

"What about this doll?"

"I'm getting there," I say. "I'd dug a tunnel under the snow. You wouldn't know this part, I suppose. But I will never forget how there was a crisp top layer, which made a nice roof. I dug fast until there was enough room for me. Then I crawled into the hole and lay there looking up at the ceiling. The heat from my breath began to melt the snow and condense around the top of my coat. I could smell the fur, that wet animal smell."

Mum interrupts here to say, "The bear coat was synthetic. It wasn't really bear."

"Now you recall," I say. How can I remember something with such visceral accuracy and be wrong? "I know I lay there and breathed in the pong of fetid bear. I stomped around to the door. I told you I was hibernating and then I sat to watch *The Friendly Giant*. You gave me snacks, then put on your coat and boots and walked out the door to get the mail. While you were gone, I put little *X*s in all the empty boxes of your crossword puzzle."

"I do recall you doing that. It was a thing you did because you hated that I was ignoring you for a crossword. But I liked them. They seemed a necessary distraction."

"Necessary?" I say.

"Like breathing."

Like breathing, I think. Maybe cryptic crosswords are to Mum like writing is to me, a puzzle that sets my mind in a trance state. It feels like floating.

I say, "I used to do it quickly whenever you left the room. I liked anticipating your annoyance at me. There was something pleasing about waiting to get in trouble in this way."

"You were always an odd child."

"When you returned, you had letters in your hand and a package wrapped in brown paper and tied with twine. 'Look,' you said, calling me over. But I didn't pay attention. When I looked over, the parcel was open and you were staring into a box. 'What is it?' I said, and I got up to take a look.

"I peered at the doll's features, its tiny rose lips, its pink cheeks, the perfect arched eyebrows, and said, 'It's a boy.' And you said, 'Okay. I suppose it can be what you like.' And I asked if I could have it and you made me promise –"

"Never to deface my cryptic crossword puzzle again."

"So, you do recall," I say.

"There was a doll, but it was not a doll like that." Mum glances away. Her face is impassive. "It was one of those dolls that walks. It was a Christmas gift, but

63

you and your sisters snooped and ruined the surprise. You also came to know there was no such thing as Santa Claus that way."

"No. It was a very old porcelain doll. I did not make that up."

But a wall has barricaded her in. Maybe this is shameful to admit, but it rushes through my body: she is despicable. We are back to being our worst possible selves. It is the only protection we have, I suppose, but still. And in this awful dynamic, I spit out that it must have worried her that I called the doll Boy and treated it like a sibling, taking it everywhere with me.

"Nonsense," she says.

And Mum and I are back to where we ever were, and in that familiar dynamic, my centre spirals out into nowhere. I shoot her the finger, but she is not looking. She ambles up the stairs, clutching the railing to keep herself steady.

"I hope the sump pump can keep up," she says.

"Yes, I hope so, too," I say, because what is the point of arguing with her? You can't win. I turn back to my task – I can nap later. I pull bundles apart, rummaging through the cellar only to find nothing, no doll, no source for that animal stench. I come up late for breakfast, and when I call no one answers, so I eat a toasted tomato and mayo sandwich, nap for an hour and head back down. I get about a third of the way through the crap, and unable to face Mum and Dad, I skip dinner and go to my room feigning a migraine. I haul the Remington up with me and try to pluck out some part of this story, but it's clumsy and the ink is more or less dry. So, I open my laptop, order ribbons and cleaner, and then, despite my exhaustion, I write until it is very late. It is as if I am writing to save my life. I write the story my mother has handed to me – the Civil War story pieced from scant archive and fabricated memory. Not the story about Wulf. Maybe it doesn't matter what I write. Maybe it is the fact of writing that will always be the thing.

It's like my mum and her cryptic puzzles. I write to breathe, to find an aliveness in myself. The day of sorting and seeking becomes, in this state of writing, a kind of dream out of which I don't want to awaken. I can't distinguish what is part of the story and what is real. People think that writing comes from the head, but it's not strictly true. It comes from our materiality as we siphon the alphabet through it. We humans are strange creatures. We require story to scaffold us. And that story comes through my hands as a subtle dance, a finger chant. Words made flesh. There is a language around storytelling, of weaving and spinning – writing is surely embodied. I'm both jangled in this other world and exhausted from the mania – caught in the grammar weeds of this war story: Wulf filtered through this imagined biography.

1864

I MADE IT THROUGH THE long week of death and dismay – miraculously. The weather had turned suddenly hot and dry. Our faces and hands were sunburnt and peeling. The heat might have been the worst of it, which is saying something because all of it was pretty terrible. I was changing in ways that made my job easier even as it ruined me. I'd been alternately elated and terrified through the whole of that time, practising, just as Bellair had instructed me, a strategy for wrathful courage that involved an elaborate construction about my father's disgust for me. In this way, I learned to be a good soldier. I learned to kill. I found that when I recalled my father hitting me, I could slash and shoot the hurt away, such that, and I am not proud of this, the killing of other men became a sort of balm to me.

My father's furious face gave me a kind of bravado to help inflict my pain on others. I have no idea what other men did to fuel their heroism. It was dismaying how remarkably easy it became to kill under these circumstances. Kill or be killed, as one of the other soldiers liked to put it, but it was not so simple for me. For example, I had to construct a whole narrative about my death in order to sustain my brutality in battle – I would die a hero! This propped me up in the moment and gave me both something to live for and a way to die nobly.

I decided that if I died, it would be glorious, because I had manufactured in my mind a death so exquisite. I will have entered the fray to save a comrade. I will be on the verge of bayonetting the scoundrel from the South who was on the attack, my mouth open in battle cry, my chest wide and heaving with promise. And then the bullet enters and I fall in valiant death. I was sure Father would not be able to maintain his hatred if he knew. I was a hoax of myself. I sometimes wondered whether we were all just so.

"I saw that the *Washington Standard* calls this business a *theatre* of war," I said to Bellair. The two of us were bone-tired and heat oppressed. We'd walked away from our bivouac and stripped down to swim. I looked at my crotch and screeched like a woman to discover a nest of wood ticks burrowing into my groin.

Bellair laughed at me and said, "With every man a hero?"

"I was thinking that same thing." I certainly felt myself to be a sort of theatre actor in the drama of my own life.

"Do you suppose that the rebel forces think they are right? Or are they also playacting?"

"I'm sure like us they've lost sight of reason."

"They at least have farms to fight for."

"Nothing feels real. I feel like a man possessed. I feel both more and less than myself, if that is comprehensible."

Bellair held my shoulder, said, "Hush," and shot me a disquieting look. He peered then at the pulse of industry on my groin – there wasn't such a thing as privacy between men in those days. We were brothers in arms. We loved one another with the ardour of the almost dead. He said, "Oh, that's ugly," and handed me his fillet knife to excavate. It was then we caught an acrid downdraft and saw that we wouldn't get in a swim after all. The swampy water hole was littered with corpses. We moved off because of the reek of it, and I tied Little Tiger to a shot-down branch to stop the cur-pup from troubling the dead. I laid my stink-sweaty trousers on the grass to sit on and leant into this new task. There were six ticks. I could feel them burrowing.

"Take the shallowest one first and don't worry about their heads too much. They will die off by and by," said Bellair.

"The Christly little agonies," I recall muttering. I was itchy all over thinking about them. I decided I would douse myself in my whiskey ration later – half down my cock, the rest down my gullet. I knew to disinfect even if the army's backwater doctors hadn't a clue. I'd read it in a British Journal back home and overheard two of my professors the year before debating the merits of clean hands. The vermin I was working on struggled against the blade, but I dug at it, forcing blood. Little Tiger pounced at grasshoppers that jumped too near, and Bellair, for amusement – his own, seemingly, and the dog's – ran the end of a stick just out of reach of her nose.

The heat never abated.

I knocked five of the ticks out in no time but had to dig and dig at the last tenacious bastard, opening a quarter-inch of flesh low on my groin to undo its grip.

"You can die from ticks or go crazy in the head," Bellair said.

I reeled over and whacked him solidly in the chest. "Thank you, Doctor." Then we were rolling half-naked in the late day, like children. In fact, we were barely men. The pup sat guard, ears pricked, watching us tussle. This was a happy memory from a terrible time. I did love that man, and I did love that dog, too. On the way back into camp, Bellair said he had heard salt was good for healing, but there was none to be found.

The next morning, we were sent with the others to patrol the field, assess damage, count bodies and begin burying. The heat had not done the dead any favours. Bodies had swollen overnight and begun to burst through their uniforms.

"I wouldn't touch that with my hands," I told Bellair when I saw him bend over a fetid corpse. "I would try not to see or smell it."

"It's Cy Marshall," said Bellair, his face dour.

I tell you all this to give you a sense of what war is. I don't want to shy away from its horrors. So many men can't talk about these things; they try to outrun them by refusing them words. To me, this feels complicit. The war was just a symptom of what we humans call history. We dug a shallow grave for the boy and used two fence poles to turn him into it. By the end, the poles were wrecked with Marshall's fluid and so we tossed them and found a new set for the next corpse. This is the system into which I had been bought for a bounty of three hundred dollars. But it was worse than that. Because as a young man, I had been taught what a hero was and how to be one. There was only one way and the war provided me with it.

But war was not a place of heroism. It was a story I had been trapped by. And because I was lucky, I did not die, not there at any rate. Though so many did. I will not turn my face from them. They were not heroes. They were corpses. Rubbish for us to clean up. I will not spare you what I was not spared.

Private Franks, Private Minden, Sergeant Haarms, Frenchie – the list went on, would never stop. By the time we reached them, days hence, some of the dead were faceless. We dragged one man to a mass grave we had fashioned to save burying time, and his legs separated from his torso. Where the rebel army had abandoned their own, Bellair and I shook our heads and walked away at first, but then realizing every corpse would breed flies and stench, we began to bury these, too, as best we could. We dug by rote until our shoulders forgot to complain, half men, half machines.

One day the field would look just like it had before the war. A bucolic, melancholy place, where cattle might graze or crops might sway in gentle breezes. Or maybe they would build a quiet graveyard here to commemorate the unknown fallen. But they were none of them unknown, were they? They were beloved pawns in a larger game. Even then, I felt the hands of some other narrator writing me into this story. That is what men are. Puppets.

We sweated through our clothes again and again, and swore to the devil as often as to God. We could be tumbling half a soldier – whatever was left – into a makeshift grave and scrape a length of wet maggots to find only bone. We forgot our manners, forgot to care about who exactly was dead – all was rot and stench and ugliness.

We did this for three weeks.

At that point, I looked at Bellair and knew he was unrecognizable from the Bellair I'd first met at training. None of it mattered. None of it.

"I'm already a ghost of a man," I confided.

The mention of spirits upset Bellair. His eyes widened, but then he began to laugh. "If you are a spectre, you are the prettiest one I ever saw," he said, and we rolled more soldiers into more holes until the last remains were buried. By then, twenty days and more had passed, and the flesh was completely gone; the clatter of dry bones was something of a delight after the weighty and viscous dead of the first few days. Off in the distance was that newsman again or another such setting up a camera to take photographs. And behind him, off to the side, another group of spectators, some of them holding handkerchiefs to their noses, some sandwiches. When Bellair and I passed them later, they moved away, like a tide receding or the way certain insects run under pressure. Bellair laughed, but I was made uneasy.

"They think I'm real," I said. "But they are mistaken."

"You are as real as anyone else, Boyt," said Bellair. He swung his arm around me in such a way that I did feel – fleetingly – human. I was surely going mad.

DAY NINE

I LIE AWAKE LATE INTO the night, unable to stop my brain from looping. That marriage story has its claws so deep into me that I can't seem to get loose. I guess in Boyt I am finding some sympathetic corollary – he is as tied to a system as I am. We all are. Fed lines. Hook and sinker. What a lie this life is. To be married. To go off to fight in a war. To be compliant to the dominant paradigm. There is such power in the neutralization of falling into a role set out for you by society.

It occurs to me that if I do not soon find a new, more palatable story into which I can inscribe myself, I will surely not *be* at all. This line of thinking has me weeping. And then when I finally do sleep, my dreams are fraught with dear friends peering at me, worried, and cars without drivers. A huge spidery robotic version of myself traipsing into the forest. Like I don't already know I'm hurting people. Like I don't already know my vectors are fucked up.

I wake to torrential rain and wind and a text from my youngest: *When can we go get me a new skateboard.* I shut my phone and open it again right away, reread, shut it, open it, write: *when the weather clears <3.* And then I lie still listening to my heart thump a wild percussion. I miss the boys. Is it weird that I miss their demands, their problems and how good I was at solving them? Who am I to be now without them?

I breathe deep breaths for a while to calm down. As I do, I recall that doll and my interaction with Mum. I remember the doll beside me in this very bed. It was just becoming light. A spider was hovering above my mouth, spinning in place, her legs fine and busy, her body almost upside down as she concentrated on her task. The thread began at the ceiling. When I breathed, she swayed in the air.

I held still, silently begging the spider to climb back up her thread and leave me alone. I reached over and pulled Boy into a hug, and tucked my thumb into my mouth. The spider dropped closer and then moved a little higher, but not high enough for me to escape. "Boy," I said. "It's okay."

We held in that pattern for a long time, the spider rising and falling, swinging on my breath like a freefall of dark dream. I wanted to call out, but I didn't dare. And so I luxuriated in my fear. Finally, when the spider climbed up just high enough, I escaped, Boy in tow, and went to my parents' room.

"Mum," I said. "There's a spider."

"Why didn't you yell?" She was plush with sleep.

"I didn't want to scare anyone."

"Oh, come on then." And so I climbed in between my parents with Boy and told them about the spider, and then I stuck my thumb in.

"Is Boy okay?" my dad said.

"Oh, for heaven's sake," my mum said. "It's only a doll."

I popped my thumb out to say, "He's not," and they both laughed.

My childhood was good enough, if I can just hold onto the moments like that. After breakfast, though, I head downstairs to the kitchen and they more or less ignore me, so caught up in their various puzzles. When I ask whether they recall this happening, they look up dazed and then look back down.

"I don't know," mutters Mum.

Mum's effacing me now, regulating me to whatever it might be that she wants – *her* creation, an enigmatic not-this, a disavowal of me as a thing at all. Her hard look makes me think: Where does the marriage plot begin? I might have escaped the fact of my marriage, but I have not outrun the way in which that story has colonized me. I have run fast from the insinuation of motherhood, the dredge and drudge of it, the web of it, only to speed headlong back to its source. Ground zero: mother. Her frown is a cryptic puzzle I could fill with Xs until the cows come home, until hell freezes over, and I'll never be able to decode it. We are meant to write ourselves into this network – quilt into the fabric of this old story of man and wife and offspring, of white picket and nurture, of tidy kitchen and breadwinner. It's not only the women caught in this story. We are meant to find what little freedoms we can eke out of the main plot points. And though we all suffer from the constraint, we also devote ourselves to that suffering, for within it, we appear somehow a little more coherent.

And I can see the allure. For my incoherence is now let loose on myself. Who even am I if I am not married? It's so destabilizing. I need a new story bad. The selkie wife who finds her skin and leaves her halfling children. She is one who dares to leave. She is one who cannot abide the main plot. We never hear much about her watery life after the story. All we hear is how, from time to time, she comes to visit her babes. She pops her pretty head out of the sea and speaks to them in her impossible seal-ish language as they stand forlorn and abandoned on the shore.

My skin now crawls. I head up to my bedroom and take a nail file from my toiletry kit and scratch along my wrist until the chafe draws beads. But blood is not ocean, blood is more metal than salt. It fails me. And then as I surface from this act, I hear Mum calling me from downstairs, then again louder, shriller, and then "Oh, for Pete's sake," and her feet on the stairs. "It's Harry on the Skype," she yells up. My son. My baby. The last of the peepers are singing in the morning. I go downstairs and there he is, looking out from Dad's iPad. Shy. Tentative smile. An eighteen-year-old bairn.

"I know you probably don't want to hear this," he says, "but Dad's being a bit of dick. When are you coming home?"

"I need to sort some things out with Grandma and Grandpa." I can't quite bear to say that I'm never coming home.

"Now don't be using us as an excuse," Mum says in the background.

"Hush, Mum."

"This has nothing to do with –"

"Harry, everything will be okay. I better go. I'll e-transfer you some money for the skateboard."

"Okay, thanks." I see the next question coiling off his tongue before it comes. "Are you and Dad divorcing?"

I don't have to coddle him. But I do have to coddle myself. "I'm not sure what's happening, honey. I just need time."

And then what I don't expect: "I hope you aren't going to take him to the cleaners."

My mind flails until I find some calm. Then I squint and grimace and laugh and say, "His words?"

"Yeah."

I repeat that I have to go, tell him to stay dry. And then the sky opens and it's like some kind of Biblical deluge – the windows of the house are awash, a crack of lightning and then the lights flicker and go out. I see Harry's forehead tighten, his eyes narrow in some realization that he has voiced a cruelty. But before he can compensate, the screen goes dark. He is gone. And I am free of it.

Dad lights a couple of tapers and gets the kerosene lamp going. He is eighty-five and beginning to stoop. His skin has thinned and he has shrunk a bit. I feel a surge of love for him as I watch him take care of us. It's the sort of tenderness that feeds a person. How love comes out of the person who loves and not the beloved. I get to thinking how I love the way he laughs, the way he walks with such method and care around the property each day, rain or shine.

And then he says, "I also hope you aren't going to fleece Matthew. He worked hard for all that you've achieved."

And my tender feelings, where do they go so quickly? "Do you hear your-self?" I say. "What *we* achieved."

"By the sweat of his brow," Dad quips. I look to see if he is joking and it's not clear.

"And what about my sweat?"

"Women don't sweat."

My parents are such a pain in my ass. "Forget it," I say. "I plan to work in the pig shed today. I can't be downstairs for another day. I need some daylight." I will tackle the myriad china tea sets that have accumulated through the deaths of various aunts and cousins. "I will take the tea sets into the forest, smash them one by one, or maybe heave entire boxes into one of the many gullies the glaciers carved there long ago."

"What have you got against the bone china?" Mum says.

Later, alone with Mum in the pig shed, I hold up this pink-and-white tureen because it is hideous and silly simultaneously.

"Why?" I say. "I mean really – why?"

"The Rose Medallion is worth hundreds."

"Think of all the women handwashing it, prizing it, being kept hostage by it. It just sickens me how it got held onto through the generations as if it has an intrinsic worth."

"There you go again."

"Did you ever read your marriage contract?" I say.

"Of course not."

"Can you imagine any other contract you would ever sign that you would not bother reading?"

"Marriage is built on trust," she says.

"And ignorance." I heave an abominable Noritake salt shaker at one of the posts in the pig shed. It misses, landing without breaking at Mum's feet.

"This was Aunt Dot's. Who, I will add, never married."

"That's not evidence of anything except how caught we all are in this ridiculous dream."

"How *you* feel yourself to have been caught," she corrects me.

I throw the pepper shaker in her direction, too. Like a madwoman, she grabs it in midair, holds it to her chest. "Stop that, will you?"

"Put it in the discard pile," I say.

She tucks the set in her apron pocket instead.

"I can't stop thinking about that porcelain doll," I say.

"Oh, for heaven's sake. I told you, I do not remember a doll at all."

"You made clothes for it. I carted it everywhere. You got it in the mail one day."

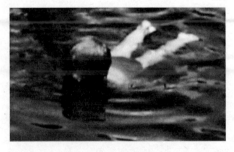

"There was no doll in the mail, honey."

I hold yet another elaborate tureen, which I immediately drop onto the concrete floor in order to revel in the smashing sound it makes. "There *was* a doll," I say.

Mum looks horrified. "Your great-great-grandmother's Spode. Fantastic of you. Nicely done."

Why is she so bent on withholding things from me? I know this feeling of being invalidated. It's the feeling of being untethered from oneself. I need to be alone, to gather in, and so I turn and go back to my room. By the time I get there, because of the bad feelings or because of the gap I have to contend with by not knowing any of the details of my dead sibling, the other story starts burbling up again, and I am undone by it. Where is my brother? Why is my own mother trying so hard to keep me from *this* family history? I know it's a bit theatrical, but I am tired. I grab my laptop and head to the screened-in porch to write. I will purposefully write Wulf in, make him up.

1864

IT WAS DAYS LATER THAT I wandered off, our regiment busy drilling. I watched the boys until I was sure they would not miss me and then in broad daylight began to walk. I had not succeeded in getting Cristiana out of my mind. I wanted to talk to her. I walked for days, having memorized the way through the bivouacs and battles of the previous weeks. In this way, I relived in reverse order all the boredom and banal dramas. I thought of Little Tiger from time to time and knew my pup would keep without me. He had taken a shine to Bellair and knew where to find scraps.

When night fell and I couldn't see, I slept wherever I happened to be. I was not concerned that I might be caught. I hoped my nationality would exempt me from being court-martialled, and for the rest I decided not to care. I made it back to the widow's stoop after four solid days of walking. The door was open a crack. I pushed it open farther. The place was topsy-turvy. It was clear she'd left with baby Charles and whatever else she could cart. Dust had settled. Some folks had gathered near the house when I went back out – two women, a baby and a young child full of mischief.

"She's long gone," one of the women said. "First she dug like a crazy person and then she tore off. She hasn't been the same since Henry passed." The yard was a disaster.

They nodded and watched me.

"She say where she was headed?" I asked. The strain must have shown on my face. I was sick with my feelings for her.

"Who wishes to know?"

"I do," I said, and they laughed.

"North is all she said."

"Thank you," I said.

"She never was all the way right in the head, they say. Folks say she was only one-half whole."

I liked to hear this at the time. I think I thought that I must be her other half. I see the madness in this now, but it was a time of madness. In civil war, are we all not split in two? I had a thought to marry her. I had a thought to make her whole. What hubris I now realize, to imagine oneself capable of such a feat.

When the neighbours walked off, I went back into the cabin and sat down on the bed and settled back. I stared at the ceiling briefly, then covered my face with my hands out of some frustration at my own stupidity if yearning could be called that. The ceiling offered no solace when I stared at it some more, so I rolled over and caught her scent on the mattress. It shocked me to find it there. It seemed a sort of spectre, and I became afraid and sat up to scan the room. Then I lurched from one item to the next – a teacup, a lace doily, a wooden rattle I imagined must have slipped out from her packings – as if in these items might be clues to where precisely she headed. And then I flung each object down in turn.

I stayed in the house pining for hours, then I slept. When I woke, I went outside, took the measure of the sun and inspected every shallow hole Cristiana Muldon had dug in the dirt yard to assure myself not one was right or deep enough. I found the pitted shovel under a dead shrub where she must have heaved it in anger before she finally decided to leave. I imagined she might have cursed my name, but it wasn't my fault. I realize now that I thought I knew her at the time. I did not. I had, in my peculiar state, half invented her. She was made up of our conversations, and the rest was just the residue of my desire. I imagined she was my perfect match in every way, my other half just as I would complete her. I believed at the time that this was what comprised love.

I paced from the corner of the building, marked the spot with the heel of my boot, walked back and did it again for certainty. She had missed the location by a fraction of a yard. I dug as the sun dropped and was never surprised, not by the huge rock I tinged midway down – the one that took a hot hour or more to shuck out of its hole – nor by the grey metal lockbox I unearthed in the pitch-black of night. Whenever I looked up, I would see the eyes of some of the village folk watching. I did not care or stop. I slammed the latch against the Christly stone Henry Muldon must have thrust down there, and I slammed it again three or four more times before the lock busted open. Then I went inside the shack and lit a candle to get a better look at what I had found. That is when I finally turned wild eyed on the onlookers and hollered until they scurried off into the night.

It was a china-headed doll, painted exquisitely to look like an actual baby. It was the size of my hand, no bigger. It gave me the shivers to think of a baby buried in the ground that I had just now dug up and was coddling. But I was past caring whether I was frightened or not, and more than a little curious as to why a doll was buried and then recounted in a letter tucked into the folds of a freed slave's Union uniform.

The doll's clothes were handsewn muslin and silk. Why would a substitute soldier have that to hide deep in the earth? I placed the doll on the mattress, with its perfectly hinged porcelain legs and feet, and then, because I felt it assessing my character – everyone and everything seemed bent on scrutinizing me at that time in my life – I turned it facedown so it could not stare into me so. Then I saw there was a tiny sewn-up pocket on the back of the dress, and so I scraped it open with my fingernails. There was a paper folded inside it, which read:

Prty of Eliza Goss, Please return to owner at earliest possible convenience. Washington.

I would not be returning it.

I took the sheet off the mattress and tore it in strips and began to wrap the doll. I noticed an inconsistency to its feel then. I stopped and carefully pulled the clothing off the thing until it was naked, just porcelain sewn into muslin and ticking. I saw there a hard wooden orifice built into the thing's back. A slit and tube carefully manufactured. I tucked my index and second finger in and pulled out a roll of bills.

"Oh Lord" is all I said, because it felt like providence. Then I unrolled the amount and set to counting it out on the bed. The doll lay splayed out beside all this. There was a quantity of hundred-dollar bills and nothing smaller, enough to take me through my medical training twice over if I was frugal. I wanted to see freedom in it, but the amount made me even more nervous than usual. I stacked it and rolled it back into a cylinder and fed it into the doll's strange compartment. I tugged the clothing over the doll's head and fastened it up, then I wrapped her in the linen bedding I had torn so that she would be safe in my haversack.

I thought I must be dreaming. It was all so strange.

And in that reverie, I grew tired and slept the rest of the night in the widow's bed, dreaming she came back and held me only to then wake in the morning screaming as she had begun to transfigure back and forth from Cristiana to a strange mechanical version of herself. In the dream, I had been so frightened that I had smashed her with a shovel, and like a doll she had never once bled. I lay there bewildered and itchy – my vermin wound not yet healed. It was not light out. I scratched at my groin, didn't care what a mess I left myself in. I glanced at my haversack, scrabbled it open to verify that there really was a doll, and began to put together a plan. Then I got up, went outside with the new stratagem on my mind and looked at the craters in the backyard. I noticed an overburdened plum tree at the front of the house and realized how hungry I was. Set to pulling fruit from its boughs and ate plum after plum.

At some point I noticed a man staring at me from a polite distance. He made a long humming sound in his throat and said, "Well, I guess you found something."

"It certainly isn't your concern," I said. I was still trying to slough the bad dream from my mind. The image of having hurt Cristiana, even if in a dream, endured, and I did not like it one bit. It unsettled me. It made me feel brain sick. I did not like to think of myself in this way.

I ate three more plums while the man walked off. When I was finally sated, I slung the haversack over my chest and headed back toward my regiment. The doll and the dream gave me pause, but I kept moving because it was in moving that things felt manageable. Whenever I stopped, I felt myself seize up in my body and in my mind.

It rained every moment the last day and night of my return, so that when I arrived, I was sodden and thoroughly chafed. The wound on my groin oozed a black muck from which the camp doctor later recoiled, then scraped mercilessly with his oiled scalpel before he compressed and bandaged it.

"I got lost," I told my lieutenant when I was made to answer for my absence. For punishment I was obliged to carry a heavy oaken log over my shoulder for two days without meals. The log reeked of tannin and wet rot and seeped a brown-black sludge onto my back. I did not care. Bellair gave me scathing looks until I confided that I'd lost my will to desert the war only to find it again. "I don't believe you," he said, looking down, "but I've been lonely hating you."

This made me smile. Within days, we were fighting again and I was granted clemency – they needed me as fodder – and put on the battlefield. I brought Little Tiger on the field to test him and because I liked having him near. I believed he was a talisman. This faith proved to be foolish. That first morning, a shell sheared off the hand of Private Henke. I watched him fall clutching his arm. The look on his face suggested that it had never occurred to him he might be hit, and that he honestly believed this war belonged to someone else.

I watched for a second before joining Bellair, who had gone to Henke's aid. We both knelt beside the man in order to tie off his arm until a surgeon could see to it. While we were working on his wrist, a bullet whistled in and we watched Henke's face recoil. He'd been grazed along his scalp. Blood was now cascading down his forehead and between his eyes like a river. I made the mistake of glancing around and saw that the field was littered with writhing blue coats. "Oh God, help us," I recall saying. The battle noises had Little Tiger shivering against my pant leg. A thin devilish whine came out of Henke.

"Don't look," said Bellair, and I had no idea what he was talking about. It was gibberish, and I wondered whether my friend had contracted Soldier's Heart and lost his mind. But then Bellair said, "Hold this," and gestured to the end of a strip of cloth he'd torn from Henke's sleeve, what was left of it.

"Oh God, please shoot me," Henke said. Bellair and I looked at each other with questions on our faces: How and why us?

"You'll be okay," I said, trying to calm him. "It's your left hand, anyway."

"Kill me," chanted Henke. "Killmekillme," over and over. His voice seemed so reasonable, so mundane. He stood back up then, swaying like a great tree. We were now separated by time and space from the rest of the regiment. Henke seemed a sort of beacon, a target standing lonely on the battlefield like that.

"Get down," I hissed. With my rifle, I pushed at the back of his knees so that they buckled.

Bellair shouldered his gun. "I got better work to do than to shoot the likes of you," he said to Henke, "and Boyt is a coward, so don't bother him about it."

"Shoot me. Oh, please just do it," Henke said, again, though with dwindling conviction. Either he'd changed his mind or had figured out that we wouldn't oblige him. His face was now a cataract of red blood.

"I'm not a coward," I said. I wanted to hit Bellair for this false accusation.

Bellair laughed and spat, and said, "Come on with me, Boyt. This man doesn't have the balls to get murdered, anyway. Look yonder, hey-o!"

And sure enough, the grey coats were right upon us; I felt my bowel crimp and loosen. I told myself that I would not soil myself, by God. Little Tiger looked up at me now and again, his tongue hanging between his fangs. The wounded were wailing to God and the angels, all around. A man could not hear himself think.

"Well, don't think, then," I advised myself out loud.

"What?" said Bellair.

"Nothing."

"Goddamn, I hate them damn rebels for getting us into this mess." Bellair gestured toward the enemy lines with his chin. "But look here." It was a poor Black soldier fighting on the wrong side, but I did not have time to wonder about any of it. The soldier made a grand sweep with his hand in order to cover his chest and fell face forward dead.

While I watched this dismal scene, a rebel came up behind us and clutched my neck so tight he lifted me off the ground. I was dying fast, my neck throttled. I tried to breathe and the breath stopped in my rib cage and scurried back down through my lungs like bad faith.

This was dying, then.

There was such confusion. Little Tiger barking madly, Bellair turning to lunge at the man.

The next is hard to recall, the way the war took so much with it. They say that everything is voided when a person dies. But I do not think this is so. I think that rather a person becomes more when they are dying. He coalesces into a self just at the moment he dies. I think that it is only in death that we can truly say we are a person.

Bellair was a hero. He lunged at the soldier to save me. He did this on the heels of trying to save poor Henke. The last thing he said was "Jesus wept," as he dispatched that rebel, and that is when a shell burst at his feet and threw my best friend, Private Bellair, in a spray of sod and black earth, his hands flailing toward the sky, to heaven, I thought, or maybe to hell.

I would miss him. I knew this right away because what was worse for me was that on his way out, he took the good part of my right leg with him, from about mid-thigh down. A negative memento.

It was a war about freedom. About the easy flow of money and resources. About status quo. About new beginnings.

I sat up and watched the lifeblood course out of me. Little Tiger was asleep. I worked quickly to make myself a tourniquet. There were any number of dead around me to rob a shirt off. When I moved to grab one, I could see my femur twist; it was cut jagged right through. I remember screaming with the shock of seeing it. And then again from the pain.

Henke watched me from a distance. He was standing with his tattered arm outstretched like a mangled Jesus. "You want me to shoot you, Boyt?"

"Go to hell."

I worked fast to stem the flow. "Oh damn," I said. I looked everywhere for Bellair, but it was as if Bellair had disappeared. What upset me most about this at the time was that I had no proper witness, no one – no Bellair – to sarcastically remind me of the lofty investment the US Army had made in me. No one to congratulate me for simply living. No one to care.

It was odd, I thought, as I stared down my pant leg, that the thing most plaguing me was not the severing – though it hurt plenty – but the festering itchiness of the goddamn tick wound I had self-inflicted. It must have gone septic. I went to nudge the dog to wake him but realized I had no leg to nudge with, and that the dog was not asleep.

And that is when I began to sob.

Henke stumbled getting to me. "Do you think you can walk?" he said.

"I guess I'll have to. Hop or drag my sorry ass. Be good to have a stick to lean on."

"I'll help you if I can." Henke looked closely at the wreck of my leg. "They say there ain't much hope the higher up the leg they got to cut. You'll likely bleed out." He flicked his hand and splattered blood across me and Little Tiger. "I'm in such pain," he said then. "It would be a mercy to kill me."

I cried more from Henke's plea than my own miserable situation. I liked Henke well enough and did not want to lose two friends in as many minutes. But I did what I thought was right. I shifted onto my side so that I could retrieve the pistol I had tucked in my belt at the small of my back. Henke's face was lost in blood so that even his eyes were red-washed. I levelled my gun at his chest and did my best to steady it while I shuddered with tears. Henke teetered. I watched the flash of some distant survival instinct begin to rise in him and waited for him to please change his mind, but he did not. He worked diligently to calm himself. Finally, he simply smiled. "Sorry about your dog," he said. "Yes. Yes, please." He had nice boyish teeth. They were healthy and spaced like ironic little white coffins.

He said, "Thank you, Private Boyt, and may God have mercy," right before I pulled the trigger and shot him straight through the heart. It was true that I right then began to know what courage looked like. It looked in this moment like a willful death. I felt myself grow madder. My blood ramped around all the coil and gear that was manifesting there in me. I was a machine, a player piano that sings only horror. I was a churning metallic dirge. The noise of the battle moved through me. I listened to the opera of it, could not stop listening.

Then, after a time, I fell asleep and slept for hours and hours, the battlefield the nightmare into which I fell. When I finally woke, that is when I saw them, the green ghostly eminences of gory death belching from the earth like hell spirits. The pain meant I was still alive. I heaved myself to sitting and pulled and dragged my body toward the flicking lights in the forest bivouac.

DAY TEN

I'VE BEEN TOLD BEFORE BY editors to pare back on violence. This always feels like a gendered suggestion to me – the parameters of what's allowed and what isn't from a female-identifying writer. I can't imagine anyone telling, say, Roberto Bolaño or Cormac McCarthy to ease off on the blood and gore. Women should write in pastel shades about love, domesticity. Leave the hardcore realism to the fellas. Well, fuck that. The fury is there; I had better write it than perform it. I'm mulling this over when I descend into the kitchen.

The newspaper is set out between them, sections being passed back and forth, first my dad and then my mum.

"Can I have the world news section?" I ask.

"No."

"Local?"

"Your father's not done with them."

"A man's need to know is somehow more urgent, apparently, more necessary than a woman's," I snipe.

"He gets first dibs."

"Why?"

"I like a virgin," he says, and stares me down. Challenging me to laugh or argue, but I won't do either. Instead I shrug my shoulders and go into the kitchen to make myself a cup of Earl Grey, what my mother calls perfume or candy tea. I've told her it's an antidepressant, but she waves me away with a flick of her fingers.

"The waters are still rising," Dad says, looking up from the paper. "I've seen this myself, in the bush, but it's everywhere. Basements in the city are filling and the sewers can't handle the excess water. This is getting bad."

"Human-made climate chaos," I say. "That's what they call it."

"Just the times; these things come and go and always have," he argues. He does not buy the stories about industry and capitalism. He does not trust the liberal news. He does not believe there is a man-made crisis. But he does believe in circular time, in the return of whatever might have once been lost. He believes in reiteration, seasons, comeuppance. He believes in the power of the Bible. And there is something to this, not that I'm a believer. The highway near the local hydro dam is washed out, people are suffering. I think about the sea creatures, the river folk, the pond people; are they laughing their last laugh?

I pull on my boots and head out to the artesian spring–fed pond at the front of the property where, as children, we were forbidden to go. It's overflowing now. I stand for a bit. It's cold and I haven't dressed properly. I clutch my sweater closed. There is a slight reprieve from the rain, but I can tell it will start up again soon. I came here once, a long time ago, and got my foot jammed under a rock. I had on my Billy boots and blue jeans and a long-sleeved navy-blue T-shirt. Boy was with me, tucked under an arm, swaddled in a cotton blanket. It's funny how I recall all these swells. How water brings memories back. I was maybe six or seven. I had this idea that I was a frog or related to frogs somehow because of the webbing between my fingers. I believed I could communicate with them. And so I went there, especially in spring, to watch them grow their little legs and arms. It seemed to be magic. But we were not allowed there for fear we would drown. Nevertheless, I snuck behind the barn and veered south to the pond whenever I thought no one was paying any attention to me, which was often enough.

This day, my father's boss and secretary were coming over. My mother was annoyed by the short notice, and so my father came home early to help with dinner and cleaning. When the guests arrived, they drank – wine and beer, gin and tonic. My sisters watched TV. Spring had a certain smell of life, of green, of sap running. And being inside was boring.

The pond shimmered, beckoning me. It was easy enough to go there. I only looked back once before I headed into the bush. No one was outside. They were busy. I skipped my way between the cedars until I arrived there. Then I lay down and leaned over a rock at the edge, talked to the tadpoles when I saw them. I put my hand in the water, skimmed the surface for the pleasure of the ripples. One tadpole had arms and legs and another only legs. They came to visit my hand if I wiggled it. Maybe they thought I was another tadpole. I stepped onto a rock in the pond. Many were rounded and slippery, so I was extra careful.

I went in right up to the red rubber stripe along the top of my boot. I didn't care about soakers. I tested the limit of it and went in a bit deeper such that the cold, spring pond water cascaded over the top of my boot and around my foot. I swore – I had recently learned the F-word – and pulled myself out of the pond, found a rock to sit on and hauled my boot off. It took a while because the boot was a little too small, and with the wet sock, it didn't want to come off. But I tugged until finally the suction popped.

A school friend had explained the F-word to me after I overheard her say it. She explained in graphic detail how babies were made and then leaned in conspiratorially and said – of Mum and Dad – that "they are probably doing it *right now.*"

That is how I came to know that people were just like other animals in this regard.

We came from eggs, just like frogs. We were amphibians. My webbing made perfect sense then. I knew the story about my great-grandmother by then, too. That she was found naked and shivering on a beach, bewildered and incoherent. Nigel watched the seals cavort for a time before he showed himself. By then he had already fallen in love with her and hidden the skin he had found lying on a nearby rock. She cried out when she saw him but could not swim away without her pelt. "You're beautiful," he said. But she did not understand his accent for she was different, from another place. I liked the look of my webbed hands underwater.

I yanked my sock down and wrung it out and then put it back on, then tipped the water out of my boot. I put my boot back on and went in the pond, selecting sturdy stones on which to balance. I was quite far out. I crouched again. The sun was low, the sky pinked. I hadn't heard the dinner bell. I planned to track back through the forest and come out on the other side of the barn so that no one would know where I'd been. Then I would toss the wet sock down the laundry chute.

But then the rock beneath my right foot tilted. I slid off it into the water and the stone slid back into place, trapping my boot. Because the water had swollen my sock, my foot was caught in my boot. I tugged but it wouldn't give this time. The rock was heavy and I couldn't move. For a while, I crouched and watched tadpoles swim in and around the rocks, waved my webbed fingers about admiring them while the stone pressed into my foot. I watched the tadpoles disappear and come back out. There were water striders, too, slipping like sprites across the surface. Then I got up and tried to shift the rock again, to pull my boot out or my foot out of my boot. The light was dying. I wondered whether my parents had noticed I wasn't around. Mosquitoes began to find me, whispering, their sharp proboscises inserting into my armpits, the soft skin of my neck, around my eyes.

I yelled a few times but the air lifted my voice and carried it deeper into the forest. I looked around at the moss on the stones beside the pond, the cedar deadfall. Boy lying on his side in the mossy undergrowth where I'd left him, tousled with the flat aromatic cedar leaves that covered the black earth there. It wasn't fairyland in this part. It was a still, forbidden place. The pond was nice and the forest was a good place for bad moods. I wondered if anyone cared that I wasn't home. I had scuttled away from their minds, receded or disappeared. I told myself not to cry. A painted turtle came up out of the dredge to dig a hole and drop her eggs. Boy watched her, too. It was effervescent at the pond. Nature was not concerned with us. To be forgotten made me not there – I was thought up and then erased.

"Kathryn?" It was my dad's voice. "Where are you? Kathryn!"

"I'm in here!" I called. "My boot's stuck."

I had to call only once. And there he was. He pulled the rock away easily and gathered me up.

"It's dinnertime."

"I thought you forgot me."

"No one ever forgot *you*."

"I thought you did."

He said I was brave. He never mentioned that I was not meant to go there alone.

For weeks I was too afraid to go back to get Boy, and when I finally snuck back there, it was with Frances, who knew how forbidden this section of the property was. And Boy was gone.

"He was right here," I said.

Frances shrugged. The pond was already half dried up, and the frogs were fully formed, googly-eyed. I'd seen many out on the concession, flattened by cars and desiccated. I looked all around the forest, but I never found Boy.

"A fox probably took him," said Frances. "Or a haunt." She peered into the forest, her hand shading her eyes as if to see farther.

"A haunt?" I said.

"Like a ghost," she said.

I did not mention Wulf. I did not say to her that I saw him sometimes, whisking through the forest or swimming. I did not say that I saw ghosts, too. What I said was "There is no such thing as ghosts, Frances."

He was named for an ancient poem, the earliest one in English. "Wulf and Eadwacer." It's a devilish poem to understand. No one seems to agree on whether it is about two lovers who are separated or a mother and her child. It is agreed that the narrator is a woman. "Wulf and I, we are different islands," it goes. It's a lament. She longs for him.

"I was thinking about Wulf again," I say to Mum when I come back inside. She and Dad are still at the breakfast table. "How you must have suffered when your milk came in. How your body must have felt all through that whole ordeal."

"It was a long time ago," she says and then just carries on reading.

Dad says, "Doctor Maes gave her pills for that."

"Still," I say, trying to be soft, to let her recall, to let her open to that old story.

"Still," she says back to me. "You're right. It was hard. I suffered. But there wasn't time. I got pregnant almost right away again. A joyous thing you were and then, so quickly, Maggie and Frances."

And then I venture too far and ask her what he looked like. I look at my hand and ask whether his fingers were webbed like mine. And she shakes her head, says she told me already. She never saw him. And what does it matter?

Dad gets up and walks away. He does not want to participate in these sharp recollections. They have edges that he is wise to avoid. But I am not wise.

I finish up my porridge and sit for a while, until it feels okay to walk away.

Then I return to my laptop, which is set up on a rickety porch table overlooking the yard to the west. The lawn is more meadow now, any plan to mow it hopeless with the weather. If we get a clear day, I will fire up the lawn tractor and save Dad the trouble.

I boot up my laptop. Ancestry.com has hints for me, which I ignore. I've been following the trail of the McIvers, the Murdochs, Boyt and the name Wulf. I've got reams of documents by now – church records of marriages, baptisms, deaths – and every one is a rabbit hole. After all this obsessive, expansive searching, I've got branches and sub-branches dating back to the 1600s. The line – via my mother – meanders back through Russell Boyt to a Jeffrey Hudson, a pituitary dwarf who famously entertained Charles I by leaping out of a pie. He was eighteen inches tall in full armour and perfectly proportioned, if the stories are accurate – the size of a doll, coincidentally. I think of Boy and the doll I have concocted for the Boyt story. They called Jeffrey Hudson Lord Minimus. At twenty-five, he fought and won a career-ending duel, and was then forced into twenty-five years of enslavement in North Africa. How much labour would have been plundered from a man not two feet tall?

I like the idea of Little Lord Minimus hauling tiny sticks for firewood and wee buckets of water. After Jeffrey, my mother's line does nothing extraordinary. They marry and work and die, leaving scant trace of their rituals and transgressions. I research until I am bleary-eyed and stupid with it. I punch in "selkie," "seal," "fairy tale" and get – predictably – nothing. It's silly but I try "Wulf Eadwacer."

"What's this?" I ask Mum, later that night. I catch her on the way up the stairs to bed.

"Can this not wait?" she says.

"Something popped up about Wulf." I show her the entry. "It's really an anomaly, the only record showing him. His death date but no paper record of burial and no birth certificate."

"Dad buried him. I was too sick to attend."

"Where? We could go together."

"I just can't think through that right now," she says. She turns and goes into her bedroom and shuts the door.

I call through the door that I am sorry if I'm too pushy, but it seems strange. It is strange.

DAY ELEVEN

THE RAIN IS SO THICK that none of us are able to leave the house. I spend hours in the basement making piles. The reek of animal is wicked, but I am determined to get this job done. Plus, I can't sit at the computer another day. I need to move and the rain has made that difficult. I stand while I work, triaging the accumulation of material objects into piles: keep, discard, donate. I do not thank any of these objects before I toss them. I am ungrateful, I suppose.

I come up for lunch and find that Dad has placed himself in front of the television, watching nature shows to assuage his yearning to be out walking the periphery. And Mum has been baking in between tirades about the "Christly weather," saying, "Will we ever get out again?" and, unkindly, "I can't wait to see the back end of you" – a jab in response to my line of questioning last night.

When I protest, she gets tetchy, says, "Call your husband, for God's sake."

I can't even with Mum, and so I press my feet into my Billy boots, grab a maimed umbrella from the back hall and head out. "I'm going for a walk to stretch my legs," I call as the door slams shut. I imagine they breathe a sigh of relief. We are all deadly tired of one another. Guests and fish, the saying goes, begin to stink after three days.

The pits and holes in the pathway are filled with rainwater. I can feel the cold of it seeping through my boots. I've never seen a more verdant spring. *Did*

I bring it on somehow? By way of an answer, the rain redoubles its efforts. There is no huddling away from it under this sad brolly, so I toss it and soak through, make it to one of the only oaks on the property, an ancient thing that stands bravely in a sway of sodden prickly ash. I keep more or less dry under the oak tree. I trace my finger along its trunk, the silver green lichen travelling there.

I received a text from Matthew this morning, offering me a financial deal as if I am a company he is buying out. And so, how to tell Mum that there is no going back, that going back would only be going forward, into some unknowable treachery? It is a case of once you know something about a person, it is impossible to unknow it.

In the hush of the forest now, the rain like white noise, I can finally hear myself think. How I need this water, is what I am thinking, despite the chill of it. It's like I am beginning to recall my roots with a liquid thirst. This business about Wulf, the fact of no birth certificate, no parish record of burial, it fuels my growing dread that he has been entirely made up. That I have made him up. That I can't stop making him up, as if his existence forms me, but I can't place how. That he is a long-dead creature who has tromped a pathway through me. That he is a trace fossil along my cortex. He was named and so he existed. Dad narrated him into something. A short indoctrination but still – and why must I miss him so?

You know, I thought about him a lot when I was young. I recall crouching in the woods, it must have been September, the year I turned seven. I was cradled in one of the cedar chairs, my hair long and ruddy brown, a rat's nest. My skin was blue-pink against the green-tinged forest light. I wore a yellow T-shirt and shorts. I'd entered the bush to an incredible stillness. I had never found the doll, and even still, I missed him, kept an eye out for him. I thought he might have been stolen by a fox or coyote and dropped elsewhere. The stillness started about three feet in, past the first trees, where daylight began to change to forest light and the smell of the air changed with it. There was a hush inside the space. It wasn't in the least gradual. It was like a portal. I was inside or outside, and there was no gradation between these places. I loved the feel of the mossy cedar cradle. Moisture wicked into my shorts. I shifted on the nubby bark, one leg swung over the languid trunk, deep in the ghost forest to the north of the house and behind the barn, where the trees were bound by the road and the forbidden pond. I liked the denseness of this kind of loneliness, the way it vibrated.

I would soon start grade two. I'd already met Miss Sally. She was nice. She wore miniskirts and white shiny boots with zippers all the way up to her knees. And now, among the cedar needles shed year after year were little shells, blanched brittle and white – hollowed out snail homes and calcified aquatic shells, and also honed shard-stones, which seemed like coins from long ago. I laid down and stared at the surface of the Earth, at all the small things there, attending them, marvelling at the particular shapes things could take and the frantic movement. The Earth was never still. It thrummed, and I had to find that entrancing rhythm in myself before I could see the creatures there.

I peered at the alien stones in the cup of my palm. I thought at the time they had been brought here, somehow imported as gifts to me. I conjured meaning for them. They were nestled in the little moss forests that clung to rocks jutting out of the forest floor. I watched a patch of moss growing on a nubbled stone, the way it sprouted little tiny trees. I waited for fairies – they moved so fast. And then the stone moved and I saw that it was in fact a beetle lumbering homeward. Doing its beetle-ish thing. It was possible to think a thing and be wrong about it. There were things that I knew had no explanation. There were things I saw that I just believed.

I knew by then that I could make things up and they would become real or real enough. That day, I began to tell myself a new story, about a giant owl. It was so real to me that I could feel the owl close by, swooping in to watch me make her up. I rocked my body on the trunk of the tree. The owl's wing tips were still fluttering on the edge of my mind when a boy – wearing a billowy dress shirt and shorts and black boots – arrived in the forest.

"Hello," he said.

"Are you Wulf?"

He smiled. "I don't know."

I told him pieces of the owl story, showed him how to track the bird along the pathways in the forest, how to notice it. And then, for days and days in a row, I met him and told him how the owl looked and what she ate and how she did not like to be seen. I grew to love the boy, could not easily fall asleep at night because my love menaced me. One day, maybe a week later, while we were deep in the property looking up at the massive tree trunk that I had decided was the owl's home, he began to cry out for fear the giant owl might bear down on us.

So I told him it had died.

"What?" he said, wiping his nose with his sleeve. "She just died?"

"Yes. Things die," I said, "all the time."

"Papa told me, too."

I was old enough to know I was being cruel with this lie, but I was so caught up in the joy of having someone believe my story that I showed him the burial site – a meadow at the front of the neighbour's property that I had just at that minute decided was the perfect site for this part of my story. "Her body fills the whole entire field," I said. I felt so good in the expansiveness of this lie. The truth would be worse. The boy would be devastated to discover his faith in my story was wasted. And so we stood at the edge of the field, and the owl story, even as it died, was amplified, for now the owl was dead and had truly grown enormous and real. All so long ago, I think now.

I am drunk now on this memory, standing in the forest where this story was birthed. Who was that boy? Did I make him up, too? The heavy rain has not stopped. It's been so exhausting, this leaving my marriage, this work of excavation with my parents. I hang my head and take deep sustaining breaths. I need to calm myself. I look up to see my dad, small and slow, walking toward me, as if he knows where I am, as if he has a kind of magnetic skill for locating me.

"Hi," I say, and when he is close enough to hear, "I wonder if it's possible to have too much freedom. To have *too* good a childhood. Was it normal that I was off on my own so much?"

"It was back then."

"I used to think I saw things in the forest all the time."

"You were always one for making things up," he says. "We should get out of the wet."

"I like the rain. It recalls the sea."

"There *was* a sea here, long before people."

"I know," I say. "I find that comforting."

"I've never been one for rain or water." He tells me then that he is going to help an old friend sandbag his place, east of here. Tells me the guy is terrified of losing his home, everything he's worked for, and what will he be if he can't even provide the basics for his family. And then we hear thunder rolling close by, from the west, a great boom coming up through the earth. And then lightning.

"This is terrifying," I say. "It's been raining straight for weeks."

"Yes, we've lost power again at the croft house."

"We have?"

"More than an hour ago."

"Does it worry you? The weather, the impending sense of climate doom?"

"I'm old," he says. He tries to leave it at that, but I jostle him.

"Come on, Dad." We are walking back to the house just as the sky cracks open around us. I know I am going to have to face Mum, talk this through, try to meet in some psychic middle ground. It will be a lie and I am girding myself for it.

"Why do you not go back? He never seemed that bad to me," says Dad.

"You've never lived in my skin."

"But how much more are you breaking things by doing this? Think of your sons," he says, as if he can read my anxiety like a treatise. This plagues me, this notion of imperfection. Not just what I have done but what I know to be true over what others think to be true.

"What about freedom?" I blurt.

But he is having none of it. "No such thing," he says, as if all of us have a binding contract to someone else's narrative. I can feel my face fold up. I work hard to veil a surge that runs rampant through me – fury, surety, future, trust that I will show them all what this perfect future can look like despite having no clue whatsoever.

"What was it like when Wulf died?" I ask.

"It was very sad," he says, a little too mechanically, too practised.

"Ancestry.com has no record of his birth or his death," I say. "Did Mum tell you?"

"The Google is not God," he says.

Earth will be moved, I think. The waters will pound the land, creatures we have never seen before will suddenly become prevalent. I will be one of them. And then we arrive home to find Mum in bed, sleeping. "She caught a fever," Dad says, tugging his boot off at the heel with the toe of the other boot. We are soaked through, have been swimming in sky. "Says her bowels are in disorder."

"She seemed fine this morning," I say.

"One of those swift illnesses, then. I'm a little worried about her. She seems suddenly so forgetful. She forgot a simple word this morning."

"What word?"

"Oh, I don't remember," he says, and we laugh about that.

Then he calls his friend. I can hear him placating the man as I walk past their bedroom to mine. I close and lock my door from inside. I do not know how long I stay there, the day so dark that night sneaks up on me. Writing holds me to the earth. It's ego, I suppose. As long as I am in control of the story, I *am*. Otherwise, all bets are off.

But forgetting words, isn't that dementia? And isn't dementia a bit like madness – without language can we even be civilized? I think about Boyt, his gears and mechanicals, as I have imagined him. The war, his bleeding leg, all that loss – civilization so antithetical to what he must have endured.

1864

MY LEG TWITCHED FIERCELY, A barometer to something I couldn't pinpoint. And of course, pain so engulfing I felt myself to be halfway dead, watching myself slip this mortal coil by degrees. I was feverish but thankful to the two privates who had picked me up and carried me to the makeshift hospital. They'd given me biscuit, which I ate lying on my back, trying not to notice the mealy worms already traversing my leg. The soldiers left me with good wishes, and I waited between a groaning bullet-ridden animal of a sergeant and a deadbeat soldier who looked more sullen than sick. I was becoming mechanical, and panicked, because now I would be assured a false limb, at least. Eb, the limb-maker, would come for me and we would further merge identities.

I waited, adjusting my tourniquet and digging out insects that had already found their way to me. I tightened the binding, peering at the shatterment that was my leg. I thought of Little Tiger in order to stop myself from thinking of Bellair. I willed myself to keep this calamity contained, despite the reality that Bellair and Little Tiger both seeped into my thoughts in horrifying ways. I was so alone. I thought about sending one of the privates back to the battlefield to try to find some trace, anything, of Bellair. But no. I would not do that. I knew I wouldn't. Each memory of the dead bled into other memories of the dead.

I thought of Eb again and wanted to laugh but nothing came of it. He would think this loss gloriously useful to him, and would make immediate material amends. The world would now make complete sense to Eb, after all. A compensatory prosthetic for my battlefield heroics. A substitute leg for a substitute soldier. The perfect twin to finish me now – his skill, my body. By proxy, Eb would be a war hero, too. I recalled the metal legs swaying from their factory hooks, awaiting inspection. What would Eb say?

"We shall have you up and whole again."

Well, I had never been whole, so that was laughable.

I imagined the scene back home. My own father would cry out when he saw me next, sure that if he'd been there, he might have saved my limb. God's work, he always liked to call doctoring. And with that came divine rights – to everything. But why would God let this happen in the first place, what stock did God have in misery and decay? There was a sound clanging about in my head, in my chest cavity, a great steel door sliding against a great steel wall. The wall and the door were ruddy with rust, and with each slide the whine of it shearing off went up my spine. The door opened and closed against the wall with furious regularity, the screeching a punctuation to the throb of my wrecked leg. This was death, I thought, the bad kind.

A farm boy lingered at the railing to get a look at the dying. I called out to him. I told the boy my name and the whereabouts of my tent, and instructed him to bypass the picket and sneak in under the flap to my cot in order to retrieve my haversack. I desired the doll and the money on my person in the event they evacuated me to wherever the half-men went to heal. In the fifteen minutes the boy was out on the errand, I became so panicked I lost feeling in my remaining limbs. But then the boy returned and told me to breathe deep for twenty breaths.

When I was finally hustled into the surgery tent, they offered chloroform. I declined even when the surgeon gestured at the tangle of limbs thrown beneath the operating table, arms and hands willy-nilly. Flies had already begun feeding upon them.

"I prefer to be awake," I said.

The surgeon was awfully young and skinny, harassed looking and bent nearly in half with some spasm to his lower back. "A poor decision, son."

"Wash your hands, first," I said. "If you don't mind."

"Hogwash," the surgeon said, "and a waste of precious time." I wondered if the doctor even had the strength to get the handsaw through me, and what would happen when his saw met with cast iron or steel. The buildup of rust I suspected was there, how my bone had accreted unyielding metal – rivets, pistons. What he might think of me then.

"Wash them even still," said I, resolute on this one point about cleanliness. I cited by page and journal volume the article from which the command I gave had been gleaned. I suddenly wondered if he was not a doctor at all but actually a butcher. I had heard rumours of such things transpiring out here in this devil's landscape.

"A medical man, are you?" said the surgeon, stepping back from me.

"Just half of one," I answered. Those attending laughed nervously because they thought I was referring to my missing leg. When I realized their misapprehension, I added, "I took an American Civil War Adventure Hiatus and have one year of training left. I'm from Upper Canada, sir."

Then the surgeon's head bolted up, his eyebrow arched. "Have you by any slim chance seen this operation performed, Private?"

"You've not?"

The doctor was sheepish. "No," he said. "I've been working from a treatise."

They devised a way to keep me seated when I told them I had seen it done once on a diabetic. They bound me to the jerry-rigged gurney and two privates were called in to hold me to the chair, so that I wouldn't, upon instinct, interrupt.

"Clean water and soap for handwashing," I said loudly.

The surgeon muttered about "time being of the essence."

I could hear the collective agony of the mutilated outside the hospital tent flaps, but what did I care? They'd pushed the hopeless cases to the side. People would die. They just would.

The doctor cut the flesh at my thigh in strips about five inches up, toward my groin. He measured with a piece of linen cut for this purpose and stained with the blood of former surgeries. The knife might have been cleaner, I thought, and sharper. The surgeon did unceremoniously swipe it on fresh linen when I wailed through my fever sweat for them to keep tidy. I saw no evidence of industrial materials in my bone and sinew, but I felt them all the same. I was ossified, thickened with matter and unhuman – a geode but with metal in place of gemstone. The war – this life – was insinuating itself into me. I was becoming a gun, cannon, buckshot, male, a man, a machine man. It was one of the first times I had ever been able to endure a whole surgery. Perhaps because it was my own.

The surgeon probed his finger into the wound and dug around for shrapnel and any obvious debris. I could see he was nervous. It hurt like hell, some stranger's finger rummaging around in me. I began a litany of citation to keep my mind occupied: "*Medico-chirurgical Review*, 1862, Volume 37, Quote: survival rates are seen to be 87 percent higher when proper hygiene, as outlined, is employed by compliant surgeries," and then I went into rote learning, the bones, the sinews: *tarsus, tibia, patella, fibula, soleus, plantaris, popliteus*. In between, I screeched out quotes from my professor, too: *Keep current with the journals, boys. Keep current!*

"Shut up, will you?"

A searing hot pain came from everywhere at once. I clenched and was wincing. It was deliriously painful. I thought I must truly be dying, but I was not. A complex mathematical calculus came to mind then. That pretty swirl of carnage in the field. Fibonacci, if memory served. Had I recalled it correctly? Let x equal x, I thought. Let me equal Eb, and I laughed with that substitution, since I would never be the same again. Eb equals me minus a leg. Eb = Russell – Russell's leg. There, that was it.

"What's your name?" said the surgeon.

"Eb," I said, and then, "Boyt."

The surgeon stood in front of me with his amputation saw aloft. "You are a difficult patient."

"I'm impatient," I muttered, thinking the pun very clever. "Corrosion, teeth, kerf, gullet, fleam." The handsaw menaced with its trace of filthy gore. "Clean that," I muttered, knowing they likely would not bother.

"Indeed."

I looked away as the surgeon sawed through the bone, then looked back to see that I was seeping fluid in spite of the tight binding they'd applied. The assistant doctor trimmed at my meat and arteries, then filed at the bone to soften its edges; they would truss me next and serve me with parsnips for dinner.

The surgeon sewed clumsily, and despite the pain, I found I couldn't stand to idly watch. So I struggled free of the reeking men holding me and slapped the surgeon off his stitching: *hough, femoral*. "Let me do it." The surgeon made noises but stepped away. After a time, he began to smile, watching me do my own needlework.

"Fine as a lady," he said.

"Did you see metal?"

"Metal?"

"Corrosion, you idiot! Gears, watch works and such."

The surgeon gave me such a look then. His clothes were gore-covered. "No, of course not, surely."

I handed him the long strand of cotton thread and the curved needle and fell back on the chair to watch him close up the last inch or so where I couldn't reach. I watched him douse the suturing with some ghastly ointment, then bind the thing in linens. "I need grease."

DAY ELEVEN

MATTHEW CALLS, INTERRUPTING MY WRITING. I pick it up before I look at the number and think better of it. He wants to know if I will reconsider.

"Reconsider what?"

"Our financial arrangement," he says. "Here's a better offer."

"Let's leave it to the lawyers," I say.

We muddle through a short conversation about the boys. He tries to guilt me by saying they miss me and are misbehaving. I suggest he parent them. This doesn't go over well. One of us hangs up. Not me.

None of the boys have my webbed fingers, I think dully as I look down on my own. They do not know how to long for freedom, I think. But that is not quite it, is it? For a selkie doesn't long for her freedom. She longs for her skin. She longs for an unheard-of autonomy. No matter what, there is loss; if she stays, she loses herself, and if she goes, she loses her children. They say my ancestor ran from home so many times that the extended family pooled their money and sent her and her husband packing to the new world. They did not admire Nigel's choice in women and felt that it might be best for them to begin a fresh life in Upper Canada. Where the ocean was but a memory.

In the old stories, the selkie finds her skin and leaves to the sea forever. She chooses the undulating life of the sea, where language fails her, where her human children cannot go. Like I said before, in some stories, she comes to visit them, peeking up at the surface of the water while they wave from shore. But isn't this precisely what it is to grow up? Isn't the mother always stranded watching her children and waving?

We are destined to live separate lives. Live on different islands, so to speak.

1864

Dear Cristiana, I am lying now in a cot in Harewood as the limb-maker I sub for has got me up here handily. And I have no one to write to. ~~Even this letter probably won't be sent for where would I send it?~~ Thank you for your ~~kiss~~ attention even if you meant it to manipulate me. It was attention I sorely needed. ~~I want to say~~ I have a photograph that belongs to you in my possession. Despite the fact that I am bleeding and bleeding and healing much slower than I should, I do intend to make it through alive, and when I do I will try to find you and I will return Henry Muldon's mother's likeness to you in person, not trusting the mails with such an object. I hope that Baby Charles is healthy and that you have found some safe place to carry on through the war. I want to make amends. I have developed some strange feelings that I cannot really understand, but if we should meet I will outline them to you. It is like a Great Gear is unwinding inside my bowel. God help me I have not been this strange-feeling in my mind in some years. Not since I was a boy at home, but that is another story for another time I suppose. Sincerely, Private R. S. Boyt, now mutilated in the leg. I guess you should know. Alack, the poor pup you gave to me is a war hero and I cry daily for him, for he was more stalwart than me.

I folded the letter and put it in an envelope. I asked the nurse to see if she could get it to a coloured lady by the name of Cristiana Muldon. The nurse's eyebrow raised in some kind of judgment.

She said, "The sutler comes by tomorrow. He would be a better option."

"What is your name again?" I asked. I found her pretty in a boyish way.

"Nurse Murdoch," she said. "Meredith, if you prefer."

I never called her Meredith. She seemed to suit the formality of Nurse Murdoch. "I'd be obliged if you didn't read the contents," I said.

"I can mention that to the sutler when I see him."

"Thank you." I inspected my swollen stump and rubbed my upper thigh; it had kept draining of pus and blood, for weeks now. "It's just a hard time or I would do it myself."

The man in the bed next to mine gave me an ugly look when the intern left with the letter. He said, "An epistle to a coloured woman, you say?"

And I made a hard face at him and said, "Mind your own business or I will smother you while you sleep."

"Why you –"

"And nobody will miss you."

I looked fierce. The man turned and swivelled his own bound leg-stumps to face the other side of the room.

When night fell and the other men slept or moaned, a kind of isolating calm came over me. I felt under my cot for my haversack and took out the porcelain doll and cradled it to my heart like it was a baby, mummified in strips of bed-clothes.

DAY TWELVE

"THE CIVIL WAR STUFF IS coming fast," I say to Mum. She's lying in her bed, looking a little befuddled. I don't mention yesterday's phone call with Matthew. I decide it's too much for her. Instead I keep to the writing news. "I worry about misrepresenting Cristiana. I mean I have loads of documentation, so I know more or less what happened. I know that Russell Boyt killed her, that he was suffering terribly from PTSD –"

"PTSD?" Mum sounds incredulous.

"Yeah," I say. "Post-traumatic stress disorder. They called it Soldier's Heart back then."

"I know what it means, honey, but he wasn't." She sits up a bit straighter in bed. I can see that her nightclothes are stained with food and drink from the day before.

"Mum," I say. "Let's get you into something fresh."

And while I root in her dresser, she drones on about Boyt and what she knows.

I'm stripping her and putting on a fresh nightie when she says, "Oh, his issues predated the war. He was unstable. He was diagnosed with Furious Mania. His parents disowned him a number of times because of incessant masturbation."

"Mum!"

"I'm not making this up. I have his mother's diary. She remarks on the diagnosis several times."

"Diary?!"

"I guess you'll want that, too, now."

"I am a bit curious as to why you haven't given this diary to me yet."

"I wanted to read it again first."

"To censor it?"

"Don't be ridiculous, Kathryn. I just wanted to reacquaint myself with it."

"Really?"

"What is your project about again? A book?"

"Yeah. A book." I tuck her back in. "Wait. Are you seriously telling me that the family disowned him for jerking off?"

"Well, spanking the monkey is a mortal sin, honey."

"What drivel is this?"

"Can I ask you something?" she says. "Do you have feelings for your characters? Is that the normal thing with writers? I feel as if I read that somewhere."

"He isn't a character, Mum. He was a real, live person." I am talking out my ass, here. Even on Ancestry.com he is a footnote, not much more than that. I have made him up, made up his fury, filled it in with my own. "We have that one letter," I say.

"You're getting worked up. It's ancient whatchamacallit."

"History?"

"That's right. Ancient history."

What Dad had said about her losing words. "Are you okay, Mum?"

"It's just a lot lately."

"I know."

"The flood. The waters."

Is she obfuscating, or has she forgotten?

"I'm so happy you can swim," she says.

"You are?"

"Yes."

We go back to our own corners of the house then. I go downstairs and reread the letter my mum received all those years ago.

And then I come back to her. "One more thing," I say.

"Yes?"

"I'm sorry I brought him up." We both know to whom I am referring.

"It's okay, honey. I'm sorry it's all such a big deal for you."

When mum says this, my heart seems to curl up into a ball to shield itself from harm.

"Where is that diary?" I finally get out.

"Oh, it's somewhere, I suppose. Must be."

Another dead end, another secret, I think. I head back down and outside. I want to sit at the pond to watch the ripple of action at its surface, to peer in and see what life it harbours, but the pond is washed out. So I go farther up and into the woods. I nestle in a cedar chair like I did when I was a kid, and in the distance, I spot a glint of white on the forest floor.

"Boy?" I say, because I am suddenly so sure that it is my lost doll.

But it isn't Boy, of course. It's a puffball, dirty and swollen with all the moisture it's getting. It is larger than my own skull. I take some sick pleasure in kicking it.

DAY FIFTEEN

I SPEND SOME TIME AT the local library on Ancestry.com making notes and putting names into search engines in the hope of finding anything new. I spend a good hour looking up Wulf, again. I find nothing. I try inputting Baby McIver, Baby Murdoch, Baby Hudson even, but nothing comes up. I do a Boolean search. Nothing. The phantasm of my brother is therefore not legible in the archive. He simply isn't. Eventually, I close down my computer and watch the landscape whir past, watch traffic trundle by the window. When I finally get home, Mum is still in bed, looking pale.

"What's going on?" I ask.

"Oh, it's so painful. Your father had to walk me to the bathroom this morning, going so slowly. Every movement, every one, is just terrible."

"Oh, Mum."

"Can we not talk about it?"

"Sure."

And then there is nothing but silence between us for some minutes. I sit beside her wondering what possible solace I can offer. "How is your project coming along?" she says, eventually. It is a wee voice emerging out of the comforter, which she has pulled up to her nose.

"Slowly," I say.

"I shouldn't be standing in the way of your process. I really shouldn't. I don't know what's gotten into me. I guess I'm scared of what you might find. Can you read some of it to me?"

I take this to mean she really wants to help. So I read her the last section. And one of the memory sections. When I am done, she is asleep, which feels bad enough, but when she wakes up a few minutes after I stop reading, the first thing she does is snort and say that she thought I was writing memoir and not fiction.

"Autofiction," I say.

"It comes across like bad faith."

"I can edit out the bits you don't like."

"Oh, for heaven's sake." She is all bluster, even in her frailty. "Eva's diary is just there in the bookcase," she says, her hand emerging to point. "I finished rereading it this morning. There's nothing much in it. It's mostly daily memoranda about what she hopes to accomplish, but here and there she writes a juicy sentence."

The diary is calfskin and brittle to open, the paper so dry it threatens to turn to dust upon touch. "Can I borrow it?"

"I would have given it sooner, you know, but I didn't want to distract you from the memoir."

"Okay, okay," I say, even if clearly her modus operandi has always been to distract me. There are newspaper clippings of recipes and a few letters tucked in between the pages. A photograph slips out. "Who's this?" I say, and hold it up for Mum.

The image is of a landscape: a few trees, an Edwardian house and in the foreground, a man in a felt hat, a woman laughing and a boy. The man is wearing a suit of what looks to be very fine wool.

"Your great-great-grandmother Murdoch," she says, squinting. "And the man who eventually married her and adopted her son by Boyt, the one he never knew existed. Nigel. Remember that the nurse Boyt knocked up ended up going to live in England to avoid her shame in Ohio, where she hailed from. And lucky for her, she found a generous financier in London to marry her despite her out-of-wedlock child."

I peer into the picture in hope of eking more information from it. The face of the boy is plump. If there is a family resemblance, it's hard to say.

"Do you think Boyt loved her?"

"I think that he was as mad as a hatter. And that she was lonely and perhaps wanted a baby."

I think about how it's Mum who wanted a baby, that this is her projection, and the image of this laughing boy and the mention of babies has me reaching too far again. "Would you ever want to go to his gravesite?" I say. I mean my brother, and she certainly knows this.

She looks up at the ceiling for a while, then turns her face to me. She begins a kind of onslaught designed to get me to leave her alone. "Nigel and his wife, her name was Connie, are buried in the old pioneer cemetery on Highway 62, and I am tired of all these questions. They may have made me sick, you know. I've had enough." And then she turns very mean, indeed. She says, "That evening your father's boss came to dinner, when you got stuck in the pond. Do you remember? Well, we had all had too much to drink. And I was so annoyed with your crying over that doll that when they left, I went out to see if I could find it."

"What? But you said –"

"I know what I said."

She waves me away with a fluttery hand. "Parenting books at the time suggested that children shouldn't get too attached to things, and that doll, well, it was so disturbing lying there by the pond, like a real dead child face down in the dirt. Imagine how I felt! I picked it up and held it for a minute. And then I went to the barn and got a shovel. I guess it's still buried out there under the crabapple tree with the cats."

The cat cemetery is at the margin of the north lawn and the bush, near the barn. Mum gave me the general coordinates of where she buried the doll before falling back to sleep. Mercifully, the rain has slowed to a drizzle. I press the blade of the shovel into the earth. The first thing I exhume is the old cat Marbles. The skull is eerie, its teeth still sharp and gleaming. After all these years, there are still tufts of fur and the few pennies we buried with her. Mum has not recalled precisely how deep she dug, so I go down several feet before I begin to nudge the earth up and scrabble it away with my hands. The earth is cold. Finally, I catch sight of some fabric soaked in yellow-brown moisture. I know it to be the receiving blanket I'd always wrapped about him.

"Boy," I say, to no one.

I use the shovel to pry back the sod and gently dig until I know I must be close to the doll. A heap of earth has accumulated beside me. Anyone happening upon me would be excused for having morbid thoughts. I look up to see Dad watching from the back door, waving. He pushes the door open and calls, "You need any help?"

"I'm okay. I found him."

I poke a hole into the earth and nudge my hand in, over the doll, and then I do the same with my other hand. I feel around until I grip the doll's outer edges and then slowly, gently pull him toward me – like a birthing. Even though I've been careful, when the earth finally gives up the doll, he tumbles away from my grasp and falls down into the area I've dug out. I worry he will be broken but he isn't. He lands face up on my Billy boots. The cloth wrapping him is a half-eaten rag. I lift him up to find much of him decayed: his porcelain hand falls away, his feet and his other hand hang by the thinnest gauzy linen remnant. I pick up his hand and put it in my lap, then I put the rest of him on the grass so that I can inspect him.

There is almost no body left to him. The jacket and trousers are worm-eaten, and the straw that was used to stuff him is wet and mouldy to the point of being compost. I turn him over and over. I scrape what I can of what has become more earth than doll. I smile at his face, though. It's just as I remember. I get up and go back into the house to get a towel. Then I return and gather up his pieces.

I wrap him in a bundle and set him on the back stoop before heading back to the mess I've made of Mum and Dad's lawn. I shovel dirt back into the hole until its filled, cover over the cat skeletons, the pennies we left there.

"Why would you bury the doll there, Mum?" I ask when I am back inside.

"I don't know, honey. I wasn't thinking straight, I guess."

And why didn't you admit you knew there was a doll is what I don't ask. She's lying in bed still, looking ashen. Dad is worried because it'll be a chancy thing to drive out in this weather, but she likely needs to see a doctor. She's getting worse, not better. "It's okay, Mum," I say. "I understand." And I mean it. She must have been pretty upset to dig a hole for a doll when she could more easily have tossed it in the trash or donated it to the Salvation Army. She hadn't been to Wulf's burial, hadn't even met him. I want to think there was some healing in this act.

"I can drive you to the hospital," I say.

She looks suddenly like a frightened child. "No," she says. "I will be okay. I just need to rest. Get my wits together."

"I'll be in my room if you need me, then." And I take Boy into the bathroom and clean him up. The doll looks real, the eyes the sort that open and close. They still work. Before I write, I fiddle with the eye mechanism until he works like new, his soft painted cheeks crazed along the porcelain. He's lovely, I think.

1864

THREE WEEKS INTO MY RECOVERY at Harewood General Hospital, Eb Wilkes showed up and stood before me, and, just as I expected, he was full of untold glee. "Can I sit?" he said. Then he perched on the edge of my cot just where my leg would have been if I still had one. "We've got to measure you up, Russell," he said. "That's right."

"I am suppurating oil," I said.

"Oil?"

"Fluid."

"Never mind. I can adjust for the swelling. I've seen this before."

"My plan," I told him, "is to head home as soon as possible." I'd had all the time in the world to think this through. I would spend the last two semesters of my medical training in style. Find a commodious apartment in a rooming house, one where they cooked for you. I had all that money tucked into the back of the doll, enough to finish my training and start something. I would specialize in the least unpleasant house doctoring I could. Man midwifery, or something along those lines. I wished only that the thin screech of dry gears would stop shuddering through me.

"Of course, of course, you want to head back north," said Eb. I watched his face contort as he peered at the knot of scar and fleshy disaster that was my former leg.

"I will need a leg of exceptional quality," I said.

"That goes without saying. You are as me. Your pain is mine. Your success is my joy." Eb pinched the measuring tape at one end and drew it along my thigh. He measured the diameter of the stump, took the inside and outside measurements of my intact leg. He worked quickly and in such a way that gave me confidence in him. My leg still hurt and I experienced horrid phantom limb. It made me realize how the things that leave us never really disappear. I began to think what a messy thing the human mind is. It can never let anything go, can it?

"It will be articulated at the knee, I trust," I said. It must have been fated for me to lose a leg whilst substituting for a limb-maker. It was like a bad joke into which I had hobbled.

"Right here will be a ball joint for utmost agility," said Eb. "The ankle – let me show you." He took my ankle and demonstrated the range of motion I could expect from my new appendage.

I wondered if the leg could be attached to my femur, where it had ossified to metal. But I did not quite know how to pose my question, so I stayed quiet.

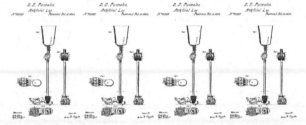

"Limb-making has become an advanced craft, Russell." Eb placed his hand over his heart and beamed. He was a really genuine sort of person. The kind that can make others cynical. "I am so very proud to be able to provide this service to you," he said, girded suddenly, it seemed, by some fantastic vision of valiant warfaring. "*So* proud."

I did not see what there was to be so proud of. I had taken a beating and had shot others. I would have preferred not to have done any of this. I would have liked to have never seen war, or even known anything about it. It had been nothing but gut ache and dysentery and watching the dead untether from this Earth, and it had been this awful grinding all through me. Nurse Murdoch walked

115

toward us, followed by the sutler, who had left his cart of overpriced trinkets to come along in person. He had a letter.

The nurse nodded to the limb-maker. "Morning, sir."

"A fine one."

"The sutler wanted to deliver the letter himself." Nurse Murdoch rolled her eyes. "He wants his extortionary tithe, you know."

"The widow Muldon asked for security," the sutler said, poking his tongue into his bottom teeth.

I was reminded of Henke in his last moments, how he paused to steel himself as if he had figured out some solution to living – and that solution was to die. The sutler's solution was money; money as a bulwark to this life. I looked at the pretty bird-scrawl on the envelope. I pulled my wallet from my haversack and handed over a coin, and then, when the sutler didn't move, I handed him another. Nurse Murdoch mouthed that she was sorry and shrugged her shoulders. What could she do? I waited for her and the sutler to leave, then I tucked the letter under my bedroll and returned my attention to Eb. "At what price does the top model come?"

"Oh, mercy me," said Eb. "My father and I wouldn't dream of charging you, Russell. Good Lord in the wild capacious heavens, no." Eb rubbed his hands over his face and through his hair. "The government subsidy for your loss you must also keep for yourself."

"That's kind," I said. I thought of my leg festering in the field and wondered whether anyone might have buried it. A part of me was perhaps already winging up to heaven; did the soul depart piecemeal for those in my situation? Was the soul dissipated throughout man's body or was it housed somewhere, in some particularly lively part – the heart, the lung, the pituitary gland – and unleashed when the whole perished? "I'm so thirsty, Eb." My moiling innards, let me be released from them, I thought; let me drink some medicine that would stop this. "Is there something that can cure this?" I whispered to Nurse Murdoch when she came back around. Eb's eyebrows came down in a perplexed squint. Had I said something wrong?

"Cure what?" she said. She was flirting, I see that now. The button at her neck was undone where normally it was not and she smiled overmuch at me. I admit to feeling that this was all very nice.

"This deliberation. This. This. This grinding, eking rasp." I glanced at my torso.

"Hush!" she said, and looked around to see if I had upset the others. "I'll find you a compress.

"That's kind," I said.

"Oh," said Eb, and it came out a shrill sort of squeak. Where he sat on the edge of my cot, the spring coils sang an ugly song, then settled.

"A leg will do," I said then, to calm the room of my outburst.

Eb swallowed nervously. "I can't help but think what might have happened to me if Father had not been able to afford a substitute."

"Eb Wilkes." I laughed, and even for me it was a sudden, unexpected laugh. "You would have fought like a tiger. You would have wrought untold havoc. The war would be won; the pastures red with your glory. There you are, and there you are, and there you are." I pointed and pointed into the distance, glad to have the subject changed.

It was madness, my gestures designed to erase the debauched and wanton killing with broiling moody cloud and undulating hopeful flags, fife and posturing. The truth was, my brain was awash in blood and effluent, but I could fake things for Eb, who should never know more than the sepia of news reportage and ambrotypes. Media drained the whole story of its gore. I did not want Eb to know; I wanted to bear the load for him if I could. "You are everywhere with your sabre and your spirit," I whispered. "There is no enemy who sees you first. Valiant man!" I was exhausting myself in the performance.

Eb stared into the nowhere, glazed over with some notion of a vigour he did not himself possess, then he recovered. He smirked and said, "Doubtful, Russell, highly doubtful," then he lifted up and fussed his clothes to straighten them out. "Good day," he said and left.

The visit had wearied me. I drowsed off to sleep until Nurse Murdoch yelled, "Stop that." I woke, trigger pressed and wild-eyed, looking around for whomever it was I must stop. But there were only men groaning and sleeping or staring, and Murdoch pressing down on me with her torso, pinning my chest and leaning on my throat, telling me to shut up, sir. My neighbour in the next bed recoiled from me with utmost fright.

Nurse Murdoch had me pinned to the mattress as best she could. A bearded volunteer appeared carrying ropes and asking if he should tie me to the bed. My brain was still sluggish in dream – there was no accounting for the thick thoughts accumulating and the swift scene changes. A nightmare but in the day. I was being strangled again and again. I could not slough Bellair's explosive disappearance. How he was so utterly embodied and then just gone, shattered, wet and nowhere. Did each droplet of viscera hold some caged soul fragment, perhaps? The nurse's pretty face hardened. I felt her push my hand away from where I'd run it up her skirt. I was still struggling against this nightmare that felt so real.

"How could you?" I yelled, thrashing around. "I will kill you! Give me that. Won't you?"

She glared at me and then said in a steely voice, "Behave or you'll find yourself tied right to that bed, sir!"

That was when I woke up fully. I found I had an erection, bone-hard and aching – what ghastly eros was this? – until it collapsed to dough. "Oh God," I said. What a sad sorry state I was in. The inside of my brain was clockwork, only rusted and behind time. It would never catch up, I thought. And then my body fell into soft weeping.

The pretty nurse petted me and said, "Now, now. That's okay. It was only a dream, private sir."

"Oh God," I said again. "A nightmare. A reliving-of-the-war sort." In my dream, I had been throttling some beggar reb to the very death and Bellair was marching in the distance, like an automaton, a huge grown man toy soldier awash in his own blood. I slumped at the dwindling recollection, felt that loss as a pin to my heart. "Have you ever felt alone?" I asked the nurse. She was neither blond nor red-haired but something in between and attractive. Her face, her arms and her entire legs, where I had felt her, were all befreckled.

"Yes, sir," she said. Her lips were so thin they made a sad cut across her face. "I've been lonely my whole life, I guess."

"What do you do for that?"

"Well, I work and I pray."

"Does it help?"

"Not always."

"I'm sorry my hand strayed," I said.

"It's okay."

She looked like Jessamine Peabody in profile. I could see the tangle of blue arteries running under her skin. I said, "You're pretty." I don't really know what had got into me. I was so untethered.

"Only to delusional men," and she laughed. "Now, settle back." She told me she would get me a cold cloth to ease my discomfort – for it was true that I was burning up. My whole leg ached again. I recalled I had but half a leg now, and I wanted more than anything to find Bellair and die with him, for surely that would ease the passage. To be obliterated together. Even as I thought it, I knew it was senseless. Nurse Murdoch left, and I pulled the covers aside and unwrapped the stump to see if I could clairvoyant a kind of future in the lumpy scars; surely, it was a tangled oracle if only I could read it.

The future was certainly bleak. I inspected the spidery suture and the angry puckers where the thread knots had been – these were hateful to me. I spent some minutes pushing the edges of the wound wherever I saw pus, dabbing it with the selvage of the dressing. There was less pus every day. This offered me some physical relief. I thought I could detect a trail of corrosion in the pus, though, and this signalled something strange – an industrial future where I would simply be the factory of my*self* – and a deep agitation arose. Could a machine die? I hoped so.

I pulled my haversack from under my cot and located my flask. I poured capfuls of whiskey onto my stump wherever the cut was not yet closed and sucked in for shock as the fluid entered the incision. Be damned if I would let it go septic.

"Wasting good drinking water," my neighbour said. I had not known I was being scrutinized. I remember I turned and scowled.

"I have such crowding thoughts," I said. The strangeness of this, or the look on my face, shut the man up. My haversack gaped like a fish's mouth and I saw the doll's white porcelain cheek. I stared at my neighbour with some awful mixture of menace and bereavement until the man turned away in mortification. Then I fingered aside the cloth that wrapped the doll's face and traced along its features – drawing across its eyes and nose and mouth as if it were a real child and not artificial. I was careful to keep the doll well hid, deep in the walls of the haversack.

Nurse Murdoch returned. "What have you got in there?" she said. She was a few feet from the end of the cot. "You have such a look about you."

I rolled the haversack to close it. "An old bundle of letters is all. Nothing much."

She perched on my bed and had me lie back while she applied cold wet towels to my face and neck and one to my chest. She had a bowl of ice – I had not seen ice for months – that she used to cool the cloths over and over.

She left the basin of ice next to me and, until it had all melted, I reached in again and again for shards to suck on and to let transubstantiate on my chest. The water tingled as it thawed and ran down my stomach and onto the bedding. It was so cold it seemed to cut me in half. It was nice to feel something other than the ache of sutures on my stump and the careening neural pain associated with the amputation.

She returned that night when the hospital was quiet and everyone asleep. I woke to find her beside me. She shushed and nestled into me. "It's true, I'm so lonely," she said, and she put my hand on her thigh where it was warm.

"I do not love you," I said, and she said that was okay. She did not love me either. We did what people do and nothing came of it. But it felt good to enter something soft for a time, and I was grateful to be undone inside of her. She was kind to me in an unkind time. She never seemed to care that I was half a man and missed my leg. She was gone in the morning as if it had not ever happened, and neither did she ever come to lie with me again. I thought for a long while that I might have fabricated it. I was not well.

The next day and the day after, I suffered this fever. In my delirium, I thought I might write a manual when I was well enough. Some of the time I felt calm, the rest of it I obsessed about gears and inner pulleys and sufficient oil and how to maintain myself in this state. I ruminated on all things: on Bellair and Little Tiger, on how very wet and dismaying death and sorrow were. I watched my leg being sawed in my mind's eye and smelled that smell all over again – the special odour of bone dust. And viscera. I thought of Eb and how clean his suit had been, how precise his measurements – crotch to heel, heel to toe, the circumference of my remaining thigh. So efficient and confident and without pity or even without really noticing how changed I was. It must be writ large. Then I thought of Nurse Murdoch and then of Cristiana's lips on mine. All these thoughts oppressed me, as if they had all happened at once and had never stopped happening. My head kept thinking and puzzling the nonsense of it all. I needed exercise, something to clean my brain out.

And then I remembered the letter the sutler had brought. I reached under my pillow and pulled it out.

> *Dear Pte R Boyt. Thank you for your letter. I am pained to hear word of your war wound and have commenced praying for your speedy recovery. My son and I have indeed relocated away from the pathway of fighting. He is healthy. Please do send the photograph of Charles's sweet grandmother, which we want for our family safekeeping. If you have any other such items that belong to me, please send them as well. Please get right with me also for your own sake. God is watching over us all. Much obliged. C. Muldon.*

She did not include a return address, but the letter was faintly infused with the perfume of her body stink. I gloried in sniffing it and was determined to personally direct the photograph to her own hand. I wanted to think that I would give the doll back, too. The money was out of the question, though. I had it spent every which way. What a man could achieve with such a sum. I read the letter three more times. I made a plan that I would heal and then would find her. I would make her understand that I would fetch her once I had set up house back home. I would say she was my housekeeper. This arrangement would be tolerated.

In the weeks before Eb returned with my limb, I learned to manoeuvre with the help of a crutch so very well that, when it arrived, the prosthetic slowed me down some until I got used to it. Eb also handed me a tidy wad of money to aid me in my studies, he said, and as a kind of hopeful retainer that I might be induced to the limb industry once my degree was to hand. But all I could think was that this sum was nothing but blood money. I tried to push it back.

"Please, I do – must – implore you," said Eb. "We can always use a physician." He clutched my shoulder so hard I had to stop from flinching.

The cash made me another seven hundred dollars richer.

DAY SIXTEEN

IT'S AFTER MIDNIGHT WHEN I finish writing. It's not exhaustion that stops me but a whine I hear from my parents' bedroom. I tiptoe to their door and it's quiet. I hold my breath for a few seconds, listening, and there it is again, a strange plaintive cry. My mum, dreaming or wincing in her sleep. I turn the knob and, as quietly as possible, go to her.

"Mum," I whisper. "Mum." When she stirs, I ask her if she needs to go to the hospital. I am still dressed, wide awake, and can easily get her there.

"Is it still raining?"

"Yeah."

"I'm fine."

"You were making this strange noise."

"Your father says I do that, too. I have no idea."

"Like a kind of sorrowful call."

"I'm fine. Go to sleep. I'm fine. Really."

I sit there for a bit until I am sure she is back asleep. Then I go to my room, power down my laptop and try to sleep. There has been so much rain that now the sump pump is running continuously. I hear it engage, the gurgle of water moving. I don't think Dad has been down there in a few days. It occurs to me that someone better check it just to make sure we aren't flooding.

The lights flicker and stay on. I go down with my boots on, which is a good thing because the floor is muck. It's looking like if the rain doesn't stop, the basement will soon be underwater. It's groundwater from farther north. The streams and lakes are engorged and the groundwater keeps rising. I heave a few Tupperware bins off the wet floor and onto a shelf and stack some cardboard boxes on top of them.

Wet has entirely seeped into the walls – they are dripping, and the smell of fetid animal is strong again. I suppose there are any number of mouse and rat and chipmunk families scrambling for their lives in this weather. But this odour seems too big for a rodent's death. It's overwhelming. I pull an old Singer sewing machine out from behind a paint-chipped table. I yank a boiled wool coat from where it's wedged on the floor between a couple of old chests. It's moth-eaten and mouldy, and it looks like something circa 1920 or so – a women's coat, purple, with big buttons and a bit of flair at the bottom. I wonder which ancestor wore it.

Stupid to have left it down here. I'm getting deeper into the hoard at this point, closer to the walls since I started weeks ago, more or less, in the middle of the room, working out in all directions. I've hauled quite a lot upstairs by now, too, and set it in a pile for when we can get a bin delivered. Behind the coat, which I have placed on the stairs to bring up, is a stash of shoeboxes filled with documents, photographs, stamps, old passports – all of it ruined by damp. The ink is cloudy and unreadable and the photographs are rotted. None of it could be salvaged even if I wanted. The whole of this business of cleaning up is starting to piss me off. Why was everything kept without any attention to its preservation?

It absolutely reeks down here. The spores of whatever is degrading this smelly thing are probably killing me right now, but I'm drawn in nonetheless. I stand and try to calm my nerves. I'll get what I can save off the floor, is what I am thinking. And quickly. The pelt smell is suddenly stronger. Maybe the groundwater harbours the dead. I scramble to pull a mess of old newspapers – tied with baler twine – away from a puddle forming on the ground. As I yank them out of their spot, a curious heap of oil, or slick, or some blackened thing reveals itself. And that smell! It's both awful and glorious. Something crammed like a rag into a mortared seam along the wall. I know that the early settlers used whatever was on hand for insulation, but this is not that. I reach in and it's soft.

Then there is a strange feeling of recognition. It's as if I have located a piece of myself. I let the smell of it waft up at me. It's a skin. I hold my phone over it and scan. I pull it out farther. It comes quite easily and I spread it on the floor and over my lap, too. It is wet in patches, black. Grey where it is still dry. Seal. The flippers are intact and the eyes are missing, of course. It's human-sized, a massive sealskin. I look at my fingers against the skin, line them up along the flippers. It is gamy and rain-soaked, and something so familiar it is as me, as my mother, my grandmother, my great-grandmother – a helix of self so old it's magic.

My whole body is shaking. Because, of course, this particular skin has its own story. The story of my great-grandmother who was herself a seal-woman, as Mum has recounted, plucked from the ocean by my great-grandfather. Stolen from her family, her watery home and all the completeness of her very self. He needn't have hidden it here, to be honest. There is no escape, no water hereabouts, only stone outcropping and clay dirt. Shield. Barely a creek that doesn't run dry when summer comes. My great-grandfather, leery of losing his beautiful selkie wife, well, he might have left the skin out in the open for all the landlocked good it might have done her here.

It's nonsense. Children's silliness. But in the metaphor, there is surely something for me, for all us women. I tuck my nose into the pelt. Hidden, secreted, a little key, it seems to me, that needs turning.

I wrap the skin into a bundle and stumble upstairs to the living room. My parents are still sleeping. I lay the skin out on the floor as a surprise for them when they awaken. Objective proof that the seal story is lively. I lie down on the couch next to it, the sun already pushing the night out, a thin orange line on the horizon that blinks out as the rain resumes full throttle. And I fall asleep to the shush of rain and wind cascading down the cedar shingle roof. I am out and gone just as my eyes close.

When I wake, the house is humming, the sweet perfume of diesel on the air. It's the generator, it turns out. The electricity has again failed; the sump pump stopped sometime between when I exited the basement and when I fell asleep. The water has meandered up the ground and wandered between the stones, lapping like an old lake against the foundation walls. The basement is deluged, anything I was unable to get off the ground either floating or sunk. And the seal pelt I laid out for them on the carpet beside me is gone.

When I ask, Dad squints and says, "What?"

"The ancient selkie lore, though," I say, something in my heart breaking. "A sealskin. I found it," I whisper. "I found it tucked in the wall of the basement."

"Twaddle," claims Dad. "You've dreamt it, dear."

"I want it back," I say.

"I'm not sure how to help you."

"I know it was there. I'm not losing it." The smell lines my nostrils with the raunchy perfume of abattoir and sea salt.

"It's gone, though."

"Please."

He shakes his head. "There's no point. It'll lead to no good."

"But –"

"But nothing. Your mother has taken a turn for the worse. I'm taking her into town in the truck. If I make it."

"And if you don't?"

"I'll die a hero."

"That's very funny," I say.

There's a terrible and unmistakable noise from upstairs. I look at Dad, who is laughing. It is then that Mum glides down the stairs fully dressed and looking better than I have seen her in a week. "I feel great," she says.

"We thought you were dying."

"Just a spot of gas," she says.

"You farted?"

"If you want to be vulgar about it, yes."

The two of them are laughing now. But I am not. I furrow my brow and tell Mum about the sealskin and ask where it went to and why they don't want me to have it. I ask them why that thing was tucked into the foundation wall. I ask them why in the hell the family has kept this thing and kept it hidden since time immemorial. I demand to know why a fairy tale should feel so threatening to them that they have to dispose of its evidence.

"Don't be stupid, Kathryn," says Mum. "Your father came upstairs to tell me that we were heading to the hospital. Apparently, I am forgetting things, but I wouldn't have forgotten that, now would I? He said you'd laid out the mouldy remains of what looked like a dead animal on the living room floor like some madwoman, and I told him to clean the damn thing up. It was the only sensible thing to do. Furthermore, lest you get more thick in the head with this, we have decided that today is the day that you leave. The way is being cut off for you. The main arteries are severed by the water. You'll be fully stranded here if you don't get out soon. And besides that, your father and I feel strongly that it's time for you to face the music."

As I take the stairs, I can still hear her ranting, but in diminishing returns. I turn into my room, slam the door, open my computer and shove in my earbuds. I crank Gould playing Goldberg's Variations on Bach, but she is outside the door banging, listing every good reason I should go home, make amends before the world ends. My parents are lying to me. My discovery clearly upsets them. The story about the selkie ancestor who left and left again is too close to home. They want me gone, and they want me to relinquish this old tale. It makes no sense, but I know how good it felt to be in proximity to that ancient pelt, to its old story. It felt as if I was entirely whole.

1865

THE LEG ARTICULATED AT THE knee. It had a strap that I could leave outside my trousers or fish up underneath them to pull on if I needed to bend the thing. It worked tolerably well but chafed the tender thickened skin at the amputation site. A piece of my soul had certainly been dismembered with the leg. I fixated on my body, replete with fury. I imagined my leg always lying beneath me – a dead thing – with the remorse a person ought to feel upon losing a close relative. I was so full of myself in those days. I curled my toes that were not there and marvelled at that magic – the realness of all things that were not real. Perhaps none of this was real at all. Perhaps my life was a prosthetic. Artifice. A made-up thing.

This was a thought I wanted to get away from. I ran my hand down the false leg. It was certainly fancy. The toes were burnished whalebone, modelled perfectly, with bucktoothed toenails carved in them. I sat up and slipped a boot over the fake foot and another over my good foot and got up, steadying myself with my hand on the mattress until I was less dizzy without my crutch. I pulled the strap attached to the limb's thigh and used it to manoeuvre my leg, and in this way I limped up and down Recovery, the other men's eyes upon me – envy, pity, some kind of hate I could not quite place. A kind of air-thick grief hung about me. If none of this was real, I would master the dream that was my life. I had no choice, it seemed. I could not shake myself awake. Or when I did, another worse dream was there to take this one's place. What a living disaster I was in those days.

I walked with my new leg three times each day for two weeks. Every night I pledged to leave the next day, but each day I failed to follow through. I knew I must bide my time until I was healed enough to set forth. During the nights, I fought sweats and all manner of demons. I fantasized or dreamed of body parts, of blistering wounds, of sudden enemies, and woke sometimes to find Nurse Murdoch or one of the orderlies lying on me, yelling at me to awaken. Once or twice they tied me to the bed for fear of what I might do. I was violent and unruly. We never dallied again, she and I, and when I once mentioned it, she looked queerly and hushed me. But I could see her shame.

Still, I could not be trusted.

I am sorry to say that I was so unpredictable that, in some way, I was grateful to be bound. I was not the only soldier with this ailment. I had seen one soldier slit the throat of another in some unspeakable delirium. I sometimes wondered whether we would ever finish fighting this war. "Tremors," madness brought on by war – "Sissiness," one of the doctors had sneered when I had trouble calming myself. Soldier's Heart, another said. Soldier's Head, more like it.

I could not keep things straight.

The day I left was fine weather. I had tried to strangle the man in the bed next to me twice that week, waking from sickening war dreams that I could not exit. They bound me those times. But on this day, in some stupid belief that I was well and hale, knowing I would escape this place, I told Nurse Murdoch I would like to practise on rough terrain. A doctor smiled and waved as I traversed the lawn in front of Harewood, and I just kept walking.

As I breached the hill that marked the perimeter of the hospital compound, the doctor seemed to suddenly realize that I might not return and yelled, "Hi!" But I only half turned and then kept going. It felt good to be moving along the vector of a plan.

"I'm grateful," I muttered, and as I said it, it seemed to me that I might really mean it. The staff had, over time, cleaned up the mess at my groin by then – the tick had left a trace fossil, its trajectory and the path of my scratching having formed a thick, coiled scar there – but I was, at least, alive. The war was over for me. I had paid my debt with a limb and a number of dead rebels, and now I could haul my ass back north and finish my medical degree, maybe do something useful in this life. I suddenly felt freedom nudging me, and with it, elation. I was in charge.

I would write a letter to Eb, keep that door open. But first I wished to neutralize another owing, so that even if sense directed me north, some spirit pushed my body elsewhere. The freckled Nurse Murdoch had apprised me of where I might find the sutler who had delivered Cristiana's letter. She warned me to be careful. I would not. I headed there. It wasn't far. I felt all through me that I *needed* to see Cristiana. Fated if fate were cruel, as it turned out. I reckoned it would be two days tramping, three with my new leg. I wished it weren't so heavy. I slept curled into dry gullies where I could find them and once in a barn. There was the newness of my injury and the fact of the prosthetic, which made me shy. I hated my loathsome, teetering walk.

When I got to where Murdoch had said I might find the sutler, the man had moved on, so I limped another four hours, my stump now screaming.

"You don't know me," I said to the merchant when I caught him up.

"I sure do." The man was wearing a black wide-brimmed wool hat low on his forehead. It was unmercifully hot and my suit reeked.

"Where is she at?"

The man just blinked until I handed him ten dollars, and then he smiled and said, "You're in luck, soldier. She's not an hour farther. I will deliver you if you hop in the wagon."

"I won't tolerate conversation."

"Well, I'm a talker," said the sutler. "Know thyself, I like to say."

"If you give me my ten dollars back, I will not kill you when we arrive." And that shut the man up until we got to the whitewashed shack.

It was not much bigger than a log piggery, and dormered along the roof pitch. There was no other house for a mile, and that was also a sort of piggery but not limed; no one lived there any longer. Cristiana was walking away from a line of laundry that looked so clean and domestic after the drudgery and dust of my walk. I heaved myself out of the sutler's wagon and listened to the clatter of hoof and wheel receding. I stood there watching the scene, Cristiana and the boy moving about the property, weeds and meadow flowers shushing in the soft wind; I thought I could sometimes hear them speak but caught nothing of their words. After a time, I walked up the lane until eventually she noticed me limping toward them.

Cristiana squinted at me and said, "What has the cat drug in?" The boy toddled out the open front door and found her leg to wrap his plump hand around.

"I brought back the portrait of Jessamine Peabody." It was a stupid thing to start with, but it was all that came to my head. We stood together on the front stoop. "I apologize for stealing and for keeping it so long. I do not know what got into me. I think I was lonely and grievously scared. For that matter, I still am."

As I pulled the little portrait from my wallet, Cristiana reached for it. I see now how she did not care about me or my feelings, but at the time I somehow managed to elide this truth. The image was an inch or so of exquisite beauty wrapped in a slip of paper. Cristiana opened it up and looked at it fast, then wrapped it back up and tucked it into a fold in her dress. "It will mean a great deal to Charles when he gets older and the war is won," she said.

"I had got to thinking of it as a good luck charm." I did not really want to think what luck it had given me; I did not feel myself to be a lucky sort of man. She stared at me, and so I said, "I walked a long way," in the hope she would invite me to sit.

"You can't stay," she said. "But come in." She folded a wheat rusk into baby Charles's hand and set him out of doors to play. "Scoot," she said. The boy looked up at me in such a way that made me want to stand up taller. "Scoot," she said again, and the boy went out the door and to the edge of the stoop and jumped off.

"Hell of a strong mite," I said, and Cristiana hissed and scolded me for cursing. She was proper. She reminded me of my mother in some ways – polite, willful, able to bring a man to his knees with one withering look. When she closed the front door, I took off my hat and she asked me to sit down.

"I'm sorry for your leg," she said as I limped to the chair.

As I sat on a hardback chair in her tiny kitchen, she recalled to me how she had dug up her yard in the old house, and the fruitlessness of it. She wondered whether I had anything else I might be persuaded to return to her and her son. She said that she was still grieving Henry. She also told me how she missed the proximity of people, of a husband, and also the sense there was some person in the world who might take care of her. She supposed this might be loneliness. "The truth is, this place is so isolated," she said, "that I have forgotten how to be with people."

It was as if she could see into my mind and read my guilt. I fidgeted and tried to keep my eyes from telling her everything. I kept thinking how I needed that money if I was to save myself. And by saving myself, I rationalized, I could save her and the boy, too. Perhaps I was a bad person for this, but I ask what you would have done in my position? She was no worse off without that money. After a time of awkward silence, I finally cleared my throat and said, "I have developed feelings." Then I cringed. I was always one for saying stupid things.

She blinked at me as if she could edit me out with her eyes, or maybe as if she was assessing my usefulness to her. There was something about her that undid me. I was frantic, I will admit. I felt such a pull to her and yet I was also selfish. I wanted what I wanted.

"I know you are rich from the money in my old backyard."

I dug under my shirt and pulled the chain and locket over my head. "Here."

She made a face but took it, dug in her dress and fished the daguerreotype from where she'd tucked it. Then she shoved a thumbnail under the clasp to pop it and nestled the portrait of Jessamine back where it belonged. She then put this around her own neck. Her mouth was set in a terse grimace; it looked like hatred to me.

I watched the locket chain slide over her clavicle and down her blouse. I thought of the hole built into the back of the doll and the roll of bills hid there. I knew I should relinquish it. I should pull the damned thing out and give it to her. A good man would do this, I thought, but something stopped me. I could not bring myself to say a thing about it. I was so selfish and in love with my future that I wished I had reburied it. I would not then have the burden of it on my person.

"Where you cried on Henry Muldon's last epistle to his dear wife," Cristiana tried again. I tried to empty out my mind. She leant onto the table, toward me, and peered into my face in a way that was persuasive. "If you truly have feelings," she said. "There was something of import written there and, because of it, I think you must have stolen an important object that belonged to my poor dead husband."

"Stolen?" Already I was talking over her, telling her I had money from the limb-maker and from the United States Great Civil War Benefaction to ease the burden of procuring a false limb. I could not seem to shut myself up. Some part of me wanting to do right, or so I pretended to myself. Also, I must have been crazed with love or guilt, for what else would propel me to such selflessness. "I got this false leg for nothing," I told her, and I pulled bills out to give her. I told her how I was "heading north to Toronto." She just watched, her lips pursed so tight, as I unfurled that money in her whitewashed house. She didn't say anything until she saw how undone I was, how wracked, how made stupid with my own "feelings" and lies, and how freely tears could course a grown man's miserable face when he didn't know a thing. Three hundred dollars sat on the table.

"It's all I got," I said, disarmed.

She laughed then and said, "No, it surely ain't."

"I swear."

"You are one big lie." She was already rising from her chair and turning away from me. She headed to the door and then opened it and held her hand on the frame. She made it known I was no longer welcome in her home.

"I have been thinking about you for months and months now," I said.

Her lips curled in a fury that frightened me. "The second Negro you ever touched."

"The first woman," I whispered. When the screen door slammed, I stood outside it looking in at her. "I do have feelings," I said. I was near to crying. "You kissed me!" It was a desperate thing to say to her.

She laughed openly at me. "You do not know yourself." Then she said how she pitied me my privilege and some nonsense about how without opposition, I was destined to be an idiot like all my kind.

I thought this was not fair but shut up. Cristiana pulled open a broken-down cupboard desk and took from one of the wooden file dividers a letter I recognized. She unfolded the letter and ran her finger along the pertinent line. She looked at me.

But now I was upset at her cruelty to me. Here I had given her three hundred dollars. "I just came by to lay out my feelings and to bring you the photograph you so wanted." My leg hurt me and I felt a tightening all through myself, like I was winding down.

She stared at me, unmoving for a time, the letter dangling from her fingertips. Then she said, "I will give you whatever I have for the object mentioned in the last letter my husband wrote to me. I will let you spill your sick and tired warrior's heart to me. I will lift my skirts." She glared at me and added, "Don't you look shocked at me!" for I had recoiled out of fear at her forwardness. "Don't you dare, Private Russell Boyt, broken and war-weary substitute." She looked with unveiled contempt at my false leg as if its falseness signified the falseness that ran through me every which way. Then she said how the Lord worked in mysterious ways, did He not?

Cristiana Muldon seemed to know something that no one else knew, something about my being, the withering corruption in me. She seemed to know it better than I did. It was as if I saw the truth just as she pointed it out. I was reminded of Father and Mother and the way they seemed to bind me in unpleasant ways.

I swallowed. "You ought to be more kind to me, Mrs. Muldon."

"Why ever for? You are a liar, Russell Boyt."

Cristiana had somehow broken free of some awful trap the world seemed to have laid out. My armpits were raging wet. Maybe if I gave her the doll, she would stop, but then I reasoned she'd keep at me until I caved in about the money, too, and then my future would lie in ruins. I am ashamed to admit that at the time, I did not think much of her future, and the meaner she was the less I considered how I would save her after I had saved myself. I turned to watch Charles, who was far off from the house poking at dirt. It was getting on for dusk.

I looked back at her. "I am a stupid man," I said. "And I am sorry to have bothered you." But I could not will my aching body to take me away. For one thing, my hips and back hurt me terribly, and for another thing, I just felt locked and rusted all through me.

I wanted to blurt how I was sure that I loved her, but I knew she would scoff and I could not bear that. Why should she believe there was something in it? She had clearly hurtled so far from the meaning of love. She did not care for it. She did not take stock in it. Love was a ribbon that was flying in the breeze for those dim enough to try to catch it. Me. I was dim enough. I suddenly saw a demure wife – Nurse Murdoch came readily to mind – and three robust towheaded children gathered into me in some future photograph. I saw my own future.

"No!" I yelled, and I saw Cristiana pull back.

"You really must be leaving, Private Boyt. And do come again when you can't stay so long."

"What did you expect of me?"

She laughed then and seemed to let her guard down some. "The only expectation there is for such a one as me, Private Boyt, is that I not pretend to have expectations."

I believe I looked dreamily at her. I had no idea what she meant by what she had just now said. I clearly did not know any one thing about her. I vowed I would stay close by this place and spend time that night thinking of a question to ask her the next day. My throat was so dry it felt dusty.

"Can I drink from the well?" I said.

"You may."

"And I am tired and hungry, too," I managed.

She told me later that she did not know why she felt an ounce of pity for such a cruel and despicable man. She would like to be rid of me as soon as possible on the one hand, but on the other she wanted the doll and the money, and had not had the company of anyone in so many months.

I believed she came to some fondness for me. But it was only what I wanted to believe, which perhaps amounts to the same thing. For over the next weeks, she told me the whole of her story, how her deceased husband was the substitute for a rich gentleman named Moser Blakey, who believed in the cause of the beleaguered slaves of the South. She told me how she now received meagre cheques from him in compensation for her dead husband, and with that small stipend she bought cloth and staple foods, enough to keep herself and Charles out of the way of things.

That first night, she said to me, "I'll make you some grits and eggs. That's all we have. You can sleep in the chicken coop out back. If anyone sees you coming in and out of this house, they will likely kill you or me or both of us."

And that was how I first came to know she had some scant feelings back. That night, after Charles slept, I told her about Bellair and Little Tiger. I felt comfortable. I thought she might begin to care for me. I wanted that. I told her the whole war as I had seen it. I watched her wince as I told her about the amputation and how I had sewn my own leg. I stopped short of telling her about the gears and the corrosion, but I did say how I was almost strangled to death. She shushed me and I could see some slight pity in her eye. And so, to save her a bother, I decided I would not mention the gears, nor the way my heart palpitated, nor the furious sounds I endured all throughout myself. I also did not mention that I woke sometimes in violent throes, that I was perhaps dangerous in ways I could in no way control.

DAY TWENTY

I CLEAN UP THE PIECES of doll and inspect the damage – crazing on the porcelain face and some chips to the ears and nose – but I am not equal to the task of fixing things, it seems. I wrap Boy up in a new swaddling instead, by way of holding him together. The body is more or less disintegrated and there is no evidence of a hole in its back, much less money tucked back there. This makes sense as I have made it all up based on a deep dive into Civil War dolls. I certainly have no recollection of a compartment in the back of Boy.

As I work, wafts of sealskin come off my hands and arms.

It is still raining, the lilac blossoms bending with the weight of water. The area has never seen so many consecutive days of rain. It shushes like a great universal pulse, this water surging and slowing, billowing up and down the windowpanes. I look outside, wondering at it.

When I come downstairs later that morning, I pretend like my folks and I are in a truce. I pretend as if my parents have not demanded that I leave. I ask Dad about the river that used to run at the very back of the land.

"The Black River," he says.

"I hadn't realized it was named."

"It's on the Google Earth, if you care to look. But the image is all wrong for today. Now, it'd look more like a lake. It's breached the shore quite handily. I read about it in the *Packet* and there was a drone shot of it. The entire back fields of everyone on the concession are washed out. Well, it was only pussy willow and prickly ash anyhow. But you'd need a kayak to get there."

"I hadn't thought of kayaking deeper in," I say.

"Well, what would be the point of that?"

"To see."

He scoffs and says, "There is no there there."

"Gertrude Stein," I say, and he shoots me a look that tells me he has no idea he is quoting her, and possibly who she even is. So I pat his arm, grab his slicker since mine is back in the city and pull on my boots, then I head out to the porch and slosh my way to the pig shed, outside of which the kayak is moored in its little wheeled cart.

I only have to haul it three fields back to finally hit a shore of sorts. There is a smell of lively animal, rot and, of course, water. The clouds are dark and full and every so often let out a cataract of rain. But still I paddle north, wondering at the changed landscape, at the persistence of nature. I wonder if the rain knows the future, if there is such a thing as a beyond-human intelligence, the sort that knows in ways no single entity could know.

"It's true," I say when I get back. Dad is watching something on TV about a cult in the wilds of Oregon. "There *is* no there there."

He nods and smiles without breaking from the television. "There's a package came for you from the Amazon."

"Very funny." It's a box with another box inside it. And inside that box are two boxes. And inside one is a double pack of universal typewriter ribbon for the Remington and inside the other is the cleaner fluid. I go back upstairs with these to find that Mum has packed my suitcase. But she is back in bed. I peer in to snipe at her, but she is fast asleep or else faking.

And so I go back to my room to unzip the suitcase and spill everything out. The diary tumbles to the floor, open. I pick it up. The entry is dated May 14, 1865. Eva writes: *I begin to worry for Russell. It is my opinion that Father works to avoid feeling. I am much alone lately. Weather warm.*

May 14 is tomorrow, Mother's Day, likely why Mum wants me gone. She abides by these special days, reckons on them. But I will not go back. I can't bear it. I think I will keep my phone off, too, so as to avoid all coerced communication. So far, I have avoided picking up messages all this week, since that last phone call. I have umpteen from Matthew and a scattering from the boys. I sink into work just like Eva suggested Russell's father did. I have put the phone under a folded-up carpet in the closet. I make it hard to get to on purpose. Happy Mother's Day my arse. I don't need their messages to remind me of what a terrible mother I am. I can remind myself just fine without them.

I try to believe that finding a self, my own self, will provide a lifeboat. That this work is necessary. That everything is connected. But that is seeming less and less likely to be true. As I write about Russell losing it, I too seem to be. Well, we are the same person, of course, since I am writing him into existence. This, too, seems like a mad thought. As I write, the sealskin smell seems to waft up from my hands, which cannot be since I have washed them.

Someone once wrote that smell is 90 percent of love. Was it Tom Robbins? At any rate, the odour gives me a small, doable mission. A quest within my reach. I will begin my search tomorrow for the sealskin they have hidden or discarded. It can't be all that far yet.

I spend an hour swabbing out buildup in the Remington with Q-tips and cleaner. The typewriter ribbon is easy enough to install after that. I set out a stack of printer paper, load the Remington, test the keys by rewriting Eva's diary entry – the mechanical sound of type plunking out meaning is its own particular thrill.

1865

AFTER EATING, I WENT SOLEMNLY to the chicken coop and pushed some straw together into a kind of bed, and I fell asleep on it gently crying. I did not know why, and I woke up shocked because in my sleep I'd forgotten where I was. I half recalled a dream of Cristiana coming to me there. It surprised me that she deigned come. I had thought she hated me. In my dream, she never said anything, just unbuttoned my woollen trousers and pushed my two hands down under her skirts. I tucked my fingers into her blouse and held her. I woke wishing it were not a dream. I prayed she would one day come to me.

I stayed at Cristiana's little farmhouse, sleeping in the chicken coop for three weeks – longer than I should have, I knew, but I was having a hard time recalling why I should go back to Toronto. All was confusion inside my head – it just got worse and worse. And after those weeks, Cristiana said she was scared for what might happen to her and the boy should anyone take an interest in why a white soldier should carry on with her, but I could see she was also scared to be alone.

"You should leave by nightfall, feelings aside," she said, and I was not certain she was speaking of her own or mine.

"Feelings?"

She did not answer, but that night I woke to her riffling through my things; it was dark out and I did not know what time. I watched her – what I could see of her – a furtive shadow moving quietly through my scant possessions, but I had hidden the doll so well, she would never find it. After a time, she stopped rummaging and sat very still. Then she turned toward me and saw that I was awake and watching. I could see a pleading look in her eyes. "I will die from lonesomeness," she said, and I believed she half meant it even if this too was a ploy.

A person is always more than one thing, I thought. Hadn't Nurse Murdoch said just the same thing before she made love to me? And hadn't she disavowed me later?

It was the first time that Cristiana and I made love. I never asked her nor did I pursue her. She took the lead. At the time, I thought she admired me, but now I am quite sure that she wanted something from me. What power did she have in that bad situation? Me, so impassive and greedy with the items I had found on her husband's corpse. And her with nothing but herself to barter. I deserved whatever awfulness fate sent me.

For weeks after that, she came to me and we did not speak, and we got relief one body with another, and then she left and it was a thing we did not talk about. I never came to know whether she sought solace from me or simply sought the doll. She might have felt less alone but I knew I felt more than that.

And then one night, I made the mistake of unwrapping the porcelain doll. I had been sleeping fitfully and decided it was because my conscience was eating at me, so I took the doll out to see if I could part with it. If I gave her the doll and the contents of it, I could be rid of my terrible thoughts and maybe the corrosion and gear-grinding might subside. I thought that I might be free and poor and broken but how that might be better than being rich and sick with my own spiralling ruminations.

It was as if the doll – the strange meaning of the doll – and the facts of my obfuscation of it had slid in between the pistons and gears of my innards. It was as if the feelings of shame and guilt were now greasing the whole mechanism. I did not want to admit this to myself but there was also the thought that if I gave her the doll and the money, she might begin to love me. That is what I wanted, that sole thing. To be loved, something I had never really known.

I got petulant with this line of thought and hurled the doll at a broody hen, its gurgling egg-making infuriating me suddenly. The doll bounced off the henhouse and lay there, straw-bound and never-changing. The chicken squawked and danced frantically for a time. Hens were just nerve endings on claws, I thought. I drew a line in my mind from one bird to the next until the henhouse took on the appearance of a web. In that moment, I was brought to a sort of solution: I would leave tomorrow with the doll and the money. I would head to Upper Canada and put a life together, and send for her once I had. I know now that I was deferring things that would never transpire. My days on this planet would cloud over in worse and worse ways.

The doll lay inert in the broody nest. I left it there instead of doing what I should have done, which was wrap it up and hide it back in my haversack. I would return to that error over the whole rest of my days and wonder to what extent I meant for Cristiana to see it and find it, to let me out of my head if even for a minute. I saw the kerosene lamp swaying and the shadows it made before I saw Cristiana's face. She scanned the henhouse, following the sightline of my agitation. And when she saw the doll nestled in beside me, she looked as if she knew she would always find it.

"Finally," she said in a way I didn't appreciate, as if her sleeping with me those times had bought her this moment. As if she had *earned* this. Or magicked it. She reached in through the matrix of lines I had conjured and dug into the doll's back with fierce determination. "Where is it?" she said. I wondered how she knew about the strange hole in the back of the doll.

"It's only a doll," I said.

"No. It is certainly not. It's a vessel made to look like a child's toy."

"Mechanical."

"It has no moving parts, Russell."

"Yes."

"Where is it?" she said, digging at the doll's spine. "Money that surely never belonged to you nor to me, neither."

"I wanted to help you," I said. It felt to me as if she was removing the money, or something – a giant metal whirring insect – from *my* spine, and I shuddered at the operation. I reasoned in that moment it would be a relief. I would be free of it. How wrong I was. I was feverish in my crazed state.

"Private Boyt," she said. "I'm not a child that needs taking care of." Her face went from disgust to pity. "I'll get you a wet cloth," she said, for she must have seen what an inexplicable heat had overcome me. I wanted to say that I loved her, but I knew she would not hear it. She had once said to me, "There is no room for love in this world, and I gave mine away to a now-dead man and he has held on to it dearly. *He will not let it go.*"

She was weeping. I found myself hating her suddenly for her vibrancy and what that did to me. I had too many feelings. I wished I could slough them all off me.

"Please, give me the money, Private Boyt."

I needed to get back to Toronto. I needed to solve this. The fact was, I would live a terrible life and I would be crippled and I could expect only hatred and scorn from my father; I was so weak. It was in this state that I revised all my plans. Or at least I acquiesced and went, in a second, from being a rich man to being a poor one.

"The money's in my prosthetic," I said.

"Thank the good Lord," she said, and she rushed to pull the wad of cash out from where I had it hid, my leg lying beside me in the straw. A kind of hostile gratitude spilled throughout the chicken coop for she had clearly not thanked me.

I grimaced watching her. My future unwound quickly. "Thank the good Lord," I repeated with treacly sarcasm. She let the doll and the money fall into her lap and kissed me long and deep. Feelings went all through me again, spun out into the space, ricocheted between the sad walls of the coop and my flesh. The lines in my mind that I had drawn between the hens attached to her and to me and held us there. We were trapped in the henhouse. Could she see it, too? I must have been so mad to think all this. I was so mad.

"Half of it would buy the rest of my schooling," I ventured, but she just looked at me.

After a long time, she said, "I knew you would eventually do right."

The lines throbbed among the chickens and Cristiana and me, jounced in the air like tramlines. They were all colours and then solid black and unmoving, then they began to move again. They cut through the air and broke the space in a pretty way. I could feel the hens settling and hear them clucking their soft hen coos.

I nodded that I understood what I might have just now done right. "My plan was to send for you and Charles when I was settled." I wished she could love me, but I could see she did not. I could hear my innards whirring. Every organ turning to ironworks. Fire dancing along my skin. I bounced my teeth together to calm things. She was pointing with some eagerness to words on a slip of paper. I had forgotten about the note pinned to the doll; it had seemed so inconsequential to me.

"This note," she said, indicating the directive on the doll's dress. "The money doesn't belong to me, don't you see?"

Prty of Eliza Goss, Please return to owner at earliest possible convenience. Washington.

"Who is – ?"

"Will you trust that I can't tell you, Private Russell Boyt?"

I would have to walk north, and I would have to beg at my father's doorstep for debts to the college and fees for my final year. I had fooled myself into thinking Cristiana might share it with me, and now that foolishness was racing away from me. I saw my father's smug lips. I would never be able to go home. The thought was so miserable that I leant into Cristiana and roughly kissed her. I thought she might owe me some affection; I wanted my mind to empty into something pleasurable. I hoped she understood I needed her help to calm down.

"I love you," I said. "Say something nice."

She would not say it. In fact, she laughed by way of answering. The kerosene lamp fell over then, and the light flickered and died. She said, "Good night," and then she was quickly gone with the doll and the money. I could smell her receding into the night, the lines stretching and breaking so that it was only me still caught there, with the cluck of hens and the warm eggs and the thought of the only kind of future I could imagine – a bad one. The darkness seemed to accumulate in the front of my skull and breed there into some pure black hell. I fought against my own wakefulness and reiterative thoughts and the trap this world had set for me by my own terrible choices.

1865

I AM COMPELLED TO COMPLETE this archive of my misdeeds. Maybe I will heal something in myself, and therefore in some small way for the world as well, by recounting it aloud.

I fell asleep in Cristiana's henhouse, a dreamful sleep that pressed on me like a train driving into my sternum; I was pinned by some horrible nighttime encounters. I swear it was not my fault. In the thick of one awful nightmare, I woke finding myself in Cristiana's shack. How I got there I did not recall even then – I must have sleepwalked my way. Charles was screaming like a rageful animal, finally waking me from this devilish dream.

My hands were around Cristiana's neck, squeezing. In my mania, I half expected to find the nurses and orderlies pinning me as they had at Harewood, but no. There was no Nurse Murdoch to restrain me, no orderlies to save me from my worst self.

I was smashing her head against the wrought-iron headboard. At first, I was not sure where I was until I saw the child sitting up wide-eyed in his bed, his small hand extended as if that gesture could contain the truth of this.

This was bad, hellish. I spent an incredible minute or more wondering what had happened to Cristiana, despite the clenched cramps through my now-open palms. I jostled her and watched this jostling only shift her, until her dead body was almost falling off the bed.

"Shh," I admonished the boy, though Charles had stopped peeping and now only stared, his fingers sucked into his mouth, his expression neutral with some kind of uncanny understanding. His face was filthy with dried tears and sweat.

"No," I said to Cristiana, for I did not then – could not then bring myself to – believe I had killed her. "No." I said it many more times, as if this could breathe life back into her corpse. It was too simple for her to be dead if all it took was a dream from which I did not wake in good time.

I recalled then the line stretching as she had left the henhouse. The money and the doll she took with her. This was bad. Bad because I had surely killed her and worse because I also loved her. I had killed myself or some important piece of myself, or it felt like that. I shuddered thinking about my fingertips and the white, bloodless clenching, clenching – my thumbs had been parallel on her larynx. If that wasn't murder, what was?

What had she said to me all those weeks ago? That I was a liar. That I did not know myself. I was crying in my stupid shame.

In some unreasonable hope, I thumped at her like I had learned in medical school, counting over my own rhythmic breathing and trying, and failing, to will life back into her body. I put my mouth on her strange dead one and tried to breathe life back in from my own lungs, but it was like breathing into a wall. Her lungs would not receive me and she was not remotely living. I kept thinking, maybe if she had only said she liked me when I had asked her to say something nice, maybe then my dreams would have been sweet and would not have run in this direction, but that was not right thinking. For the dead could never be blamed and dreams were just powerless ghosts. There was a terrible smell coming off me, of burning rubber, oil on fire, a shriek of metal on metal and the hot smell of that, too.

And then the child was feral, storming at me tooth and claw. I made myself soft and let the boy have at me with his small fists. He deserved that much. The boy landed punch after punch, screaming his fury. "Mama," he said. "Mama." These were near the first words I had ever heard him utter. He sank his teeth into my arm and could not be shaken off, nor would I have shaken him off. When Charles was spent, he curled against Cristiana and whimpered. I inspected my arm and found small teeth marks – exactly like gears – and congealing blood.

I did not know how I did what I next did. I was like a machine throughout. I told the doctors this later, and they looked at me as if I was evil. I think that evil must be something very normal then. Because all I could think of was to clean this up. I wanted it not to have happened. I swear I loved her, in my capacity. I did.

I left the cabin and found a shovel and started digging. Charles squatted down beside me and watched for a while, until I told him, mournfully, to "scoot," and he wandered away toward the chicken coop. I just dug and dug, snagging the spade's footrest on plant and tree roots until I had to curse to hell under my breath. It was full night by the time the hole was big enough to hold her. Then I went inside and pried Cristiana's body away from the boy, who'd fallen asleep. She barely weighed anything. I cried because I thought my own self-horror might be love, and because I began to realize that I hardly knew her and what had I done with all the feelings I had developed but this awful thing. This nightmare.

Love was surely an evil instigator.

I slid into the grave with her and laid her down and then climbed back out, filthy, her scent on me. She was so tiny deep in there. It sickened me to throw dirt on her, but I did that, too. I watched the dirt slap her dress and face, and then I thought I saw her twitch. I cried out to Jesus and jumped down into the pit to lift her up and listen to her chest. I shook her and moaned out, "Please, Cristiana. Please. I'm sorry." But she was dead and would never be able to forgive me – and why should she?

I vowed I wouldn't ever forget the crescent moon above me, everything so quiet I thought I could hear the wee boy stutter-breathing in the house. And myself down in that grave – some hell I had come adventuring for. She would haunt me to the end of time. This ex-slave who, once having gained freedom, would die by my loving hand. She would extract payment for this, I knew. She had every right.

I clambered out of that sorry ditch and swung that shovel fast until she was covered. Then I scattered leaves to hide my awful deed and said, "Our Father," and then went back into the house. I wrapped a scarf around the boy's silken neck, tucked his arms into the jute coat his mother had sewn for him, pulled a pair of red woollen mittens onto his hands – they dangled from a crocheted string inside the coat's sleeves – then tugged a hat over the kid's head. It wasn't cold out but it would get cold later, when night fell, and again every night that we travelled. The boy was lost-looking, his lips cherry red, chapped. I hurled him up onto my shoulders. He weighed almost nothing at first.

"Hold my ears," I told him, shouldering my haversack, then putting it back down when I saw the doll. I checked its back cavern for the money – she had tucked it back there. "Mama," said Charles, and let go my ear to reach back as we ducked under the doorway. "Mama."

"Charles." I tapped the boy's leg and set to walking. "She's not here anymore," I said. I pointed into the nowhere and told him, "We will search for her out there." A whirring started up in my ears again. "We'll find her, okay, Charles?" My voice was cracking miserably. Any idiot would have sensed I was unreliable.

I muttered sorry over and over again, but that salved no one and nothing. Sorry to Cristiana and to myself and to wee Charles. What had I just now become? What did sorry get me, though – what did sorry buy anyone? I had failed miserably at manhood; it was writ on my skin and cranking all through me. I wondered how I might fix this thing that there was no fixing and came up with, if I could only live and make a life for this child it would be some recompense for everything stupid I had done so far. Which felt like the biggest lie ever concocted. I had no choice but to keep living. I had no choice, or so it seemed to me.

After an hour, the prosthetic began cutting painfully at my thigh-flesh and I sat down. The boy had fallen asleep again on my shoulders, drooling into my hat. I let him slip onto the grass before I pulled my limb off to tend to myself. A laceration had developed from chafing and was oozing a little pink blood. I patched it from my kit and cursed the false leg under my breath, then wrapped my arms around my haversack and tucked myself around the boy to try to sleep a time. Once or twice I began to feel nauseous and thought maybe I ought to go back and dig her up and check her pulse. Had I really checked her pulse? Maybe she wasn't truly dead. Maybe I should go back and see, but I didn't. Me – a medical man. I kept thinking that perhaps the deed I had done was a dream, too. But I pressed on. I walked all night and had to ask where I was of the first person I met in the morning. The boy whined how he was hungry and thirsty and where was his mama. A new responsibility was coming at me.

"Call me Papa," I said to the kid, and shook him too hard. "Say it."

DAY TWENTY-ONE

I SEARCH THE PIG SHED thoroughly, and the hayloft of the big barn – I find a single egg in a massive turkey vulture nest but no sealskin. I look in the basement again, and in my parents' beat-up Volvo. Nothing. I'm beginning to wonder if Dad threw it out with the garbage, but I can hardly believe he would dare. It would amount to an egregious family treason.

At lunch, I say, "If you were a seal, where would you hide yourself?"

"In the ocean," says Dad, without looking up from his sudoku.

"In the well, maybe?" says Mum, and Dad shoots her a look. But she does not receive this since she is scribbling on her cryptic crossword.

"Thanks a lot," Dad says. He then proceeds to get up, pull his slicker on, his Billy boots, a straw hat he has taken to wearing since a friend's cancer scare some years back. He is in a hurry and fuming mad, but it's raining, of course, and he is above all else a rational man.

I am ahead of him. I am barefoot and don't give a rat's arse about wet feet or wet anything. I'm in a nightdress that needs a good rinse anyhow. I can hear them behind me as I cross the lawn, Dad scolding Mum and then her whining, "How was I supposed to know?" and Dad's huffing at me as he shuffles down the front porch, "Oh no, you don't!"

But I do. The well is as old as the house, 180-odd years. Moss and lichen have found hospitable locations in the pitted ancient concrete. The lid is a rough bevelled cube, held in place by its sibling bevel on the concrete top of the structure – likely built as a renovation to the water source sometime in the 1900s – and the lid handle is a simple, corroded, thick wire bent and jammed into the cement. Every few years, Dad pumps this well dry, throws a ladder down, unhouses the snakes there and scrubs the walls with lye before letting it fill again. He brings a sample to the county to perform an E. coli test. Despite the snakes, the water always comes back clean.

I have about thirty seconds, I reckon, to find the sealskin before he storms me. I stand on the top of the well, legs spread, and heave the lid up and over. Then I jump down onto the grass and peer in, tugging at the ropes hanging down from the top, the ones that hold the pump and (I'm hoping) the prize skin. Neither of them has much slack, so I think maybe he has just tossed the pelt in, let it fester down there for all time. I take my iPhone out and swipe the flashlight app, to try to shed some light on this problem. I'm too late, of course, because Dad is hovering.

"It's not there," he says, huffing, but I do not believe him. Why should I? "It's just an old story," he adds.

So why race out here after me, I think. What's his reasoning?

"She's just silly. She forgets things. She can't keep a story straight anymore."

"How so?"

"The story goes that the selkie went back and forth. Left and returned. Left and was caught."

"Like an animal?"

"Never to be free . . ."

"I won't be caught."

"I just wanted to save you the bother of looking and maybe make you see some sense. Have a look –"

I scan the walls of the well and try to get a read on the metres and metres of water. The thing is up to the top with water. I think I see a water snake swimming deep down. I should be repulsed by this but instead I am jealous. To be a creature riding current – this appeals to me. Dad is standing over me, but I have more or less excised him from the scene, so focused am I. But no deal. No sealskin. Mum has fabricated this or else he has moved it. I stand. I'm crying and trying not to, in a way that I'm quite sure makes my face seem ugly, distorted, corrupted.

"Matthew sent a lawyer's letter through my email," I say. "He's 'not wasting time,' he says. He's been advised to be swift about this lest I spend more of 'his' money. I got the note on Mother's Day. He waited to send it for the optimal suffering he could inflict on me."

"No rest for the wicked," Dad says.

"I suppose not," and then I realize he is referring to me and not Matthew. And so I get a bit testy. "It's like you don't feel my pain. It's like you haven't an ounce of love left for me. What did I ever do to harm you? You two obfuscate at every turn. Why are you hiding this old relic from me and what is the story of my dead brother? Surely you can shed some light on one or both. It just makes me want them even more. For why should I care about a smelly old pelt?"

I need some – freedom – space – room to breathe.

"You'll get in your car and you'll head back to the city. Those bairns need a mother."

"Those bairns are full adults."

"They need a mum. They've been messaging after you for days and days. What did they ever do?"

"What did they ever do to deserve me, you mean?"

"If that's how you want to put it."

"I don't. It's how you implied it."

"You've been weeks away. What do you suppose they're eating? It can't be good. You've a duty to perform."

"I don't recall casseroles being part of the marriage contract."

"You've always been so bloody high strung," he says. "What would it cost you to go home? And besides that, your mother and I are missing our privacy. Your poor mum is at the end of her rope with you."

"Her dementia is not my fault," I say.

I think of the rope that is the umbilicus. I think about how she won't let me go, how her secretive ways are just ruses to hold me in place. So I fume. "We should cut that rope, then, Dad."

"That is not what I meant and you know it."

"But you did say it," I whisper.

He has not heard, I realize. His ears are not what they used to be. "You'll do best to head out today," he says, looking down at his boots. They have sunk into the earth by his weight. He looks old suddenly. Much older than he did a week ago. The rain has thinned, but the grass is sodden, fully soaked, and the yard is now a bog. "Soon enough, we'll all be trapped in our houses. There's not been water like this in my lifetime. Gerry has taken to paddleboating from one outbuilding on his property to the next, and there is nothing for it but to wait for the sky to close." Gerry is the neighbour two farms over. I've known him since I was a young girl.

"There was a terrible rain in 1869," I say, but Dad is already walking back to the croft house. It rained for weeks then, apparently. It's something I've come across in the latter pages of Eva's diary. The weather consumed her. She notes it at every entry. Her penmanship is elegant and tight, the script a mirror to her unpoliced inner thoughts. She speaks of rains inundating Toronto for weeks that spring, her heart heavy with worry for what had become of Russell, her only, the one upon whom she and her husband had pinned such hopes and through whom they had endured such heartache. *To be a man in this brutal epoch,* she wrote, *must surely be calamitous.* And I wonder as I read it whether there was ever a time in which it was not calamitous to be a man, and how we should perhaps clamber back to that pristine moment and start over, write a better story for humanity. One that is better for everyone, better for the planet, too.

The whole time I've been thinking this, I have been watching my father's hunched form picking its way back toward the house. He is skirting puddles and muttering under his breath. Once or twice he turns to glower at me, to see if I am following. After a time I do follow. When we reach the house, standing on the back stoop, we face each other. I see that he is actually worried, not about his and Mum's privacy, not about Matthew or the boys, but about me. "What is it, Dad?" I say.

At first, he just looks furtively away, down at a sad, water-drenched peony, its flowers still tight little nuggets for the ants have not been able to find it. I imagine they are clinging to the roofs of their underground warrens, in utter terror at the flood. Finally, Dad shakes his head and says, "It's unspeakable, what I am thinking." Then he adds, "I just wish you'd come to your senses."

But I do not. The storm ebbs and flows and then, as prophesied, it is too late, my Prius's wheels are underwater, and the road out is officially closed.

1865

THERE WAS A LETTER WAITING for me at Wilkes' Manufactory of Limbs. Eb Wilkes showed me the letter and told me it had been forwarded by a nurse at Harewood. Wilkes then gazed at the child.

I made a face by way of stemming the tide of his inquiries and then squatted down and tugged the boy's woollens into some kind of order. They were soiled, I noted, and smelled strongly of urine. I looked back up at Wilkes. "Sorry," I said.

Eb just waited for me to continue, his eyes flickering first to Charles, then to me. Eb couldn't quite look me in the eye. What was it about me, I wondered, that made me so unpleasant? "Am I sickly?" I asked. Gears. An awful sound travelling my circulatory system, like crashing waves. "I have killed someone," I muttered leaning toward Eb.

It felt like a respite to announce this, even if Eb misunderstood.

"War is a terrible thing," he said, and I just stared at him. Concern creased his forehead. "It's uncanny to see you here with so young a child. I hadn't anticipated it. And so filthy."

Uncanny, I thought. "I found him," I spluttered.

"Found a child. These are strange times indeed."

"May I?" I said, by way of deflection, and gestured to the letter in Eb's hand. This made Eb all business, made him happy for something to do other than deal this uncomfortable interaction.

He said, "My office is behind you. Let me take the boy in the meantime."

The office was small and smelled of city men and paper dust. As I took a seat at the desk, I could hear the boy's thin, anxious wail receding down the hallway. There were files stacked everywhere and what I assumed were plans for limb prototypes rolled and stuffed in an umbrella holder. In front of me, on a sheet of parchment, a sort of prosthetic was drawn, one that would turn a man into a bird. I looked it over and then pulled open the letter from Nurse Murdoch. There was a scant note from her that tersely told him she was "badly" and would be sailing to England soon.

Enclosed in her letter was another letter that had come to the hospital after I had run off. It was from Cristiana. In my madness, I quickly surmised that this was fated. I began a narrative that was so incongruent to reality that I am ashamed now to enunciate it. I told myself that she must not be dead. That I must have dreamed the last days, and in so dreaming somehow come to believe it. Cristiana had once held this paper I now held, had impressed herself upon it with ink and the pressure of her hand. The letter seemed to crackle. The dead did not write. Therefore, surely, I had imagined her sorry death. Surely, she lived still. I peered at the envelope for some clue, a date, but there was none. I felt her words creeping through me and wondered: Could words change a person?

> *Dear Pte RM Boyt, If you know the whereabouts of a certain child's toy, the back of which is hollowed out to a cavern – that doll is the very missed property of a colleague who much requires its swift return. This is an important matter about which the orphaning of Charles is at stake. Do not question me please, but send along the information on return letter, and the toy if you have it in your possession. You cannot take what is not your property. C. Muldon.*

That the letter clearly predated my arrival at the cabin did not sway my thinking. I became convinced that she was alive and was upset with me for having taken back the doll and the money. She was tracking my whereabouts. Even the sense of her hate made me happy, for I would have taken anything from her in those days. I was thrilled to have in her still an object to adore. She lived! The awful thing *had* indeed been a dream. I dug into my haversack and pulled out my writing kit, which was, of course, not mine at all but Henry Muldon's. I wrote one letter and then copied from it for the second and third.

The words, as they emerged from my pen, seemed everything. I was exultant to spend words and more words, for they seemed to oil me. I know now that storytelling is a kind of illness for me. That madness is wordy. The line between fiction and paranoia, for me, had been blissfully eradicated. I wrote and wrote in those days. I left the office and wandered through the three rooms that comprised this strange artificial charnel house – body parts everywhere I looked – in search of Eb. I handed the notes to him and asked him to kindly post them for me. Eb nodded and handed them to a young man who scurried away.

"Is everything in order?" he said.

"Yes," I said, not at all sure, while running my hand through Charles's dirt-thickened hair. "Yes! Perfectly in order."

The boy had shoved his filthy thumb into his mouth and was suckling on it. I looked up at the row of prosthetic arms that dangled from great pocked iron hooks; some of the limbs exposed strange entrail-like mechanisms. My head churned and there was a kind of pressing fury at my skull, which I worked very hard to keep in check. I told Eb that I should like to keep the boy, bring him north to some normal life. "I have a responsibility," I said. "And a growing fondness. Besides, with that Godly halo of blond hair, he will pass as sure as day for my son." That his grandmother was as white as a cloud I did not mention.

"But wherever did you come by him?"

"I found him wandering. So many are war-orphaned. If only he could speak," I said, "he could tell his awful narrative."

"How old is he?"

"As young as five, as old as seven. He won't speak."

Eb watched me shudder, steadied me by holding me with both his hands. I did not quite know what I ought to do.

1865

MY MOTHER HASTENED TOWARD WASHINGTON once the letter I wrote was received. It was deemed incoherent and "frankly worrisome" by my father. They now knew my precise whereabouts. It had been tactical on my part. I had hoped just for this outcome. But on rereading the letter much later, I realized how much of my delirium had seeped into the discourse. It must have worried them terribly. The letter read:

> *Ah, Mother – the strangest creatures lurk in the battlefield. Out they come in their many hundreds, a separate siege it is, all at once from the tangled stomachs of the dead and dying. The creatures hover and scream their ghastly screams across the field. They are tiny, misted-over men, all sloe-eyed and bewildered, which then feed with ravenous intensity on those bodies which are not fast enough removed from the field. They feed and feed before dissipating into the ether. They are green and filled with light, and they scare us men until we shiver in terror in our tents. I never saw the like before, Mother, and recounting it to you now must be indeed my worst transgression. My writing is only to give ventilation to a vision that returns to me by day and night. My plan as it stands is to hobble back north to finish my studies and give some education to a young freeman I have rescued from certain orphanhood. He wandered in a Virginia forest until I saw and took him. He is bedraggled and too*

young to speak proper. I thought he was a doll lying there abandoned. I have brought him to my original landing at the Limb Manufactory in Washington. I suffer regular fever but am otherwise well. Have mercy. R. Boyt. PS I have lost my right leg at the knee. Things are not well for me.

The second letter I wrote was delivered, I heard later, to a desolate and empty house, the front door of which had been left ajar. I now know that the messenger left the letter tucked under a ceramic butter pot and closed the door behind him. This letter was half the length but otherwise substantively similar to the first. The third arrived to Harewood Hospital and was never delivered to Nurse Murdoch, who had since left her post.

In Washington, Charles and I were given a spare room in Eb's expansive home – in a servant's quarters no longer in use. Within a fortnight, my mother arrived by train to fetch me and take me home. She suppressed her own rising eyebrows at the sight of the little boy. "He's very thin," she finally mustered. I believe she stopped herself from saying "Black."

The boy prodded at me when he was hungry, said, "Papapapapapa," and my mother smiled.

"He is certainly not your pa," she sniffed at the boy.

She sat poker stiff the entire train journey back to Toronto. She did not break her stare out the window, not even when Charles got up and off my lap so many times and made such a spectacle that people stared and shushed. After all the wanting to get home, I already felt disgusted with myself for my desires. Being in Mother's vicinity was like a corruption to my body and to the body of the child. I could see that my time at home would be temporary and that I would have to leave and set up for myself in a part of the city away from my parents' scrutiny. I would not like to subject Charles to them for overlong. I watched my mother blanch with embarrassment and so I incited the boy further to goad her. This was not mature of me, but at the time I wanted to get rid of my bad feelings and this seemed to mitigate them somewhat.

When the boy was finally asleep, I watched as my mother tensed her jaw and held herself from crying. My conscience dug at me. I wanted to open a conversation with her but couldn't settle upon a topic. After a while, I fell into a kind of half-sleep and dreamed of the doll walking toward me.

The trip took two days, Charles and I occupying one sleeper and my mother in separate quarters.

"Mother," I said when I woke, "you know why I left."

She petted my hand as if it were a small dying bird. "It's going to be all right," she said.

I nodded. I glanced back at the boy and then at my leg, which she must have seen me do. "I had a dog that died, too," I said. "It was a crying shame."

"Does it hurt?" she asked.

It hurt almost continuously, as if it were still there. It hurt all up and down; haunted me excruciatingly. "I wish I could tear it off," I said. "Tear it off all over again."

"Russell!" she said, her pitch high enough to cause other passengers to stare. She dropped to a furtive whisper. "What a horrid thing to say. You mustn't say such things. Not aloud. Not in public." She was glancing all around. People were watching us.

I leant toward her and touched her arm. "I lost my head for a second," I said.

"That's all right, Russell. I wish –" and here she must have fought hard to contain her emotions. "I wish that you'd not left home." She swallowed a number of times. "You never would listen," she added.

"No," I admitted. "And look where it has landed me."

My mother looked out the window. Her face slid between fury and despair. It was as if she had lost the limb and not me. When we finally arrived at the Front Street station, the boy stood between my legs smiling in wonder up at me. Charles had not smiled in days, weeks.

We hailed a taxi, the boy fixating on the Negro man driving the horses as if some half-formed memory came to him. I thought of Henry Muldon, though my own memory of the man's face was a blur. I recalled the tattered mess of uniform and some deep craving in myself between terror and eros. The interaction between the boy and the driver made my mother uncomfortable to the point that she tugged the boy away and enticed him to look out at vendors hawking food and flowers. It made me strangely pleased to see her engage with him.

When we arrived at the house, even as Charles gaped at him, my father pretended not to see the boy. I felt made small by this. I never could seem to stabilize the rise and fall of feeling in myself. I wondered if this same problem plagued others, if this was why other people – why my father – drank spirits. This had never appealed to me. I wished father would give the boy a proper look, but he only scrutinized me. "You're in a fever, son," he said, pulling down my eyelids, first one and then the other.

"No," I said. "I am not," else I had been months in this fever.

My father, Martin Boyt, tsked and let it go, but by the next morning, like a prophecy winding out its sordid truth, I was pinioned to my sodden bed, writhing, not always knowing where I was nor caring.

"Am I dying?" I asked my father. I was so suddenly undone by simply arriving back home.

"You will anon," my father said, tugging the cloth binding from my stump and recoiling at the seepage and the foul smell. He called to my mother for a basin of warm water. "It's suppurating, Eva," he said. "I shudder to imagine what those butchers have enacted. It's never yet healed. And look at this mad stitchery."

I was too inchoate at this time to admit my own piece in that tailoring – how I had not trusted the surgeon, how I had fled Harewood and walked away, and never bathed the wound since. How I had defended against my own rotting body by ignoring it, listening while it accreted with iron filings and rusted shards of metal, the tailings of some ill-favoured ironworks.

"And bloody hell if it isn't a creeping gangrene. Jesus Himself wept."

Mother was a shadowy spectre in the doorway, the boy tucked behind her at her skirts. "There's a letter," she said. "It might cheer him."

"Not now, Eva, please! And keep that peeping child away."

I saw a flit of light and they were gone. I fell into a sort of stupor and dreamed that father removed a shiny golden Minié ball from my chest and then hacksawed me directly in half, entered my chest cavity and beat me from within quite severely. My father loomed over me at my bedside all that day and night, pressing along my limb to keep the circulation going. This likely saved me from a second amputation. There were more days and more nights like this, such that I lost count of time. I woke to screams – my own – and Mother trying to pin me down, my stump waggling up and down as I struggled to torque my body to sitting. How long I had lain.

"Charles," I cried out. "Charles. Don't let him – Oh, Cristiana!"

"He's here." The boy appeared out from behind my mother's legs. I blinked – I had conflated Cristiana and my mother in my paranoiac dreaming, and the fear of God shot through me. A ghost and also real – could a person be both? She wouldn't ever leave me alone. I suddenly knew this all through my body. Cristiana was all over me and in me. If I lived then she also lived. I was scared and grateful in equal parts. But there, there, okay, okay, okay, it was just my mother. I did not like that I needed to be pinned down.

"Who is she?" my mother said, handing me the daguerreotype of Jessamine.

It was bewildering. Wee Charles touched my arm. His eyes were so shiny and open. He nestled close so that he could look at the image with me. "Where did you –" I said.

"It came by post," she said. "I wondered who she was."

I counted to twenty and then again. I whispered that the person in the image was "wee Charles's grandmother."

"So, you did not find him wandering in a forest."

"No, Mother, I did not."

"Is she living?"

My blood beat at me, a kind of liquid accusation. "Mother," I said, "I have killed so many."

"It's okay."

"How can it be okay?"

"In war it's different, they say," and she handed me the note that came with the image.

"You have no idea," I said, meaning the carnage, the wreck of men, the stink of ammunitions and blood and mud and bodies decaying. Cristiana's awkward form in the gaping earth came to mind. "Where are my things?" It came out rough because I had a sudden fear that my parents had gone through my haversack and discovered the doll and – who knew? – the money. I could sense a barrage of questions limning the room and I got scared, my body shivering with it. My mother found my bag and handed it to me.

"I will call the priest," she said, which got me cackling for overlong like a crazy person.

When she left, Charles trailing after her, I sat clutching the haversack, rocking to calm myself. By and by, this succeeded and I was able to pull the letter from its envelope. It read:

Dear Private Russell S. Boyt, Please be sure to give this to Charles when you deem him old enough to make good use of it. Love, C. Muldon.

Love, she wrote. It did not occur to me then that she must have written these notes after leaving me in the henhouse and before I did what I did to her. I reckoned her still alive because that is what I surely wanted. But even still, in that sliver of time, she had written "love," and it was this word I now fixated upon. I had elicited this articulation. A person loved me. I would hold onto this for some time. A shiver danced through me – I had finally achieved the love of this freewoman. A tear fell, for I could not help the thought arriving that only a ghost might care for such a man as me, as I ever was, as I ever would be.

I drew out Muldon's writing kit and commenced to write. In that first day after my fever broke, I wrote seven times to Cristiana, as if to write to her meant she must surely be alive. How I believed this is hard to now fathom. I think I must have thought I could bring her back by the will of my carefully chosen words. I was as mad as a hatter then. Now I am merely mad.

Dear Cristiana, Charles is in good hands as you know. Even my father is now won over by his antics, though my mother bides time, more suspicious by nature. Thank you for the memento.

Dear Cristiana, I recall with delight you whispering to me in the henhouse post coitus.

Dear Cristiana, Do come north at your earliest convenience. I will set you up with some intelligent work such that your spirits will actively rise. This is a good town.

Dear Cristiana, I long for your correspondence.

Dear Cristiana.

Dear Cristiana.

Dear Cristiana, I dream day and night, and never do the dreams feel less real than when I am not dreaming. I don't know what I do and what is simply done to me. I have taken to reading Walt Whitman, which

*my mother has brought to me. He must have been born of some strange
god. I hear he was in Harewood about the time I was also there, but I
do not believe I ever met him. I wonder at his multitudes. The world is
capacious, I have learned. To me it is miniscule and cramped. Does he
know the strange battle creatures? Have the wounded informed him of
that splendid horror? I worry about dirt, Cristiana. And being so still. I
worry I am too sedentary and this cannot be mind-healthy. I worry all
the time. Have begun to pick myself to scabs. Write soon.*

As the months passed, I worried that I would not be able to return to school,
to sit still enough to learn a thing, to take in the thoughts of others. It was this:
I longed to be moving, longed to have Charles's weight pushing down on me,
and missed the incantatory sense of achievement in the nothing of walking
away. I wanted the feeling that moving gave me, the way it shot through my
thoughts and brought some calm to my confused mind. But I did not go. I was
still in pain. But that was not why. I stayed on until a machine-like inertia took
complete hold of me. I was a factory of nonsense. I barely ate, I let corrosion do
its slow work through my organs.

One night at supper, my father cleared his throat and said, "There is the
matter of schools." Maybe school would provide regularity and structure, and I
could find a way back.

I looked down at my false leg – I could see the line where it met my body
through my pressed wool trousers. It was a sign of having endured something
monumental, but for others, I knew, it was a sign of my consummate incom-
pleteness and failure. My mother insisted I wear the prosthetic to mealtimes,
and so, while I eat, I must negotiate the metal and leather clamped to me. I must
be careful not to let it scrape along the floor, where it might leave a blemish on
the hardwood. "I'm properly re-enrolled, I understand."

"I mean for Charles," my father said, and nodded in the boy's direction.

"Ah." I felt anxiety clench and wane, bad weather coming.

"I've been investigating boarding opportunities. You'll be in school, too, as
you mention, and too busy to attend to a child." There was the tonal inference
that suggested I wasn't mentally equipped for the task. "Your mother is otherwise occupied and I've my patients to consider. I won't have Charles underfoot,
and besides, he needs an education." Father droned on in this manner. While he
did, I half rose, cupping a tureen as if to clear the table.

"Where do you suppose you are going, sir?" Father said. It was a sputter between one absurd rhetorical point and another, about how this particular school was highly recommended by – of all people – his own old childhood friend, Howard Spence. I knew how these boarding schools were; they were all the same. Charles was staring up at me, reading me from under the table, where he would sometimes slip down and hide.

I hurled the dish.

There was a short lull before impact, the food having spiralled off in all directions. Then came Father's rising bluster. I glared and swept whatever I could off the table with one arm, then grabbed at anything I could reach to hurl – acutely aware of my mother pulling Charles out of the way and then out of the room – until I was breathless and wondering how this rampage of mine had started and how it had ended, certainly with untold expense.

The next morning, my father was not able to bear the sight of me and another doctor was brought in to attend. I wished this doctor would say something, but he merely came in and waited. The man was a redhead who looked curiously like Bellair.

"Dr. Oswald," he said, reaching out to shake hands, and then he happily admitted he specialized in cases of insanity. He sat quietly by the door to my bedroom, me standing, and we stayed like that for an inordinately long period, despite the unbearable heat this day. My father was in the room, too. He had taken a chair in the corner and sat poker-faced, head cocked in the direction of the doctor, away from me. The hottest spring on record.

"Do you see faces?" Dr. Oswald asked eventually. It was like a languid interruption to a dream I had not realized I was having.

"Faces?"

"You are welcome to take your jacket off."

"I mustn't," I answered. My mother insisted I wear a jacket. The breeze from the window where I stood mitigated the heat but only just. The doctor began a gentle goading. My voice sounded dead where it never had before. The room oppressed me. It is a strange thing to say, but the way madness worked I was only able to see it when I was no longer mad, or at least, less mad. The madness had a sureness to it. A certainty.

"Ah," said Dr. Oswald. "Yes, of course," and noted something down.

"I'm not completely ignorant, you know," I said.

"No, of course not. A medical man yourself, I understand."

I sniffed derisively and fixed my gaze on a shrub in the garden that was about to flower.

"It must have been dreadful, an awful thing."

"What?"

"The battlefield. Over twenty thousand dead in a short week, I read. Thousands more wounded. They say a person couldn't see the ground for miles."

"They," I blurted. "Who are 'they'?"

"The newspapermen, of course." Oswald's eyes were like blue glass alleys, pure and unblinking. He was a slender man, without spectacles, which made him look ill-suited to doctoring. He looked to be a banker. I laughed when I thought this.

"Is something amusing?"

"No," I said, and I sobered, noticing Henrietta, our maid, crossing the yard with a wicker basket of laundry while Charles skipped behind her. I had tried to intercede the other day, to get Charles to do something with me, but the boy preferred her. She'd scolded me and said, "I don't mind him tagging along, Russell. You were just the same. Do you remember?"

Had I ever been a child? I could feel Dr. Oswald's intent stare along my back. There was a part of me that desperately wanted to talk, but I worried what would spill out if I started. Finally, I said, "My father must have outlined the incident in the dining room yesterday evening."

"He mentioned something."

Oswald got up and came to me, put his hand on my shoulder. I did not like this. It seemed to release some old taut thing in me, and before I could regather, I was blubbering, trying to keep my body from convulsing in obvious grief. I recalled the pleasing arc of the dish such that even as it flew, I wished it back on the table. "That tureen had the most beautiful painting upon it, in grey and pink. When it shattered, my mother said to us – to the room, really – how it had been her great-great-grandmother's. She did not raise her voice. She was stoic in her loss. But when I held the shard in my palm, I willed myself into the utopic scene depicted there. I have it somewhere."

I hop-hobbled to my writing desk. The shard had two young entwined seals on it. My mother had wept late last night, when all had calmed and she was able to take the measure of the damage I had wrought. She wept not because of me but rather the discovery that the seal lovers, which had perched atop the lid, were fully split one from the other. She held a piece in both hands and made the strangest face. I had yelled at her for forcing me to wear the leg at meals, and she had reacted by leaving the room. I leaned down then and pocketed the porcelain seals and wandered away, my father berating me though the words made no sense.

I used the banister for support up the stairs, hating the way the damned false leg ate into me with each tread, cursing Eb Wilkes for his shoddy workmanship even while knowing he meant well, that it was the best leg on the market, that Eb thought of his work as *useful*. In that moment, standing in my room with Oswald and my father, I decided to forgive Eb. I would write him – at any rate, I ought to keep the avenue open for the future, a future I now knew was fast approaching, for I could certainly not stay here much longer. I could not see the boy boarded away at the school that had been my own undoing. Halfway up the stairs, I recalled the boy smiling up at me from under the table, laughing at the ruckus, before Mother hauled him away.

Oswald nodded at the seals. Father scoffed. I shoved the busted piece of tableware back into the writing desk drawer.

"If you'll excuse me," I said to Oswald. "I've paperwork to catch up on."

"You write?"

"Primarily letters," I said.

The doctor nodded, checked his fob. He looked perplexed. "I've one last question."

"Oh?"

"Yes," said Oswald. "Do you defile yourself?"

My lip curled. I preferred not to answer such a question. I was well aware that he was implying I should be institutionalized. Then my father would find a way to sideline me and put Charles away in school. I stared at the doctor until he left but would not say another word. And then I wrote so frantically.

Dear Cristiana, ///// ///// ////// /////// /////// ////// ////// // / ////// /// /////// //////
/// /// /// ////// //////

I wrote letters like this every day for weeks after this. I also ripped them up and threw them away. They were a code. I believed that then. But now, thinking back, I believe they might have just been the jottings of a sick man. Meanwhile my leg seemed to finally be healed. The black spot turned out to be a withering infection and had withdrawn after weeks of rest. I fevered it out. The flesh webbed itself together.

And then healed enough one afternoon, I had two letters to mail and got myself downstairs. One to Cristiana. One to Eb, advising him of my improving health and my academic plans. *The boy is hale and hearty, a vigorous lad, and quick-witted*, I wrote, and asked him in return for any news of medical interest. I told him how starved I was for communication of any sort.

Mother interrupted me at the front door as I set out. "There are two appointments scheduled pertaining to your recovery," she said. I didn't like the symmetry of these two schedules and my letters and thought I must destroy one or hobble upstairs and write a third letter. But to whom? I wished I were stealthier, faster, so that I might have avoided this encounter with my mother. I loathed speaking to either of my parents these days.

"When?" I said.

"Tomorrow: a carriage ride to Dr. Oswald, and from there, to a local prosthetics man to make you a spare." She gestured to my leg. "This one begins to reek."

"Oh," I said. "I hadn't noticed. I am sorry for the inconvenience."

"It's not me," she answered. "Your father requests you get a new leg, which he will pay for. He tells me that great strides are being made in prosthetics. Dr. Oswald expects you at three o'clock."

"Strides," I muttered and then laughed, but my mother only looked baffled at the joke. "Oswald is extraordinarily rude, Mother."

There was something in her manner, the way she tilted her face toward my leg, the guardedness of her answers. I smelled some lie.

"A short journey," she said.

"Where?"

"Offices on Queen."

"Ah." I pushed the door open to leave. "I'm off to the post office. I won't be long."

Her body seemed to collapse at this. She watched me walk down the walkway, and I became acutely aware of the mechanistic way I moved. I was a kind of machine, certainly, flesh and bone and leather and springs. I could feel her looking upon me pityingly.

"I can take the letters," she called, her tone sprightly and false. "I'd be happy to."

"No." I half turned, my smile more a grimace. "The exercise pleases me."

I felt the pressure of tears, so I made sure she couldn't see me.

There was only one medical facility on Queen Street, for lunatics. I wasn't an ignoramus. What must the good doctor have pronounced upon me? Insanity by mania? Insanity by masturbation? The appointment was surely a trap. I would be forced to go there and then I should never leave. The boy would be sent away to school where he would be harassed in all the ways one could expect to be harassed in such places.

I began to plan. The boy, the haversack, walking. It formed around me, a strategy for leaving, and I let it. I knew everything about it by the time I reached the post office doors. I would allow the boy to abscond with some small token from the house if he wished, something he'd grown fond of and whatever was on his back. I suddenly realized that I had been planning since my debacle in the dining room, but now I saw I must act. This night. The idea made me sick, a necessary illness that crashed through my body, set my brain in an icy turmoil. It was a kind of fuel. I began to move faster. I helped my leg along with my arm, a technique I had honed.

In the post office, I asked to borrow a pen, pulled open the letter to Eb and added a few lines, to the effect that I was on the move, looking for work, heading to Washington and would certainly come directly to the manufactory. The additional lines calmed the feeling of unease I had been unable to shake regarding the coincidence of twos. I felt relief to pin the letter down with this new plan, and I knew that I had, with these few lines to Eb, broken a spell my mother had cast on me.

DAY TWENTY-FOUR

I SLEEP ALL DAY – rather, I hide in my room in order to avoid my parents. I've been told that the city's storm sewers have hit capacity and that there is a likelihood that my boys and Matthew are stranded in the house. I wonder if they have made use of the canoe that is tucked in the rafters of the garage. It's strange to me that I have had no word from them, but then, why would Matthew bother? The past is past, from his perspective. No point in going back. Not over his own history and certainly not over mine. It is women's work to dwell.

And dwell I do. On the past, on this ancient Civil War story. It's funny, the word *dwell*. Funny how it implies obsessive rumination but also living in a place, as if the two things are contiguous or even precisely the same thing. I'm aware of the extent Boyt's story is just me working through whatever I am working through here in this old childhood homestead.

I suppose it is natural to mourn the dead when we feel the least like ourselves. I have this feeling that if only Wulf had lived I would be complete. I have this feeling – something about the way Mum and Dad are stonewalling me – that the sealskin is the key to him. But feelings are not facts. I look down at my hands, the translucent webbing between my index and second fingers. I used to be teased about it. Classmates liked to call me ducker and duckwit. It used to bug me until a babysitter told me it was like a superpower. It's true that I could swim faster and with more efficiency than anyone in my class, my hands like little paddles scooping the water behind me. I still love that feeling of moving through water. I wonder if perhaps my selkie ancestor was just like me, enduring a birth defect, something locals explained through magic and folklore: she had webbed hands and feet, she must be part seal. But why keep a skin like that? A talisman, maybe? A joke? Something perhaps entirely unrelated. Uncanny to find it lodged in the house like that, dwelling in the dwelling, like a dream object. And then, so odd that Mum and Dad won't let me have it, won't speak to me about it. What had Dad said out at the well? That there was something unspeakable.

Unspeakable. That word itself so potent. What is unspeakable resides in the folds of the unconscious. These things – this material – is tucked in there like little seeds harboured under a sidewalk. If you tamper with the environment there, nurture any aspect of it, you incur composting – those seeds are liable to sprout. The unspeakable thing that unfurls will break you open, form all manner of cracks in the pavement.

Nature always prevails.

I'm realizing suddenly that my parents are in pain. Their whole bodies and minds are contorting in order to hold this sprout, this latent seed, in place. They think they are protecting me, but they are barricading me inside their trauma.

Also, they are pissing me off.

I know the unspeakable thing. I live it all through my body. It resides in every crevice of my nervous system. Trauma is body just as writing is. I know their trauma even if I don't have words for it yet. For they, in their huddled attempt at protection, have bequeathed it to me in every way. By their shifty silence, by their fury, their whispers, their guarded emotions, their particular and idiosyncratic habits, their scorn, their very bodily being, they have given me the gift that their parents gave them, and their parents' parents.

It's so sad.

In my body, I am Boyt and also Eva. It goes back generations, I suppose. I am the sensitive, queer son, the selkie wife, the settler, the privileged, the racist, the struggler, the landlocked. I am Wulf, my sisters. I am Cristiana and Charles, too, in the way their story intersects with my family. It's a swirl of laughter and decay and horror and hope. And it is unspeakable only because of the fear that holds us prisoner.

I see him, my brother. I am seven or eight. He walks the edge of these woods, over where the bush gives way to the neighbour's old horse pasture. I stand still so, as not to disturb or frighten him. I don't want anything I do to influence his movements. I also don't want to frighten myself. It's the way the sun glances off his skin through the foliage. He's dirty, his clothing tattered.

If I were to walk only a few steps back and turn, I would see the pond through the branches, the water high this time of year, already the tadpoles growing legs and arms. The moment of evolution, I know, is fully alive in the frog – how it was a fish, and then a creature that could come and go from water. Like a seal, I think now. Flippers, webbed.

He is coming from the neighbour's side, as if from nowhere. He's coming to find me through the woods. I imagine bringing him home, but I already know this won't be possible. He moves carefully, picking his way in between the scattered cedars, stepping gingerly, watchful, skirting bracken and deadfall.

It's late spring, and the forest floor is black and dappled with green. I love the way the ground seems to thrust up at me when I walk on it, like a sprung gymnasium floor. This boy makes no sound and does not crouch; he has mastered the forest. I ache to be like him. I already love him so much my heart expands until my rib cage hurts. I am so still, so still – forever – for so long – until he is right in front of me, and I know I have won this moment.

"Hi," I say.

"Hi."

His jaw is already square like a grown-up boy, and his hair is blond and curled tight. He's got a wool dress-up outfit on but it's been wrecked from some wild game he's been playing, or so I think. His eyes are huge. His eyelashes are like a doe's, thick and straight.

"Do you want to play?" I ask.

"Sure," he says. We find sticks, spend an hour or more traipsing through the forest, heading deeper and deeper into the bush, toward the back of the property, where I show him all the secret places – fairyland, a small round meadow surrounded by a copse of trees. The butterflies are thick there. We smash puffballs and watch their spores plume. This is the work of serious play, and we take it on, searching for more and more puffballs, like skulls peeping up out of the earth, until we can't find any more. Then we take to whacking at the trees as if they are enemies. We smash at last year's standing hay, whatever frothy milkweed has survived the winter; we smash everything.

He taps me on the shoulder with the end of his stick and I turn. I know this is a duel. We touch stick ends and bow, then scrabble and lunge, hitting each other so hard. Our legs and arms are bruised and cut. We bleed. After a time, we sit on a stone that juts out from the ground like a shelf. It's a favourite of mine, almost perfectly flat. I marvel at the infinite greens of the lichen that grows there. The bruises bloom.

"How old are you?" I think to ask.

His brow furrows, he leans in and tracks a finger into the cuff of my cut-off jeans, trying to figure out what manner of clothing I am wearing. Then he smiles. "Ten," he says. "Ten or more. No one ever wrote my birthdate down."

"How can that be?"

"They just never did."

"I'm going home now," I say.

"Sure, okay," he says, and he watches me get up and walk away.

"I can bring you a sandwich," I say, because there is a hungry look to him.

He is not there when I return that afternoon. But I see him again, curled up and sleeping in the forest behind the barn. This time it's winter and there's plenty of snow. He isn't dressed for winter, is sleeping in the middle of a circle of thawed ground on a bed of leaves – oak, elm, maple, willow – all of which look freshly fallen. I stand over him and try to wake him, but he won't awaken. His skin is warm and, after a time, I become a little afraid to be seeing things that are not there.

When I mention it to Mum, she tells me I am making things up. "Your brother never lived," she says.

"He must have," I plead.

"No. It's sad. But it's the truth."

This should reassure me but instead it makes me cross. And so, the next day, I take the sharpest knife from the kitchen and go to the forest behind the barn to get a stick. I plan to make a gun. I find a stick and sit, stripping the bark from it. My whole body is humming with the movement, of tucking the knife blade under the bark and sliding it along the shaft of wood. It's a cedar branch, for there is nothing else in the forest but cedar. I love the resin smell.

It is the straightest branch I can find but still not all that straight. It will be an act of the imagination to make it into a gun. I do it in secret. I'm ten and too old for such games, but I don't care. I take the fake gun and climb a tree. I see our cat ambling over near the barn. She stops and lowers her head, for she is also hunting. I tilt my body and squint down the length of the gun, swing it until I'm aiming at Marbles. She's looking in the wrong direction. I wait until she turns her body sideways. I have a good chance then and I shoot. She bolts at the sound I make. She has dodged my bullet. She has escaped the story I tried to write her into.

I climb a little higher. At the top, this tree sways like crazy, and I have to hold on by wrapping a leg around the trunk. There is a mouse or a mole nosing the underbrush far below. Marbles crouches and scrambles toward it, her nose twitching, eyes never leaving it. I think of the boy's hair, the lean muscles on his rib cage, like a hound's. I look down at the rodent and the cat, make quiet *pow-pow* noises so as not to ruin Marble's fun. She is so close to catching whatever it is. And then she pounces, has it in her mouth and is shaking it. It's a pretty mouse. Marbles drops it and puts a paw upon it, then releases it to see what it will do.

The mouse makes a fumbling escape before Marbles sinks her teeth into it again. She tosses it a few more times. The fun of it passes, the mouse wet with blood and cat saliva. It's certainly dead. Marbles has it in her mouth still, its tail dangling, and she trots off toward the house. She'll bring it to Mum, the kind of sublime animal gift that humans can't fully understand.

I drop the gun, watch it hurtle to the ground. I climb down the cedar like it is a simple ladder, not caring about sap or scratches. I fetch the gun and prop it against the trunk. I straddle the low bough of the cedar tree now, the one that yaws out horizontally to the ground, then I take the knife and scrape off a circle of bark. It's work doing this, and I have to press my body into it until I have made a nice bald patch. "Fuck you," I say. "Your brother is dead and gone."

I go to Mum in her room, where she is holed up, feeling sickly again. I ask her now if she recalls my pestering her about a boy in the woods when I was young. She looks over her coverlet at me, and says, "I recall so little of when you and your sisters were wee."

"Do you think it is possible to see or recall things from times before, like ghosts and things?"

"No," she says. "The past is past. We only have now."

"It must have been annoying to you that I kept bringing him up."

"Annoying?" she says. "No. It was worrisome to both of us. Your sisters never mentioned Wulf. But *you* were fixated."

"How did we find out?"

"You just always knew. You were always the intuitive one."

"Was I?" I'm thrilled at this acknowledgment and feel, for the first time in years, seen by her. "I love you, Mum. I'm sorry I'm such a pest."

She wrinkles her nose and asks me to make her a cup of tea, and when I get back, she is asleep, shelled up like a turtle. I put the tea on her side table and stand at the window in her room. I hum as I watch the rain catch itself in drips down the glass. Then after a time, I leave and go to my room. I sit at the Remington and pluck out Boyt's strange letters to Cristiana. They feel true sitting in a stack on the desk, as if I can make history by merely placing one word after another. Then I open up my laptop.

1865

MOSER BLAKEY, THE MAN FOR whom Henry Muldon substituted, took the train from New York City at Chambers through Portland to Montreal and bought a ticket directly on the Grand Trunk Railway to Toronto, where he arrived at the squalid station as the sun was rising. This I pieced together much later from hearsay and anecdote. I was half raving, a sad case, and whatever instability I now bring to this narrative must therefore be forgiven. This is what I heard and cobbled together and invented. Is this not the essence of history? Gossip and fact and the imagination of the author intermingled.

The night of travel had exhausted him, and so he took a red-and-yellow taxi, delighted to discover that the driver, a runaway slave ironically surnamed Freeman, owned a fleet of these vehicles and was by all measures a fabulous success. Blakey considered himself a friend to the ambitious and successful. He identified firstly as an abolitionist and secondly as a human. He gave generously to the effort and invested in ways he felt were progressive. As a stakeholder, such stories of entrepreneurial success energized him. How delightful he must have found this taxicab owner.

The driver brought him to the closest inn, Queen's Hotel. Moser tipped him excessively, asked him if he would be so kind as to wait for him. He then spent twenty-five cents on whiskey at the hotel tavern to wake himself up. He secured a room, intending to leave early the next morning. He put his travel chest on the floor next to his bed, locking the door behind him as he left. By the time he arrived at my parents' doorstep, it was not yet eight o'clock in the morning. He knocked and waited for Henrietta to locate my mother. When she came to the door, and he asked for a Dr. Boyt, Mother told him that Martin was "not at home," it being a weekday. He was surely at a house call. He worked incessantly.

"Martin?" said Moser, confused. "But I am looking for a certain *Russell* Boyt."

"Oh?" said Eva. "My son is Russell. Whatever is it?"

"Well," said Moser. "It's a long story."

"I am afraid he is not here." She knew by now that I had left in the night. I had scrawled a note and left it on the dining table, the broken shard of her favourite tureen holding it down. The contents of the letter showed I had not gone to my appointment with Dr. Oswald and that I was run off with the boy. I was bound by train for Washington. "I do hope there is no trouble with him," she said, a shrillness edging into her voice. "He's very ill."

"Your son is a friend of a friend, I believe." Blakey wore a brown bowler and was done up in tweed. He seemed extraordinarily wealthy to her and smelled of spirits. She could see a Negro man in a similar hat standing beside his taxi just beyond.

She said, "It is very nice to make your acquaintance –"

"Moser Blakey."

"Mr. Blakey, won't you come in?"

"I have such a diminishing amount of time," he said, and looked back at the cab driver. "I arrived early this morning and must return as soon as possible. I had hoped –"

"I wonder if you happened to pass my son in the station on your way in," she said. "You might have noticed him. He is remarkable, I believe. He is maimed in the leg and walks limping. He has coal-black hair and is boyish in face, can barely grow a beard at twenty-three. The boy with him is tousle-haired, blond and wearing a blue peacoat. An orphan my son has grown fond of who is called Charles. We believe him to be five years old or so."

Moser's eyebrows raised at that. "Orphaned?"

"My son found him wandering near Petersburg in a disoriented state," she lied. "He hardly spoke a word at that time. He is nowadays much improved."

Moser reached into his coat – it was fine Scots wool. He enjoyed the silken feeling of the lining as it brushed his hand and wrist; it felt rich, and he liked to be reminded of his own wealth. The feeling of righteousness was equally silken, he found. There was a wholeness to feeling right in one's politics. He pulled out a packet of letters, all of which he had previously read.

Their seals were torn. Eva recognized the letters as written by Russell – she herself had posted many of them. "Oh dear!" A wincing sound emitted from her. She excused herself and reached for the letters. "However did you –" she said, but the man pulled them away.

"Maybe I had better do come in, after all?" he said. "I do not like to delay the driver." He turned and went to the man, and opened his purse to give him some money.

The taxi was already clipping away when Eva let Moser Blakey into the parlour, called to Henrietta to set tea despite Moser's protests not to bother on his behalf. "It's no trouble at all," Eva said. Badness bloomed in the pit of her stomach.

"I'm obliged first to apologize for bursting in upon you, madam." Moser settled into the only hardback chair in the room, as if determined to be uncomfortable. "A mystery has presented itself, and I feel I have a moral necessity. I hope this conversation will clarify events for me. You say your son is ill. May I intrude?"

He set the letters down on the low table. Eva resisted reaching for them. She missed me so already. "He is unwell, you must truly understand," she said. She would have liked to tell him about Dr. Oswald's diagnosis but was embarrassed to say the word. She felt as if she herself had somehow led me astray but how she could not precisely fathom. She had been just the sort of mother hers had been to her. Had she failed me somehow? Martin had assured her this was not so, but she felt responsible. Had she coddled me overly as a boy? She knew she had. Martin insisted that she had been a dutiful mother.

Blakey shifted about in his chair. "I hired a substitute at the conscription. You must know, I could not leave my work to fight. I hired an ex-slave to fight in my place. I paid him handsomely, more than the amount suggested for such an arrangement. He died in his first skirmish, so I am told. May his soul rest in peace."

Eva reached again for the letters, out of some instinct to change the course of the conversation. It seemed to be going nowhere good. "My son was also a substitute. He wanted, in his own words, an adventure. He lost his leg there."

"I'm sorry to hear this."

"Yes, well."

"I can let you read them," Moser said, gesturing to the letters again, "but I must insist on keeping them until the details are sorted. I have some atrocious news, and you had better be sitting for it. Is your husband close by that he can be fetched? It might be prudent."

"He never returns in working hours, I am afraid." Eva was not sure Martin could manage the news, whatever it was. He was still unaware that I had left, and to think of all this overwhelming him was more than she could process.

"My substitute's name was Henry Muldon," Moser said. Eva's skin prickled at the oddness of this. This whole day was turning odd. She felt cold creeping under the skin on her forearms despite the warm day heating the parlour.

"Mr. Blakey," she said, finally, "what is your business?"

"Investment and exchange," he answered.

She had meant his current errand, not what he did for a living. Still. A banker, and what that must mean, she thought, was that I must owe some dreadful debt. She said, "We will not hesitate to compensate for any debt our son –" and here she heard herself whine out "– that our son may have incurred."

"No," said Moser. "No. I'm afraid it is more serious – more esoteric – than money. It would have been so helpful to us all had the boy been here." Moser shifted. His nerves were frayed, and he would have liked to sleep. He took a breath. "A body has been found. It seems a woman lies murdered." He let this horrific information waft around the room, a hard-edged bit of news untethered, now filling every corner, and watched how singularly it unnerved my mother. He watched her carefully. She seemed to physically diminish. "The deceased's name is Cristiana Muldon," he said. "The widow of my substitute." He leant in and riffled the letters on the table between them, a movement that created the slightest mouldy wind in my mother's direction.

"What?" she said. She recalled Dr. Oswald's prognosis and thought: insanity, insanity by mania, exacerbated by self-defilement. The doctor's written statement in perfect calligraphic penmanship, the *f* of *defilement* flourished and mocking. What might I have done? Her own heart was whinging. And what of the wee boy? It was all jumbled. She felt her blood ebbing. And there was Moser's slick voice.

"The body of an ex-slave. You must have heard this name. The letters your son wrote seem to suggest love and secrets. Perhaps you saw something. I am not one to judge."

And my mother woke up. How a person could not know she was sleeping her whole life until that moment. "It wasn't him," she said. "It can't have been." It came out as the throaty expulsion of a protective animal. An ex-slave, Eva thought, the notion bringing some relief that it wasn't a white woman, for that would mean certain jail time or even a death sentence. She began to assess value against punishment, thinking if she had read of a similar case in the newspapers. My mother was no abolitionist, but she treated her help as well as one might expect. She always said so. Hadn't she cared for Charles? He was surely a halfling, so light of tone. Her whole body flushed. She wanted to scurry out of the room in fear, like a small rodent. She turned to the man in her parlour and said, "Are you a constable?"

"No. My interest is moral. As you yourself said, your son was also in substitution for another man. I wanted to let your boy know about Cristiana. He must be made to know she lives no more. And I must take the poor child back with me to bring him up as my own. I have a certain clear responsibility to the family of my substitute who fought in my place. You see, don't you?"

Eva slumped back on the settee with some relief, but when she looked back into the eyes of Moser Blakey, she saw he was obfuscating what he really believed: that I was not really safe from his scrutiny, that things would only become more and more devilish. Moser thanked her for any help she could provide and left her flustered. He left his calling card and information as to where to find him should I return or make contact. She tried to imagine what I might have done and how it was that I would continue writing to this murdered woman. It did not make sense, her mind could not line the story up, but then little about me lined up anymore, she had to admit. I had killed a woman – how could she not take this personally? She went to her bedroom and wept until she felt some equilibrium returning.

At the Queen's Hotel, or so I have heard, Moser opened his throat and swallowed down another whiskey, then ordered another. A gaunt rebel soldier tried to engage him in conversation, but he put him off, saying he was exhausted and preferred to sit alone. He removed himself from the bar to a table and feigned watching out the window at the comings and goings on Front Street. It seemed to him this town was made of dirt, or else a kind of filth had clung to him all the way from my parents' house, all the way from Virginia, more likely. He shuddered, recalling the scene he had found at Cristiana Muldon's address. That whitewashed shack.

A terrible stillness, first of all, one that made him shake along the skin. Under a ceramic pot on the sheltered porch was a packet of letters, many scrawled with my manic hand, and then there were Moser's own letters – seven of them, one for each month he'd sent money. He berated himself for not growing suspicious sooner, but his own affairs had occupied him. It had certainly niggled at him that Cristiana had not sent receipt, since she has been so routine, so hygienic, in her correspondence prior.

He knew she needed the money, for she was alone with the boy and had no way of earning enough on her own. But he'd pushed his concerns aside, keeping his head down with work and his patronages and philanthropy until he simply couldn't ignore his intuition. Then he finally did put everything else aside and made the trip, telling his wife he had business and would simply be away. Why worry her? He rented a buggy out of Washington, once he arrived there, and manned it himself. He had such a terrible feeling now, recalling all of this.

The shack she lived in appalled him, for even in the small time since he purchased it, nature had overtaken it. The battens were covered in creeping plants and the whitewash was chipping. Foliage had grown up all around it. He should have located her in a town and not in so isolated a place where anything might happen to her. Immediately, when he noticed the letters and read them through, he began to puzzle out what had transpired. The inside of the house, when he went in, looked as if it had been hastily abandoned. Moser reasoned Cristiana may have run off, pushing northward for her own reasons, but why would she not have informed him? And then he peered through the window and saw the henhouse, one scrawny bird pecking in the yard, and beyond it, a section of disturbed earth, a remarkable quagmire with all the rains they'd had. He started, his body passing through an awful veil – could one die of fright? He'd heard of this. The ghostly stillness of the place made sense in that moment, an awful kind of sense.

He walked toward this strange sighting like some sleepwalking creature and found the corroded shovel I had left there. It was stupid of me to leave it there. He dug. The soil was red and cakey and heavy – this part I know. It took him hours of apprehensive work, for he did not want to find what he knew must be there. Halfway or so he began to weep, the kind of weeping of men who are taught not to ever do so, and so it wracked his musculature like a pummelling. Thank God he was alone.

And now, sitting in the sunroom with his beverage at the Queen's Hotel, just back from his curious encounter with Mrs. Boyt, a new puzzle, a new horror really, emerged. He knew now that I had the boy, Charles, with me, and what could that possibly mean but that I already knew, had been writing letters to a long-dead corpse, a corpse who had left behind an orphan – yes, Mrs. Boyt had used the very term *orphan*. The last thing he had said before he left my house was meant warmly.

"Your son, madam. Some of his letters are worrisome –" and he trailed off for fear of offending. But what madness in those letters.

Eva said, "I mentioned that Russell is ill." She looked so defended and shock-stricken. "He runs an occasional brain fever."

Moser beckoned to the barkeep and ordered more whiskey. The reb soldier, in near tatters, headed toward him and sat down. "There was spectres misting up all over the field," he said, and then, as if reading Moser's thoughts, added, "I ain't drunk. I swear it. They most certainly did rise out of the dead, and their blackened teeth menaced the bejesus out of me." He reached over and drank Moser's whiskey. "Even out of the coloured soldiers. I didn't know as no one never told me that darkies had souls. Proof right there or I am crazy," he said. "Or I am right insane."

Moser said, "I'll buy, kid." He would set him straight over a whiskey, he thought, for all men had souls, even the stupid ones. Even this one.

DAY TWENTY-FIVE

MY MOTHER STAYS IN BED; my father is quietly worrying, walking the ever-shrinking perimeter. I think he might be praying for a break in the rain but his prayers, thus far, remain unanswered. Once a day, I plead with him to tell me where the sealskin is. He is tight-lipped. He acts as though we have a truce, but we do not have a truce. I am vigilant watching him. I just know he will slip up. That I will catch him in his secret. Meanwhile, Mum grows stronger. We feed her soup and tea. But she says odd, feverish things. This morning, she said, "What has become of your sisters in your story?"

I say, "They asked to be left out of the story."

"But do they call?"

In fact, they have each called twice and she has spoken to them. They live far away and send love.

I haven't mentioned, nor has Dad, that the basement is completely underwater. There is nothing to do but brood. Lean in, the current terminology is, and leaning in I am, to this story that has fully obsessed me. The lineage I imagine to belong to me or I to it. That network of DNA and life experience, the way Boyt carried out his life within the structure he was born into. And how badly he managed that. And how we all now pay for it. I wonder if it is possible to re-narrate the whole thing – not just Boyt's story or mine, not just the small stories but also the larger one, the paradigmatic one, the shitty colonial one that seems so solid we can't begin to topple it. Hundreds of thousands of people tried a few years ago and nothing much came of it. Is it possible that money holds this story in place?

I tell her about it – the bits about Moser that I have extrapolated from the diary. She looks at me through watery eyes. When I ask why she is crying, she says, "It's just so moving." She falls asleep so fast, I get scared and shake her awake.

"I forget," she says then. "What was your brother's name?"

"Wulf, after a baby in an old poem."

"He lived on an island."

"That's right."

She smiles grimly. "He was a sweet baby."

Dad's at the door, hushing her now.

She's grown old so quickly. Dad is acting as if this is it for them. Yesterday, when I came to make porridge for them, Dad was hunched over his accounts book, scribbling numbers. He twisted his head to acknowledge me and said, "There will be nothing to show for it."

"What do you mean?" I said.

"I wanted the house to be left to you girls. To sell or keep. There's no money to leave you. Just the house. And now it'll be ruined, and I am so sorry."

"Oh, Dad," I say. "Never you mind about that. We're all just fine." I'll get the separation agreement money in a month. "Maybe I can buy a place for us all. I can take care of you. It's not the end of the world," I say, even if it might be.

"Still," he says. "It was my hope."

I give him a little hug. It's all he will let me.

I kayak out into the fields, just past the lawn, and there is almost nothing left of the old forest – just cedar copse rising from the horizon like little shrubs. The property is a sea. I dip my hand and drink the sweet water. It's cold and refreshing. There are terns swooping overhead where there have never – at least not in living memory – been water birds. How quickly nature comes.

Story, too, comes to fill a void. I have run out of research for Boyt's story. Ancestry.com is a wash. I have made a few calls to some archives, but what I come up with wouldn't fill a shoebox. Little quilting points of "facts" and the rest is fabrication. I am making something out of nothing. I pull out the diary.

So far it hasn't given much. The penmanship gets more and more cramped as if Eva knows she is running out of space and doesn't want to start a new journal. I've been flipping through it, using it like an oracle. I open it backwards and read now for the first time its final entry, dated October 1892:

> Cold. Blustery wind. Martin died yesterday. And in the mail a letter from a woman name Meredith Murdoch. There is a grandson, she says. His name is Nigel. She enclosed a photograph of him. He was always contrary, she writes, and now he comes to Canada with his bride and daughter. I'm a great-grandmother, it seems. I wish Martin had lived to know. Perhaps they will reach out to me. Murdoch says he will build his own house out of stone with skills he learned in Fife. The bride is odd, she writes. She tells something truly mad then, that the woman comes from a small coastal village and that she longs obsessively for the sea, and that already twice she has tried to run off from her duties. I freeze all through myself when I read this. I can't help but picture her bound by the hands on a ship heading here. Captive. And then I think of Russell and Martin, both dead now, and this big house and all the things I might have given up for this life, and the way that safety cuts one off from truly living. And from oneself. I think of all the choices I never got to make for myself. And I find myself sympathetic toward this odd woman who longs for the sea. I find myself in a fantasy about daring to run off, but where would such a one as me go? And now that they are dead, what is the point? There is no longer a self to find.

That is the entry in its entirety.

1865

EB HAD MOVED HIS PROSTHETICS manufactory onto the hospital grounds. A convoy of ambulances meandered in the dirt with maimed soldiers inside of them. I knew I must look a wreck. I had taken to rubbing and worrying the skin on my face such that I was pocked and scabbed. My eyes were rimmed red with fatigue, and even I could feel how furtive I'd become. The nurses at the front desk gave me queer looks until I showed my prosthetic to them, and then they pointed out where I and the boy should go, a building on the grounds set off and to the side of the main hospital.

Eb saw me almost the minute I walked into the new manufactory. I shook his hand vigorously.

"Sorry for the inconvenience. We moved locations in a hurry."

I clenched my jaw. I was in bad shape. "So much of me has become constructed," I mumbled. I could hear my thoughts as I thought them, a valve on the pressure. Charles moved closer.

"Excuse me for asking," Eb said, "but are you perfectly well?"

I tucked my chin down, shook all over. The boy clutched the fabric of my trouser leg.

"You should sit," Eb said. He pulled two chairs close together so we could talk on the same level.

"All these dreadful things hanging," I recall saying.

"Prosthetics," Eb reminded me. "For soldiers."

"Dreadful." The place was replete with death.

"Legs and arms," said Charles, looking up as if he had just noticed them dangling all around him. This brought a grim look to Eb's face.

"Business thrives," I said.

"You are in want of work, I understand," Eb said then.

"If you can replace a man's leg," I said, "why not a torso? Why not a whole person, piece by piece?" I was half or more crazed.

"Your words are oftentimes dismaying, Russell."

But he set me up in an office and I worked hard for him. As I said, we slept in a spare guest room in his home. I kept busy to keep sane or to hide. I felt hunted. And then it came to pass that I was hunted.

Two weeks later, near closing time, Eb was out front supervising when a man in natty business attire arrived at the manufactory, flanked by two Irish police constables. Was a Private Russell Boyt to be found? A warmth bloomed along Eb's skin, he told me later. It hit his back first and then prickled over his whole self.

"And who's this?" the man said to Charles, peeping out from behind Eb's legs.

"An orphan lad," Eb said. He nudged the frightened boy. He was bent on teaching Charles how to be polite, how to shake hands with acumen. He despised a shyness he saw in the child, for it reminded him of the aspects of his father he had loathed – the shrinking isolation of him, the failure to speak his mind. He felt these were antipathetic to manhood. "Put your hand out to shake, boy." He looked at the man and then at the officers. "Because of the war he is behind in his education, but we are doing our best to catch him up."

Charles only gaped at the visitors. The man crouched down to eye level and held out a candy sucker, and said, "Howdy, sir. It's Charles, right?" And the orphan's eyes lit up.

"It's surely Henry Muldon's boy," the man turned and said to the police. The coppers sidled into the workspace.

"We would like to see Russell Boyt," said one of the police officers.

"Who is Henry Muldon?" Eb said. Then, with the tiniest hint of sarcasm, he added, "And do come in, why don't you?" because of course they were already in, had bustled in with no invitation.

The policemen smiled grimly, because nothing was ever really funny in these sorts of circumstances.

The man said his name was Moser Blakey. "Henry Muldon is the now-dead man who substituted for me." His palm shot out, and Eb took it and shook it vigorously to show who he was, his confidence, even in the face of what might be a disaster. "I have an ongoing responsibility."

Eb was thinking hard. He, too, had a responsibility, but what was it? He had never been more confused. He said, "I'm sorry to hear about your loss," because whatever else came to mind, a man had died for his country, but that wasn't precisely it. There was something dead in this man as a result of the death of Henry Muldon. A ghost seemed to fly between them, chilled the air as it condensed around them. Eb watched Moser Blakey's Adam's apple clench and loosen repeatedly.

Finally, Eb spluttered, "Has Russell Boyt done something?" To his mind, if Russell had done something, then he too must bear the responsibility of it. They were connected – they had common history, and he had a moral obligation. He and Russell formed a sort of contiguous personhood. They were one or something like it. He had said this before. He must protect Russell as he would himself, for hadn't Russell done just this on the battlefield for him? The man had taken Eb's place in war, and now Eb must make good their contract. He owed Russell his loyalty at the very least.

His heart was pounding. Fate had twinned them, had it not? They had found each other, and Russell had fought valiantly as him. Or maybe, more strictly speaking, for him. But it amounted to the same thing. He owed a debt because, well, he himself had not lost his leg or his mind, like Russell had. He had exempted himself by the glorious trick of substitution. For this he was most grateful. How far did this gratitude extend? He was beginning to see how it might extend indefinitely. And an infinite debt was not something he wanted.

He shrugged off the thought that it might have been easier to lose the leg himself.

The walls seemed to breathe tighter while Eb waited for an answer. It was the hardest question, his heart sodden with it, as if he already knew. There was a dread to Russell since he had come from Toronto, a bewitched thing shadowing him. Wind passed through the still-open door and a line of arms hanging from the rafters clacked against one another, a morbid game of dominoes. Eb exhaled too fast, an uncanny fear having grasped him. He wondered suddenly whether each part of the body had its own soul – his thoughts lingered on all those amputations.

"He's lost a leg himself," Eb blurted. "And I sometimes wonder if he didn't lose half his mind with it." There. He'd said it.

The cop's upper lip spasmed. It was in that stupid moment that I leant my face out past the door to my office. I had heard my name spoken and wondered at the sudden shift in energy in the manufactory. This strange pause to the normal industry I was used to hearing in that space. The workers were gaping at Eb, who looked bewildered.

"Come," a man said to Charles, who was now strangling Eb's right leg in some instinctual terror. The kid wouldn't have it, so the man scooped him up, prying them apart. Eb protested, holding the child's shirt at the back.

"He doesn't even know you, sir," said Eb.

"Do not 'sir' me," said Moser. "I have a massive debt to pay, sir. A debt that weighs."

A primal part of Eb wanted to resist more deliberately, but another wanted to be done with it all. He considered whatever I might have done.

"Hey, there," I called out, standing awkwardly at the closet doorway from deep in the manufactory. Between myself and them were a hundred false limbs. "Let my boy down this instant."

The kid was gathering to scream, his cheeks red, eyes welling.

"Yours? No, certainly not," said the man.

I got myself over there quickly and stood amid them, my leg sending such an ache up along my spine. I grabbed for Charles, who was kicking, but the man held him tight. I could not gain purchase on him. "Let him go, sir," I said. "Please. I know his mother."

"Are you Russell Boyt?" said the man holding Charles.

The cops moved very close by me, their hands soft on my clothing, but I could tell they would clutch me hard if I tried anything they did not like or want. Eb was right behind, so there was nothing to do but just stand there and try to reason. One of the cops repeated the question more emphatically: "Are you Private Russell Boyt?"

I made a feeble last attempt to pry Charles from Mr. Blakey, grabbing at him with a frantic impulse.

"Give him the boy," said Eb.

Moser Blakey glared at Eb so hard he looked away. Eb discovered then that everywhere there were glares. He declared to me later that it had made him feel culpable.

One of the cops was fiddling with his cudgel, to look busy or to intimidate Eb, I could not be sure. He looked at the other cop and they nodded back and forth. Then he said to me a thing I will never forget: "You are under arrest for the murder of Cristiana Muldon." They took me by one arm each, their hands like vices around my biceps, and I didn't even struggle.

"Who never did you any wrong," added Moser Blakey.

"Oh God," Eb said.

The cops hauled me off then like a dead thing. Moser Blakey left with the boy, or so I heard. He held him by the hand but with such a tight grip the boy had no chance of evading him. Moser tipped his hat and said, "Sometimes the right thing can feel just as if it were the wrong thing," but Eb was not convinced.

The floor sweeper and the last of the lingering shift stood, giving Eb peculiar looks once the manufactory had emptied of this scuffle. Eb hid in his office. He sent messages out through the hole under the window, like his father before him, he was ashamed to admit, on torn bits of paper with directions to his staff: buy leather, submit receipts before four o'clock. When the staff left, Eb curled into himself frowning with worry. Nothing could stop it but time. He did not go home that first night but slept on his bunched coat on the office floor. All night he witnessed partial spectres, arm and leg ghosts rapping at his body and hugging him, and in one horrific waking dream, a single digit traced his face with clammy insistence. The next morning, he worked up the nerve to visit me.

"I won't leave before seeing him," he said to the police secretary.

"Then you won't leave," she replied insouciantly.

When hours later he was able to talk to an officer, he made the case point by point that I was not a murderer. That I was instead a madman. "And besides," he said when he had exhausted all other logic, "who will miss her?" In the end, because I was infirm and a war hero by virtue of my stump, they agreed to assess me for lunacy.

1865/66

IT DID NOT TAKE MORE than a day for the medical staff at the Hospital for the Insane to declare me unfit. After that, it was room after room. In the schematic, which was the way of this new world I was in, I would either one day leave cured or I would die here, shuffled again and again through different hospital rooms – measurements, tinctures, needles and assessments. It was like a board game and I the token. I was days and days through a series of startling white rooms. My fitness was tested, my teeth; I was checked for vermin. Even if there was some humiliation, still I found that I liked the quiet of the place. I had not expected madness to be so contemplative. I commenced to write as soon as they left me the time. I was given a room and allowed to move about the gardens and property.

I thought: If I am mad . . . I couldn't seem to finish the thought – or better, I couldn't seem to articulate the finished thought. Too many things mobbed me. It was Charles. It was her letters. Some responsibility to carry on, but even these, the hinges that ought to tether me, broke even as I thought them.

If I was mad, then madness was Godly. Was I mad because they decided I was mad, or was I always already mad? When did it begin, and where was the boundary of madness? There was some relief in the way sense had begun to fall away. It meant I didn't need to adhere to the ways of the world. I could enter my own skin. I could be comfortable in it. And yet, the paradox was, of course, that I was in a government institution, declared insane, not fit for society.

Who in his right mind was fit, though? There were many war heroes in this place with me. The nation was overwhelmed with a new sort of person, written through violence, incoherent and babbling. We knew death.

A year is a long time and also no time at all. I spent that first asylum year cataloguing the dead – I wrote and drew them assiduously, as if by cataloguing them I could hold the horror of it all in place. I documented how they had fallen, what I knew of them, what I surmised. I was a castaway and my island was the room they'd given me in which to fester. Misery was an infection, I knew, not less than a septic wound if you could not clean it. Anyone would do this, is what I thought, to try to bring some order to the forget-pit the madhouse surely was. Rarely did a doctor visit me during this year, and when they did, I made myself proper and they tried to trick me – to get me to answer questions by strange wry lines of questioning. I would not be tricked. The staff fed me and left me for the most part having assessed me as not mad enough nor sane enough and, therefore, minimal risk. I kept in this margin – this hinterland of insanity. I could bide my whole life in the stillness of this nowhere place, cataloguing the dead, the act of which brought me solace.

One. A rebel soldier dressed in the shabbiest of home-dyed wool, barely visible in the quagmire of death and mud that was this war. I said, "Where is your weapon, man?" The soldier gestured to his waist. He tried to form his mouth into word-shapes but sound would not comply and nothing emerged. Perhaps he was too battle-weary or too wounded. I did not know. I collected a rust-bitten knife and a mock rifle, whittled from oak and rubbed black with charcoal. I also collected a wallet, the removal of which caused the man to whine like a horse, but he did not want to die so he suppressed this, too. He sat slumped slightly, like a child playing at jacks. I pulled his chin up and did him the favour of slitting his throat, for why should I trust the enemy?

Two. Walking off the field, Bellair shouting at my back to get the goddamn-fuck back and fight like a goddamn-fucking-man, I hurtled down an incline – it turned out to be a dry creek with the thinnest trickle of coagulated mud-water.

I scurried up the opposite bank and headed away from the noise and mayhem, thinking above all else that I required a minute to myself. I had to shit, a problem that plagued me all through my service. I crawled then walked for upwards of an hour, until all I could hear was wind and insect chirr. There was no house nor barn nor other menace in sight, no hedge of green camouflage to hide me, either, so I pulled my trousers down and out shot everything – my bodily fear made manifest. My stomach was embroiled all the while. I hung my head and closed my eyes with the small relief this exertion afforded me. I felt fleetingly better. When I opened my eyes again, there was a sudden shadow. I looked up to the face of a frightened enemy.

"Sorry to disturb," the man said. And then, "I see we suffer similar ailments."

"The ailment of stupidity."

"If you like."

"Well."

The man put his hand upon my arm and crouched to eye level. He shifted his trousers down and grunted his own misery. "Such is democracy," he said. He clenched my arms so tight I couldn't move.

"You ought to shoot me," I said. I saw then that he was not a man at all but a mere pup of a boy. Younger than I was but twice as big, certainly.

"I studied history before history overtook me," the soldier said, this huge overgrown boy-man. "We are pawns."

The man pulled his trousers up as he stood, and then pulled me up to standing. He looked back in the direction of the battle. "I will not go back there."

"I will not return, either," I said, "and you can count on that." I was sure the boy would murder me.

The boy flicked his finger at my dagger. "May I?"

It was almost erotic, this waiting. I smiled and nodded, for what could I do? "Just hurry," I said. I knew what was to come.

But instead he slid the dagger from its flimsy sheath and plunged it so fast into his own stomach, I almost missed it. But then such a stink arose, such an awful stink.

Three. A baby I had seen lying in the grass curled mid-wail, clinging to its dead parent.

The list went on like this, and every day, I added to it, requiring more and more paper and ink. The nurses were happy to keep me busy and placated thus. I showed this to Eb when he visited. He looked pained by it, and by the illustrations I'd made – I had decorated the entries with renderings of corpses and of other dead I had seen or half seen. My mind was filled with death.

"Why do you draw this?" The dead and dying seemed entirely made out of prosthetics – even their hearts ran by gears and pulleys.

"What a strange question," I said, and squinted at Eb, who I thought would understand even if no one else did. I drew by way of a purgative. I gave these drawings to Eb for safekeeping. The staff here were thieves. I missed Charles like an ache through my whole self but did not dare speak of him. I wanted to ask if any mail had come from Cristiana, but I did not; I recalled the one time that I had asked, Eb had frowned and his lip had twitched, and he had said that I must stop "pining for the dead woman." But surely she had written to me more than once.

DAY TWENTY-SIX

MUM IS UP AND ABOUT and back to her crusty self. I get her over to the pig shed under cover of Dad's golf umbrella and set her up in an upholstered chair that has seen better days. She's muttering to herself while going through a box of bric-a-brac. I start out sorting a similar box but decide to toss the lot of it on the charity pile. I just can't summon the energy to look at another mismatched, chipped salt-and-pepper set. Who will grieve the crocheted toilet paper doll?

I glance from time to time through the window cut out of the back of the building, at the rain flitting on the water that has accumulated there. If I suspend my disbelief, it seems a kind of coded song, the tempo of which ebbs and flows. I see it as colour – teal, orange – and am buoyed by it. There is that scent of carcass on it, and I imagine the animals who have been unhoused, lost loved ones, those teeming at the door, begging to be let in.

The water is now threatening the outbuildings. There is a soft grassy shore (the lawn) to the north, water edging up the trunks of the ancient white pines there. I know Dad sits in the farmhouse living room, defeated by the prospect of the weather overtaking us. The cellar is flooded, the legacy being literally washed away. I wonder if the foundation will withstand this. How long it will take for the currents to make the homestead a pile of rubble. How quickly the industry of mankind can be undone when nature has its way.

Last night, I mentioned the reek of death all around us.

"You've brought this," he said.

"Like Jonah," I said, to egg him on.

"Yes," was his response, which was not exactly the answer I expected. So, I flounced off to bed, where I failed to sleep and instead wrote into the night, with a chaser of bad, bad dreams. The scent of animal decay seemed to cling to me all through the night, and now again it permeates the air. Time is so strange these days. It draws out into infinity. The water promotes a sense of eternity, so that I feel suspended, static, claustrophobic.

"Maybe death is like dreaming," I say to Mum, now in the pig shed.

"What?" She was lucid now that we've been at it for a bit but seems in decline again now. She does not have her hearing aid in.

I laugh at the universe for putting me here, then choke because the air I draw in is sick with carnage. The whole landscape around my parents' farmhouse is fetid, composting with bloated rodents. I come closer to Mum. "Can't you smell it?" But she shakes her head and looks bewildered, holds up a canister of ground coffee from the year of my birth and asks me what she should do with it.

"Charity or Keep?" she says.

"Throw," I say.

"Soon the world will be entirely underwater."

"There are droughts in Europe. The highest temperatures on record. Paris is burning."

"I always hoped I wouldn't be around anymore to witness this," she says.

Me, too, I think. The hoarded objects will be mere treasures, traces of some past and backwards civilization for the archaeologists of the future. Our fossils dug up and mused over. They will be able to ascertain our sex, our eating habits, and come to believe that we fetishized Spode and silver plate, Tupperware and drinking straws. The minutiae of our lives will be obscured from them. They will never know the neurotic turns of our minds, our privilege or our victim-hood. Our books will decay, our technology will moulder in landfills, the digital cloud will disappear into the ether.

For some reason, this troubles me more than anything. Humans want to leave their mark on society, die having done good deeds or invented something useful. I'm the worst. Since running out of material, I have become obsessed with expanding my archive. I have written to the archivist of the Government Hospital in Washington, and just before the cell service kicked out, Joi Carmichael replied that there was evidence of a small shoebox of ephemera attached to Boyt's name. And then the landline is also non-operational. We are on our own. I am on my own.

With such scant material, I am beginning to wonder how to end things – for a story must have a finale. I posit that after a time, sometime in mid-1865, roughly after the war, unable to bear it, Eb stopped visiting Boyt at the Government Hospital for the Insane. By way of compensation to a responsibility he understood he had failed, or so I extrapolate, Eb went to several burial parties in Appomattox, where he participated in what he viewed as his own atonement, and some wrong-headed notion of hygienic nation-building. There he dug mass graves, lost his virginity to a whore and witnessed first-hand the depravity of war. He ran his business by telegram for three months before returning. When he returned, out of lingering and unassailable guilt, he went to visit Boyt at the hospital, and while there he demanded to see Boyt's files.

I do not know precisely what happened to Boyt from 1865 to 1869. I have only this dubious patient record. It reads: *Boyd, R, Furious Mania. P. 22, 1867, pupils normal, patient secludes himself, and writes and draws what appear to be corpses, or people sleeping. Today patient is calm, but is generally prone to bouts of melancholy alternating with rageful explosions.*

It's possible it belonged to a different patient.

For a time, Eb continued his occasional visits. He prayed for compassion. Perhaps the war had made Boyt insane, or perhaps it was nestled in his blood from birth – Eb would never know. He decided that the project of substitution had ethical limits. But he knew how he felt when he did not visit. In the end, he allowed that visiting cost him less than the chewing guilt he suffered when he did not visit. Still, he went as seldom as his guilt would afford him.

I keep thinking maybe no one will ever read this. Humanity will be extinguished before it is printed. I think of all the books jouncing on an open sea that covers the entire planet.

Dad's Biblical Deluge. Did Noah get to rewrite the story after the flood? I love that story trope where future civilizations find some old paperback and believe it to be sacred. Is not all writing sacred? If we had found a different, better text to believe in way back then – not the Bible but, say, *Gilgamesh*, or even a weird poem like "Wulf and Eadwacer" – might things have turned out differently? Might we have been more careful in our friendships, might we have been more prudent with our forests, might we have understood the gorgeous centrality of womanhood? Might the human story not be now teetering on the brink of tragic endings?

Maybe someone – the last of our kind – will find this strange text when it washes ashore, when things dry up, and decode it toward some hopeful new way of running things.

I wish I could talk to that archivist and get at that shoebox of ephemera. But as it stands, I am in a pig shed triaging the garbage of human folly. Mum has nodded off in her chair. I can hear birds landing for a rest on the roof. I'm turning out a bin of old accounts and magazines when a small scallop-edged photo shoots out. Two swaddled babies side by side. The photo is circa 1960, the sky behind them that azure blue that one wishes actually existed. They lie on a ragged lawn. I pin the image above the pig shed door.

I leave a note on the kitchen table while no one is paying attention, and then I hightail it, kayaking off the property and down the gravel road toward town. On the note, I tell them I will be gone less than a week and that, if they want to reach me, text and cellphone are best if the service comes back on. When I hit dry land, I tuck the kayak into a copse and hitchhike the rest of the way. My phone pings that I've got a text so that's working now. It's from Mum: *Say hello to the boys for us,* and then a series of unrelated flower emojis. I write back that I have gone south. Not home. I tell them I have a lead I want to follow. What I don't tell them is that I can't bear the stifling energy in the house, Mum deteriorating, Dad ruminating on the misery of having to stay at home, water-bound. I rent a car once I reach dry land, throw my one bag filled with my clothes, computer and documents into the back and go.

Navigating out by map is a challenge, but once I hit the bridge, the weather shifts. It's windy and dry, the roads are clear. It takes me seven hours to get to the outskirts of Washington. Long enough to ruminate on marriage, on fairy tales, on my brother. I've got a note from a lawyer sitting in my email. I sent the boys each a wad of money, some appeasement I'm sure they are thinking. It's hard to be generous when people think you owe them. And maybe I do. Maybe I owe them for leaving, I don't know. I wish I had a wand that could make everyone see what is going on for me. I think they would know then that this is larger than me.

"Listen, sons," I want to say. "Be happy, pursue that line of being. Especially where your happiness intersects with the happiness of others." But is that enough? Does that cover responsibility? Does that hit the limit of what we mean when we say, I love you?

I'm just like Eb and Moser. I cannot live someone else's life. I cannot substitute for anyone, especially not myself – or that cipher, that dutiful wife and mother that I have become over time. If I could, don't you think I would do it? But it doesn't work. I can't be everything. I tried. And trying got me precisely where I am now, chasing the story I need to write.

And the story, like a great snake eating its own tail, is just another way of seeking myself. You see, you can't escape the duty you have to that. You can't exit the matrix of whatever it is in you that needs healing. Either you stay in it and suffer, or you exit and suffer less. And by you, I mean me.

What is it like to feel the sun glancing off one's face through a windshield after weeks of rain? It is Godly. It is hope.

The box waiting for me at the archive in Washington two days later is a standard shipping box, roughly the dimensions of a couple hundred sheets of 8 ½ x 11 printer paper. It is only a matter of luck – and a phone call – that I have discovered what turns out to be essentially the asylum effects of my great-great-grandfather – and incorrect to use the word *effects*, since Russell Boyt did not die at the Government Hospital for the Insane, an institution that is now called St. Elizabeths, in Washington, DC. We do not know where and how he died.

But we do know that he went on to lead some sort of a life after he left these premises sometime in late 1869. He wrote a letter to his mother in which he claimed a miraculous healing and "a sense of great new beginnings." I know he briefly reunited with Charles Muldon and took up a sort of custodial parenthood, however unstable, and that he struggled on and off with his ability to "carry on" from the time of his release until his presumed death-date in 1870. And though it is unusual for such extant material "effects" to be traced, I am persistent in my search.

Joi Carmichael, when I meet her, tells me that she herself is descended from a freed-slave janitor of the original hospital, a descendent of a plantation slave who toiled on the acreage the asylum later occupied. I ask Joi whether her ancestor knew Russell Boyt.

"It could be," she replies, though her tone suggests some skepticism. She has spent hours in a vault looking through dead files in order to locate a shoebox with the name Russell Boyt pencil-scrawled on its lid.

"I appreciate all the work you've put into this," I say.

"I'm just doing my job, honey." She tells me to come back the next day, giving her time to photocopy everything. She'll send the originals to the federal archive because, as she explains, protecting and preserving the history of the era is a mandate of the hospital.

The box she puts together for me has collated photocopies of the many pages of Russell Boyt's mostly illegible journal, as well as pencilled images of his ornate gear-and-pulley inventions – madness or mere fancy, who can tell? There are several high-resolution scans Joi has made of photographs, most of which are given with no explanation, and I am left to surmise they have been merely

flung into his file, for reasons no one will ever know.

One photograph, though, has a pink sticky note attached to it: *R. Boyt is catalogued as having worked almost exclusively, during his years at the hospital, in the kitchen as a preserver, and in the laundry as a boiler.* This information is later borne out through a nurse's note dated August 1867, which mentions rail tracks throughout the building designed specifically for laundry and table busing carts, and extols the joys Boyt felt in their "efficient and hygienic" systematizing of work in the establishment.

In a second, much later entry is mention of Boyt's affection for pickles. In an image of the laundry room, which I have located digitally through an open resource, and which is dated 1897 – taken many years after my great-great-grand-father died – the tracks he describes with such emphasis are still in situ. The tungsten bulb hangs bare and a little forlorn in precisely the same way in both

photographs. There is little to be learned from the sheets of pho-tocopied paper, the notes, the photographs, even the prosthet-ics catalogue I find nestled at the bottom of the box. It is the mer-est outline of Boyt's time at the Government Hospital – possibly  one of the most consequential portions of his life.

In a letter included with the package, Joi writes about one image she believes may be Boyt himself. The photocopy shows a figure approaching the camera, but it is so blurred as to be unidentifiable. If it is Boyt, he is either in some sort of a fury or else the camera operator has gaffed, the shutter opened overly long. The aperture has captured only energy. The room itself is pristine – a bedroom, with almost no adornments, as if the occupant is wary of outward manifesta-tions of the self, or perhaps the hospital forbids trinkets, homely touches and representations.

Of some ongoing interest to me are several letters, nearly destroyed due to what appears to be manic folding and unfolding. I imagine Boyt reading the words and surmising some truth between them. I can barely make out some of the sentences because of the handwriting and the rough usage. I resort to slow reading under a magnifying glass and still get little out of the endeavour: *My mother misses me father suggests bromides.*

There is something equally distressing and compelling about all this. The let-ters lead nowhere, just as the rest of the material leads nowhere. It exhausts me to look through it all, and also overwhelms me with its retroactive call to some uncanny familial duty. One cannot go back to stem the unfurling of fate, yet there is a sense reading the letters and diary entries that my great-great-grand-father was in no way well enough to be discharged from the care of the staff doctors in 1869.

It is Ebenezer Wilkes, the prosthetics manufacturer, whose signature stands out on the discharge document, because it was to him, and under his responsibility, that Russell Boyt was released. I put the photocopies in a banker's box that Joi's given me, thank her and head out again. I should go home, but I do not. It's a fool's errand that I seem to be on, trying to make my fiction into reality. But then, I am a fool.

"Mum," I say, when I call, "I'm in Pennsylvania heading back to Toronto. I found her house!"

"Whose house?"

"Cristiana's. Boyt's mistress."

"Why?"

"It just seemed necessary. I don't know. I sent a picture to you in a text." I

can't seem to articulate the feeling I have of floating, and as I am unable to achieve this, I also feel it ebbing. Actually, it feels like joy is scuttling away – a prosthetic monster rushing from me into the forest beyond the highway verge. Cars are racing past. "It just seemed like a good idea at the time," I say.

"I'm happy for you," she says, and I know she is distracted, elsewhere.

"Mum," I say. "Are you there?"

"Yes, yes. I'm here."

"I don't know. I thought you'd be interested."

"Well," she says, "I just keep wondering what this is really all about."

"Wulf?"

"No. I keep wondering if this is more about Matthew."

"Mum," I say. "Please." And then I recall the photograph I pinned to the pig shed doorframe. I wonder if they have noticed it. I am about to ask when the phone cuts out and, though I try to redial, and then to text, I get nowhere.

She's right, my mum. This expedition is another rabbit hole. There is no there there. The truth – whatever that means – resides somewhere between the research and the fantasy. The archive is only productive insofar as it is spurring my imagination. And so I go back to the rental and drive like a fiend. I have a box of nothing – of the useless past – in the back seat. I know Boyt got out of the institution. I try to puzzle out why Eb would have made this terrible decision to release him, and all I can come up with is Charles coming back into their lives. That would provide an ample limit to Eb's sense of responsibility. He would have no truck with becoming a parent. I write in my head the whole way home. Again, I go back to my story, the one that I am now wholly making up. I haven't a clue about Boyt or Eb, and Charles is a mere cipher to history. A friend. A boy. An orphan. I am curious about him, decide to enter him, do something a little different. Who am I to enter the dead? But I do it anyway – what else do I have?

1869

I, CHARLES BLAKEY BOYT MULDON, watched Mrs. Blakey's face collapse when she heard news of Moser's untimely death. He died sitting up at his desk, and right in front of a client, the messenger told us. It was "a most embarrassing demise," Mrs. Blakey asserted later, dabbing at her eyes. He was not my real papa, she liked to remind me. He was a false papa. Untrue papa. There were many things I read in the particular way the widow's face caved, and one was that she never did really love Moser, or if she did, this love was an easily torn shred tethered primarily to his fiscal holdings, all of which, she had just learned, were bankrupted due to inconsistencies of accounting.

"Run along, Charles," she said. "I can't bear the sight of you at this instant. Moser is gone and won't come back. He has died, and we are now alone in this world. Me more than anyone because I was contracted to a moribund marriage and now I am quite literally wed to death. It clings to me." She began to weep in earnest for herself and the lonely days ahead in which she would have no one to blame or nag or despise – no one to whom to devote her temperamental misery.

Yes, I have come to understand that she was wedded more to her misery than to Moser, whom I loved unequivocally.

But in that very moment when she told me that my fake papa was dead, I knew that I no longer had a home in this place. And so a plan began to solidify in my mind – I must leave and try to locate Papa Boyt, the second papa who had always been kindly to me, and whose face was a blur to me now. It had been four years since he was institutionalized; Moser's lips had thinned nervously when he told me of this papa's Soldier's Heart.

I think not everyone is lucky or destitute enough to have three papas. I am such a one. Surely, in this great world, if the Lord was a saviour, He would deign to save me, his poor again-orphaned child, of unclear age between seven and ten, and motherless (for she is in Heaven or so I had been told). What a life!

And so, within days, I set out. There were folk heading in both directions – people like me clad in raggle-taggle clothing, as well as lost soldiers moving homeward after years of illness or I did not know what adventure. I peered at them, hoping to find Papa Boyt, but I never found him in these men.

Sometimes people passing spoke to me. Sometimes if I did not trust them by their looks, I pretended deafness and they swarmed past me, but not always. I will admit that I was not much of a judge of character. I was lonely, I would admit this, and I soon discovered loneliness could make me do stupid and dangerous things.

A sickly looking man said, "Howdido." I smiled up at him.

"I am as well as can be expected after losing my pa to an early battle, and then my ma to some untimely death, then my second pa to my third, who stole me away and tried to treat me well. I have been handed from one to the next like so much coin."

"Is that so?"

"Yes, sir.

"You must have some currency, then."

"I have twenty dollars on my person, sir." A dunderheaded thing to tell him – like Red Riding Hood telling the wolf the coordinates of her grandmother's cottage – and one I immediately regretted. So I tried to compensate by adding, "I can read. And I am not stupid."

The man had a deceptively friendly face. "Which way you headed?" he said.

Mistake number two was telling him. "Papa three up and died, and his wife hates me, so I am headed to Papa two. He is a war hero."

The man patted my shoulder then. "Why don't you walk with me some? I could use the company."

"I am fine by myself."

"A young coloured orphan is bound to raise suspicion."

I knew from Moser that my grandmother was white, and I imagined her to be a sort of queen. I imagined she was looking for me. Much of my head was filled with imaginings like these. I told him what Moser had always assured me, which was that according to some I passed as white.

"I doubt that," said the man. "Not in these times no more."

I bit my lip considering this and then hauled myself out of the ditch and we were walking. In the late afternoon, after the man told me how as a soldier in '65 he disinterred and reburied more than a thousand reckless dead from the fields of Spotsylvania and Wilderness, and how each skull-find was duly noted in a book until the number rose so high, he left the counting to the lieutenant in charge and tried not to think of it more.

"Petersburg, I believe, is where my father, Henry Muldon, lies buried. He was a valiant substitute hire," I told him.

"I may have touched him, then. I would be good luck to you, I guess."

"Really?"

"What did he look like?"

"I don't know."

The man shook his head, either in dismay or kindness. "So many dead," he said. He then shared how he had a wife and children in Washington with whom he hoped to reunite and move north, where he reckoned they would have a better future. He was convinced of this, and his conviction made me insecure again about my own scant information.

I said, "Where do you suppose I might find a place where arms and legs dangle clanking from the ceiling?" I had this strong recollection.

The man stopped in his tracks. "Arms and legs, you say?" He looked a little afraid of me in this moment. "You must've dreamed this."

I knew it was no dream and that I had been in a place like this. "I have a strong and clear memory of it."

"It is one of two things, then. Either it is a slaughterhouse where they butcher cattle and swine brought in by farmers for this purpose. You can find this place near where the troops muster. Ask anyone once you get to Washington. Either that or else it is some madness worked up from I do not know where."

"Do they hang arms and legs in a slaughterhouse?"

"They do."

"So, that must be where."

At some point, I could not walk any longer owing to being tired and, also, I had begun to mistrust this man and wanted to get away from him. And so I crossed the ditch through a foot of muck and wet to find a location where I could sleep hidden. The man called after me from the road when he noticed I was missing from his side.

"I am bone-tired, sir," I called. "You go on without me." There was no reason to trust him. There were thieves everywhere in those days, desperate people, and people who were just plain mean. I had twenty dollars and that was my whole fortune.

"I do not like leaving you," called the man.

I pretended that I was too far in to hear him; the wood had closed around me and all was quiet. I fell asleep quickly then, and I woke much later to find the same man straddling me and clenching a hand at my neck.

I had been right in my gut feelings about this man.

The pressure was unbearable. I knew it was possible to die so young. I was well aware of Mrs. Blakey's dead children. She never had brought one to full life and it was her paramount sorrow and, according to Moser, one of the chief reasons she so resented me but also Moser, too. She blamed him.

"A cuckoo child," she called me, because they were the birds that snuck their eggs into the nests of others.

As I began to die, I recalled her disapproving face, and I am happy to report that it gave me courage. I scrabbled the man's hands loose and then bit him hard on the cheek. I got up then and ran and ran. I heard the man weep out some weak apology about his dire need of money to get his wife and children up to safety. It was then that I checked the inner pocket of my jacket, to where I had shifted the money.

It was still there.

I could already feel contusions forming on my neck, and I rubbed there. I had lost my stick, my kerchief, my water jar, but I had not lost my wits. I turned back into the forest and backtracked until I could hear the man softly weeping. I listened to him gather his things and crash out of the forest, heard his boots churn up the dirt road as he lumbered away.

I was very careful after that – careful all the next day and the one after, until I reached close to Beltsville. It was there that I saw something strange swaying from the bows of a blooming maple tree. It was far off and shifting side to side. It was a silhouette and reminded me of something, of limbs hanging. Which must be a slaughterhouse, according to the man who tried to rob me of my only fortune. I thought about Boyt and finding him. He had once taken me to a zoo, and I had fond memories of this occasion. He took me on a train, too, and let me be free there. I held him in some esteem, I suppose. I could not recall a time that he was not decent to me, even if Moser had insinuated bad events. I walked faster, to see the hanging thing up close. I could make no sort of sense of it for it was a woman's body. Her clothes were dusty from hanging there, and her face was cocked and distorted into Godly repose. She was surely dead. There was a thick rope around her neck. How did she get there? She had the same colour skin as me, not Black nor white but a pretty shade of brown. She could be my mother by her age if my mother were not already long dead. I did not really recall my mother.

"Ma'am, I'm sorry," I said without expecting a reply. I wondered at the illogic of someone hanging a dead body from a tree, but there was no one there to ask. So I stood there thinking it through and getting nowhere. After a while, a group of people walked by and a woman gathered me in and said, "There, there."

And I admit, I was stupid. I asked, "Why would someone hang a dead body like that?"

And a boy who must have been my age or so laughed out loud at me – I was truly stupid, I guess – and said I must be simple.

The woman looked into my eyes as if she could not comprehend my innocence. "She was good and alive when they hoisted her up there, son. Someone's mama, or grandmamma by the way it looks."

I did not know I was innocent until she said this. I knew then that I must be the most ignorant child that ever was. I liked these people, and so I sat nearby the mama or grandmamma for some length before I could dare myself to trek away alone. So it was that I set out again for Washington.

It was late into the next day that I came upon it – a tent so large I could not fathom how it did not fly away in the formidable wind that day. I had always loved tents, since the one and only time Papa Boyt and his mother, Mrs. Boyt, took me to the circus. I remember the tigers and clowns who romped there. The memory of that spun into me out of nowhere and I stopped to catch my breath. How could I forget this, and what else was likewise hidden away from me – what things did I not know I knew? The mind was fearful terrain. I did not want to think what it might do. I brushed my trousers down and was surprised at the swell of dust rising off me. I pulled my jacket off and snapped it a few times to get rid of this strange memory of Papa number two.

There were people milling about. I came up to a small group of them. "Sir," I said, tugging on the sleeve of a pasty older boy, tendrils of black hair growing from his chin. He had on a blinding white shirt and black wool trousers with suspenders. "Is this the circus?"

The boy turned and sneered at me. Two more boys turned toward me when I asked, too. They looked all alike, though varying heights, and I wondered whether they were brothers. The boy I had asked nudged the boy closest to him and they stood there for overlong and gaped at me, so I decided to walk on.

"Thank you, anyway," I said.

"It ain't no circus," the boy called after me. He said it with some tinge of remorse, like he yearned for something more in his own measly life.

I looked back. "What is it for, then?"

"You ain't never heard of a tent-church, boy?"

"Tent-church," I repeated, dumbly, and laughed because I could not believe my good fortune. Tomorrow was a church day and I had been anxious to locate an Episcopal venue.

"And our daddy the preacher." The boy spit such a wild thick hork toward me.

The sun was nuzzling the horizon. I was so hungry. Here was a church, just what I was looking for, and a lucky day early. I nodded in thanks when I was far enough from those boys to feel safe, because if nothing else I was polite and they did not notice to nod back.

"I'll be back for early mass," I muttered, but there was no way they could hear me now. I was talking to the dust.

I walked into Bladensburg in search of something to eat. I concocted a lie about who I was and for whom I was in need of food. I decided that I would call myself after Henry Muldon, after my father who had died so long ago that it seemed only a story. I lamented not knowing him, wished that I could recall the line of his jaw, but this was nonsense. I rejoiced that I could at least use the name.

"I would like a loaf of that rye bread," I said to the merchant woman.

She parcelled the bread in a brown paper wrapper and then also a hunk of cheddar cheese I'd selected; my mouth was full of wet desire.

"That will be ten cents," she said. She did not ask into my business, for what did she care? But since I had spent time on the story, I was keen to tell it. It would be a relief of sorts to have a listener. I liked to make up stories. I had a talent, Moser used to always say.

"It is for my poor mother who is too ill to walk," I said, "by the name of Muldon, fully devastated by bankruptcy in the war. Through no fault of her own," I added, "since she never took sides and always felt a keen ambivalence to the owning of soulful persons."

The woman smiled at me and handed the bread and cheese over the counter. "Where are you from?" she said. "I never heard of no Muldon."

I ignored the query as if it was rhetorical. "I am obliged to you," I said, and gestured to the food. "My mother will also be so pleased." I handed the woman some coin, but she had changed her mind and wouldn't let me pay.

"A simpleton, are you?"

"Oh no," I said. "Oh, certainly not." I left the money on the counter.

I found a lonely spot to hide in while I ate, and when I was done and had packed up what was left of the bread and cheese, to keep for later, it was beginning to be dark. I headed back toward the tent-church, curious about it and in need of a place to sleep soon enough. I stood there watching for hours until the lanterns were snuffed and the whole place went still. Then I slipped under the tent flaps and made a little bed for myself under the wooden bleachers, using my jacket as a pillow of sorts. I would be first in the tent tomorrow morning.

In the night, a noise woke me. It was near pitch-dark inside the tent, but I saw the glint of white and thought it was the boy I'd spoken to earlier in the day. And then there was a higher-pitched giggle and I knew there were two people. I crawled under the bleachers toward the front of the tent where there was an altar of sorts.

At first all I saw was clothing, a clump of it, black and white and flashes of some otherworldly fabric that made me think again of the circus. There was the palest skin, and now I could make out the oldest boy. He had his hand over the mouth of a red-haired girl. He had her skirts pulled up so high that I saw her full rump, almost blue in the darkness – it was glimmering blue-white and prettily dimpled.

And then the oldest boy covered her with his body and rammed into her much as I'd seen the feral cats and dogs do in the outskirts of New York as they humped and screeched their dismay at this breach of solitude. I had never imagined humans did this and watched out of pure interest.

The boy was no longer covering the girl's mouth but had his fingers stuck in there. She arced her hips and made a sort of moan that would dredge up the darkness. I did not know what I was seeing but it felt bigger than the church, it swallowed me into it. I was completely unprepared for the boy's furious beating that followed when he finally caught me.

The girl laughed through it while the boy slammed his boot into my stomach and then my head.

"Git," he said. "This ain't no circus."

I played dead so that the boy would stop.

"Get out," the boy said, and he prodded me until I rose and slunk away.

Because I was both stupid and curious, when things quietened again, I returned rib-sore and ignored any more rustling I heard or thought I heard through the night, for though this was a strange place, I wanted to be at church come morning. There was not one unbruised bone in my body, and I was thoroughly supplicant when the boy's father read from Corinthians and sang and waved his arms until the entire congregation was flailing and swaying in rough proximity – the white people in front and the Black people tucked in behind a barricade (I stood amongst them feeling estranged and familiar at the same time). I had a wretched ache in my head, but I pushed my way in between folks to get to the front.

The mean boy noticed me midway through the service. He grinned and gave a wave, as if he'd never thought ill of me in all his livelong days. He made his way over. "You little coon dog," he said. "And what did you learn last night?"

"I learned to mind my own business," I said, and he laughed.

The truth was that I had learned much more. I had learned how big the world was and how inconsequential I was within it but also how important, or else why beat me for learning this?

"I am Mace Rose," the boy said. "What's your name? I ain't going to bite you."

"Henry Muldon," I said.

"Sorry I got so hot and wild last night. You look a fright. Did I do that?"

"Yes, you did."

I had made my first friend in the whole world.

The next day, Josephus, the preacher-daddy, touched my hair and said, "You look like an angel. Your hair is like a fairy nimbus of light, a halo of spun sugar. Mace, if you can practice him looking forlorn, we will have got something of value in him."

"Yes, sir."

And so I was employed to look pitiable and collect the offering and, when the congregations had left or not yet arrived, to break down and set up the tent. When the preacher discovered my passable singing voice, he got me to sing "Sitting at the Feet of Jesus" and "The Lion of Judah." It was a kind of circus after all. Entertainment church.

It took all of ten minutes for me to capture the visage Josephus desired. It was precisely Mrs. Blakey whom I mimicked, her face at the news that Moser had died and left her not a red cent. "Woebegone," said Mace. "That is right on the nail. The folks will pay for that, as it feeds their self-possession."

Because they called me Henry, I had my father's bravery working through me. We were headed in two days to Mount Rainier. I thought the name of this town was hopeful. I told Mace I was searching for my father, by the name of Russell Boyt, but Mace did not know this name and seemed genuinely sorry not to be more helpful. I longed for Boyt as one longs for a half memory that seemed once to hold promise. I was conflating a sepia recollection with wishes that could never be fulfilled. I was a stupid little boy in the throes of his fullest abandonment. I recalled his hands most of all, their tension, and the dirt under his nails. He had carried me on his shoulders, a lumbering gait. He never swore. He was pristine in his dealings with me.

I was determined that when I got to Washington, I would find the slaughterhouse with its limbs hanging and there Boyt would be. He would love me. He would feed me. He would coddle and remark how well and diligently I was becoming the gentleman he had always known I would become.

"How is it you is Muldon and he is Boyt?" Mace asked.

"Boyt is my second father. Blakey my third."

"You got more names than a duke. Plus, that is an awful lot of daddies." Mace was laughing and the others joined in.

"Two of them is dead," I said, which sobered their laughter somewhat. I did not want to say or admit that the surviving father – Papa Boyt – was a madman, or so Papa and Mrs. Blakey had always argued, and that furthermore I might never find him. It could be that Boyt, too, was dead and buried. And that would mean that in fact I had no daddies. That I was indeed an orphan and a vagabond. I blinked some tears back. I would not cry, no I would not.

"Do you know where there is a slaughterhouse?" I asked.

"Why?"

I wouldn't or couldn't abide this question and started walking in some cruel and hopeful direction. "I'm leaving. I got to go. Thank you to you and the good Reverend Josephus for the fine eating."

And then Mace and the others laughed so hard they sounded like they might die from it. I heard it and it cut me hard in my chest. I had no friend at all and never had. I was spitting angry, and so I turned and called Mace an "ass-cock," and the boy came running at me.

"What did you say?"

"I saw what you piled into the mayor's daughter's butt," I said. "I can fathom what you were up to."

Mace turned back to see whether his brothers had heard and then landed a fist right at my face. My nose bloomed a bloody flower that dripped fast and dramatically into my cotton shirt.

"And she will have your inbred baby and it will look like a mule," I spluttered and then ran out of reach.

Mace horked at me twice but missed. "The slaughterhouse is thataway," he said. "You stupid quadroon fucker shit. I will tell my father how you fingered yourself in the Lord's house. I will tell it all to him. Now, go and burn in hell, why don't you?"

"Your momma run off I guess," because this seemed evident to me in my upset state.

"My momma never run off."

"Where in hell is she then?" I was far enough that I had to yell this and far enough that Mace would not easily catch me if he wanted to.

He scowled and retorted that "she caught a devil's bullet watching drill on Monument Hill and up and died."

This news made me feel as bad as I could possibly feel. "I am sorry to hear." And I truly was sorry since now we had even more in common because his mother was dead, too.

Mace wiped snot from his nose. I left and did not look back.

DAY THIRTY-THREE

DAD IS HUNCHED OVER IN the pig shed. He has the photograph of the two little swaddled babies in his hand and is crying.

"Dad," I say, "is everything okay? I found that picture while sorting the other day. Mum was asleep, so I pinned it up hoping she would see it."

"Thank goodness that I found it first, then," he says.

"Why?"

"You don't want to know," he says.

"I think I do," I say and I sit down.

"He was perfect in every way," Dad says. I have never seen colder tears than those cascading down the grooves in his old face. It seems as if tears just like these have formed these lines he has. "He had little flippers like you, only his feet were also webbed. He had the sweetest black eyes and –" He's pointing to the baby on the right.

"It's Wulf," I say, and he nods. The little picture shakes in his hand. I lean over to pull it from him. I want to see it. I wish it was digital so that I could open it up, get closer, really see him.

"He was born alive," I say.

And Dad nods.

"Is that what the big secret is? All that withholding?"

He nods again. "It was just easier for us to never discuss it again by saying he was stillborn. It was an unbearable loss for your mother but also for me. The doctors had called me into the delivery room, as you know. Your mother was unconscious, they were giving her blood and antibiotics. She looked – dead."

"Oh, Dad."

"But think of the responsibility. I would have to murder my own son in order to save my wife."

"A terrible dilemma to be in, Dad. I am so sorry."

"But then he lived." He peers up at me with such pain in his eyes. "He lived a while."

"Mum saw him?"

He shakes his head and it is all he can do to contain his feelings. His face is wracked with the work of not falling to pieces. He shakes his head to whip the story away from him. He lifts off the chair and ambles past me to the door.

"Dad," I say. I have grabbed the sleeve of his pyjamas.

"I came out here," he says, "after supper to turn the light off and see what progress had been made. I was feeling a bit more myself when the rain stopped. I thought that perhaps we would have a reprieve from this inundation. And then I turned and there he was. It was an awful thing to have to relive."

"I had no idea," I say. "Of course, I didn't know." I am wondering who the other baby was and I muster the courage to ask.

"Yes," he says. "There were two babies. Twins. A girl and a boy. It's so sad."

His eyes fill again, and he turns and walks into the night.

"Dad," I call.

"Yes?"

"What happened to the twin?"

He shakes his head. "I can't say it," he says. "It's very bad. And we won't speak about this again. Your mother would never forgive me."

"We do not speak of sad things," I call out to him, but he won't answer. The conversation is over. I follow him, take the image with me. There were twins. I have two siblings who died. "Dad," I call. But he won't answer. I hear him going up the stairs, his door close and with it, this chapter.

I have this little insight, now. This brother who did live. A little story. He lived for a while, Dad said. He looked like me in the hands, at least. I can't fathom Dad's pain, and I can't fathom Mum's, either. I go to my room and I lie down. I stare into the photograph, at the little bundles that barely lived. And I fall asleep for a time, drooling onto the bed.

And when I wake, the rain has resumed.

I don't want to think about Wulf, but his little body comes to mind. I see him, his webbed hands and feet, and I see him swimming. I see him swimming in the foundation hole that filled up all those years ago. This vision enters me like truth and I can't bear it, and so I lie there for a bit until I locate Boyt's voice and I sink into my addiction, the wordy cure, the thing that saves me from myself. Maybe if I solve Boyt's story, I can find my way.

1869

IT WAS A TUESDAY, LATE in the year, when it was announced to me that I had a
visitor. There was no time for me to fluster about it, but I could feel my heartbeat
up in my throat and a slow crawl of nervous tension along my chest and face. I
think my body knew it would be news. My skin and nerves were preparing me
for this.

I was a bad lover of people to be sure. I was terrible at being a person. But let
it stand that I did love them – the boy and his mother – however poorly, however
ineptly. Things had not gone well for me in any corner of my life. And now I was
scared and pressed my face into my fresh sheets and breathed in the starch to
comfort myself. I did not want a visitor, and I did not wish to be disturbed at all.
I scratched my cheek until it bled, a thin mess on my bedding.

Already Eb was at my doorframe looking awkward. "Well, Russell," he said.
"What have you done to your cheek?"

"I scratched it."

"Stop that nonsense."

I scratched all day long and could not stop. I had tried. They made me wear
mittens at night when it got bad. They told me it was a terrible compulsion.
One of the nurses had said ruefully that if I wasn't scratching one need it was
another, and I shot her a mystified look. Despite the diagnosis, I had not defiled

myself in years, and even yet the madness had not abated. I believed myself to be fully weighed down by my corroded workings. I was a machine inside the larger machine of life. I saw the world in its entirety as mechanical and me a gear of sorts helping it run its course. Dismal. I could not shake that I was a moving part of some awful war-machining endeavour. I was a piston or a pulley, depending on the day and the weather. But I was surely not my own man. I had no say in my behaviour nor could I alter its momentum. I had tried, believe me. Writing and drawing helped but it was inevitable, if they would only see. I pulled my bedsheet closer to my nose for stability.

"I would have come sooner, but the manufactory is awfully busy," said Eb.

"So many maimed." It came out as a squeak. I did not like this visit and tried to keep calm by clenching and unclenching my hands. "I do get out of sequence sometimes, Eb. It is the fault of an overprotected situation."

"How do the doctors find you?"

"They believe me irrecuperable. But I am fine." I gestured around my barren room.

Eb nodded, braced himself for the news he would give. "I had a strange visitor yesterday," he said. "Do you recall Charles Muldon?"

I began to rock back and forth on the bed. I'd carted that boy for miles and miles, could recall the very odour of him, sweet milk and piss. I shifted from my position lying on the bed to sitting, my one foot on the floor. A new sensation coursed through me, something like hope. "I knew it," I said, and then with baleful eyes asked, "Is he safe?"

"He is triply orphaned."

"His mother was dear to me," I mentioned.

"Moser Blakey is dead, it seems."

"Oh?" I said, rolling it on my tongue as it rolled through my body. I got a picture in my mind of Henry Muldon then, that first death, and wondered if Moser Blakey had died similarly; if one equalled the other, if history repeated itself in precise ways or in some other sort of strange puzzle.

"A heart infarct."

"Of course," I said and sighed with the perfection of that death. "A man such as that. Such a tender-hearted man as he. It is a right death."

"Don't be foolish, Russell." Then Eb was droning on about how "the boy walked for days to find you. He recalled the prosthetics hanging but thought them real. It was the abattoir manager who made the connection to my manu-factory. The boy seems to think there is some future in your alliance."

"But I live *here*," I said, within the hundred square feet of space of this one room, where I felt safe, and where I could contemplate all the things that crossed my mind. "It's very regular," I added.

"I don't believe the hospital will allow a child to live with you here, Boyt."

There was metal track to the laundry, the dining hall, the kitchen; to the communal shower and the bathroom down the hall. I developed a full feeling of disaster in the moments I stepped off this pathway through the building. The truth of it was that I lately deigned to only leave this small space if I knew I would be allowed to follow the building's cart-track network. The last time they forced me outside, the panic attack I incurred looked to all those who witnessed it precisely as death.

Eb wondered if he should call for someone. "I'm not here to rile you, Boyt. I just thought you would appreciate the news."

In that moment, I could not bring myself to look at Eb. I stared down at his legs and then looked over at my hands trembling on the bedspread. I was near to tears. "I *am* trying," I said.

"Russell," said Eb. "You journeyed to this place, surely you can claw your way back along the same path. Surely, by degree and for the affection toward this lost boy, you can muster the sort of stability you will need to be released from this egregious prison."

"I like it here."

"If you would only –" Eb was clearly repulsed by me – his substitute – and also reviled by his repulsion.

"I would like to see the boy," I stammered. I was not sure this was true even as I said it. I had torn the skin on my forearms, my face. Blood was pebbling along these scratches. I couldn't seem to look up at Eb. What would it take to appear healthy? There was not enough bromide or salve in the world.

"– if you would only make some small efforts –" Eb cleared his throat. He looked as if he was trying to calm the creases on his forehead. "Have you seen a priest in all this time?"

"What?"

"It might serve you to talk to one. Confess and have it done, man."

"Confess what?" I rubbed at the blood on my cheek, then squeezed my hands together into a ball. "I have been receiving letters from her."

"She was a poor unlucky woman." Eb couldn't even look at me. "They dug up and reburied her sad corpse. You strangled her. And now she is dead."

It is true that I had regular nightmares recalling my tightening palms on her neck, the look of dismay on the boy's face and the long trek, but any fool knew that a nightmare was not real, that there were no such things as ghosts and that Cristiana may have been poor and unlucky, but she was precious to me.

I would not ever hurt her. I exulted her. I worshipped her.

And she wrote me still because she knew this to be the truth. It was also true that I had not received a physical missive from her in some years, but still she nowadays wrote to me through my own hand, directly into my journal. It was as God's own voice into my fingertips. A frothy dictation from her right into my skull. I did not want to believe anything otherwise. I wanted an enduring sort of love. I wanted that. It sustained me somehow. I was devoted to this lie, I see now, but devotion has a way of seeming a lot like truth.

"Bring the boy," I said, turning my face up toward Eb's. It took everything to hold it steady and to stop rocking and appear up for the task of this. "I will see him. But tell him, in advance, that I disbelieve in the nonsense that his mother is perished. Tell him I am not skeptical. That I *know*. I will confess my dreams only."

Eb, I understand, told the boy nothing of this. He went away and some days later an orderly came to get me.

Some of the men working gaped at the boy and the man as they made their way toward us. They had never seen a child in this vicinity. There was always some foreign doctor or other coming. The men themselves muttered and joked and sang about it under their breath. Together we were less mad than when we were apart. Some of them near sane, I reckoned. What were the rules of sanity? Who decided what the contour of civility might comprise? Hadn't grown men and women – the wealthy, the doctors and barristers and, who knew, the minis-ters, too – brought their picnic baskets and their children to watch the slaughter at the battle at Wilderness?

My fingers barely peeked out of the sleeves of the suit jacket. I was so far away, how could Charles be sure? Did he even see me? But they were approaching, skirting the rectangle of garden and growing larger and more real with each step.

When they got to me, I was twitchy, unable to stop my face from jumping all around, even as I suppressed a smile. For here was Charles whom I had resigned myself to never see again.

I nodded like a fool and then was also weeping. I could not stop the tears. How unmanly and shameful of me. I put my hands to my eyes to wipe them. I was so happy to see Charles again in this lifetime. I shuffled closer in the dirt, so that we were right beside one another. I looked at him and grinned.

"Wee Charles," I said.

Charles looked at my hands. "Papa Boyt?"

"Yes," I said. "Yes." I looked about, acted as if I were fascinated by the men working when, in fact, I was nervous. I made a strange sound in the back of my mouth. I said how I had to go in.

Eb made a sour face. "Russell," he said, and smiled such a small smile and nodded.

"I can't," I said, and then I said to Charles, "It is good to see you." I put my hand out for a shake. "You're a fine little man," I said.

DAY THIRTY-SEVEN

WHEN I GO DOWNSTAIRS IN the morning, I see that the main floor is damp. I call up to tell my parents, but my dad says they are fine, they will be rescued soon.

I have the photograph tucked in my bra. I can't stop thinking about my brother and, now, my sister that I never knew I had. I've woken up intermittently in the night, heart racing, heart breaking. This story I wanted so badly I am not sure I want anymore.

"What time is the rescue mission?"

Mum says, "Eleven in the morning."

"By motorboat," adds Dad.

"We had hoped for helicopter," my mother says. "But we weren't deemed high risk."

I gather whatever food can be eaten without cooking it and store it in the linen closet upstairs. I tell them that it will all be okay, and my dad says not to patronize them, that they are old, not stupid. I tell them I'm sorry, that I've been writing all night. I give Dad the puppy eyes. "I'm a mess," I say.

"Why do you write if it upsets you so much?" Mum quips.

I wish it wasn't such a good question. "It makes me feel better than I would if I didn't write."

She looks at me as if I am mad.

"Did Dad tell you about the photograph?" I ask. I can feel the scalloped edges of it along the skin of my clavicle.

He glares at me. They are still in bed. And when I ask them why, Mum says she's infirm and Dad grimaces. "It was a bad night," he says.

"What photograph?" Mum asks then. She does look frail.

"Never mind, Mother," he says.

"Of the laundry of the Hospital for the Insane."

"Oh, I'd love to see that," she says.

So I fetch the banker's box, sit on the edge of the bed and show them both.

"I'm filling the gaps of his story with made-up stuff. He was sprung from the place in 1869. They think he died within the year."

"Read to me."

I tuck her into bed. I've brought the electric kettle up as well as a hot plate I found and an electric frying pan, the rubber wires of which are broken and taped. At a certain point, the elderly make due. What's the point of buying new things you won't enjoy, Dad always says. I make us grilled cheese sandwiches and fill up a couple of hot water bottles. Dad is asleep again in no time.

I read to Mum about how Eb signed Boyt out of the hospital, how Boyt took the boy and went to try to find Cristiana who Eb believed to have died despite Boyt's emphatic argument to the contrary.

"Why was he set free like that?" Mum says. "He was incapacitated."

"I think Eb wanted him to deal with Charles."

"Right."

"The limits of responsibility and all."

"I see."

"In this section, Boyt is telling Eb his plan to take Charles to his dead mother's shack.

> "Here is the thing," Eb said. "You are free to go, and I am not about to stop you, but there is a bill against you that tells a story. Moser Blakey believed in it, and so did the constables who let him take the boy. Luck is swerving in your direction right now, but that doesn't mean a thing if you don't keep it all straight, Boyt. I am telling you now that Moser thought you killed her and stuffed her body full of black-earth and buried her badly under a spindle tree in her own backyard. All the people

from around that area believed the tale at the time. There was no one
there who does not know what you were purported to have done. It may
be that even Charles has caught this story on the wind. You are the only
soul who does not believe it, I think."

Eb turned toward me so our faces were very close and said, "She is no
longer alive, Russell," and I reeled a little and then turned to look at the
mansions being built and the destitution all around where forests had
been cut, at the march of progress.

"She writes me," I said.

"No, Russell. She is long dead."

"No."

"You killed her yourself."

"It's quite a romp how you've rendered it," Mum says.

"Shall I read on?"

"Maybe later." She pets my hand. "I am too tired for now."

Soon the rescue mission will arrive, and I will be done with this story. I want
to leave the manuscript here for the waves to send it forth, a story no one needs
about some old dead relative of mine, myself a nobody.

1870

THE INSIDE OF CRISTIANA'S HOUSE was thick with dust. There was dry mouse turd along the floorboards and all the preserve jars were cracked and spilled. The front door was shoved in and the floor bulged with winter wet. Charles and I stood outside for a time not daring to enter the house. Eventually, I trekked down the hill to the old henhouse and pushed my way into the space. The coop was dry, the straw sweet smelling, but admixed with the sour dust of chicken shit. My entry plumed up stray feathers. I could see precisely where I'd once slept and recalled the warm places of Cristiana's body comforting me. I breathed in deep but there was no lingering perfume of her. Charles was behind me. I felt the boy's hand on my arm and looked down, following his gaze. There, shy and stuttering, was one old bedraggled hen and next to her, brashly crowing, was a rooster. Under her were some eggs.

"Well," I said. "Well, well." I looked through a cut-out in the coop barnboard and spied at the edge of the bush more feral chickens dancing in and out of the dark. They had been breeding wildly all this time.

Charles petted the broody hen. She stayed so still it was as if she was dead, but I could see that it was fear. I slid a hand under her and stole three eggs, but when we broke them for lunch, we found a bony embryo curled into each one.

"We will have to steal them quicker," I said.

Cristiana's house was in order after a day or so. In a bad and makeshift way, I repaired the fence around the henhouse, and when it was secure, I used fir branches to herd the bewildered chickens toward the enclosure. The whole enterprise made me skittish, but when we had some twenty fowl in order, we clasped the gate and pinned it down so that the birds could not escape.

I was not a good pioneer. Over the next few weeks, Charles heard me rage at the bread that would not rise, but he stayed clear and was ready to applaud when things did work. One bad night I could not sleep, and at dawn I left the house and discovered that the apple tree was blooming such that it looked like a pinky white cloud. I climbed into it and stayed there until I saw Charles at the doorway to the house.

"I'm here," I called. He laughed, and I felt better than I had felt in a long time.

Charles ran to where I was. I reached down and helped him up into the tree. "It's nice," Charles said, then we climbed higher to get the best view. We could see the village three miles off or so in one direction and, in the other, the house.

"What else can you see?" I asked Charles, he being a little higher up than me. Charles squinted. "Someone is coming."

I pulled myself into the first fork of the tree and looked to where Charles was staring. A nebula of dust roiled up from the wheels of a brougham. I saw a top hat and a second person inside the vehicle. I could not tell who it was, could not even see if it was a woman or a man. "It is perhaps Eb Wilkes."

"In a lavender gown?" said Charles.

"Then someone must have perished."

I will tell it how I imagine it must have been. I will tell it as if I know more than I do. I knew nothing then as I watched it. I only knew as the buggy approached that she looked familiar. I only knew that my heart juddered in recognition and, more so, in love.

It was like a dream.

We watched, entranced, as she arrived at the hill approaching Cristiana's house early in the morning, dawn-pink glorifying the horizon. She took in the henhouse, the solemn gloom and the shack Cristiana had called home even before she noticed us watching her from the upper boughs of the tree. She pretended not to have seen us and asked the driver to wait, then scrutinized the house and peered into the windows. I watched her through all this. I watched the driver dismount and stretch his legs. He was doing something with his horse, and she could hear him muttering, the harness jingling behind her. She watched the tree now and again, wondering whether the people in it would dare to come down. The wind brought their voices up to Charles and me.

The driver muttered that "time is money." She ignored him. She did not much care about his time nor her money. She seemed to be the sort of person who would settle when she was ready to do so.

Her gown was full lavender – for she had revised her attire for mourning once she learned from Mrs. Blakey of Cristiana's death – and she smelled delightful against the odour of farmyard. She knew the driver was dismayed to be accompanying her, that he hated her with a certain kind of blind hatred with which she was familiar for he was white and she was not.

"This is my dead sister's abode," she asserted, but he did not really care. She walked along the rough porch and tried the door, which soughed open at her touch; it had been left unlatched, and she entered just far enough to look around. The house was tidy and clean, which was something.

"I have heard it is haunted," said the driver just before he left her.

And then he was gone and it was only us watching her. I thought she was Cristiana. I swear to God I thought this and a longing set in on me.

She stood there overlong in the threshold to the house peering in. I know now that there had been little pleasant to recall except that there was a smell to this memory – of hay, of sleep and of a sister's love. Her name, I discovered, was Eliza.

Prty of Eliza Goss – yes, that Eliza. The one whose name was pinned to the porcelain doll.

DAY FORTY

WHEN MUM WAKES UP, SHE comes into my room. I look up, still jangled from being so deep in the writing.

"Is it okay?" she says. "Can I come in? You can read to me more."

"Of course," I say. And I catch her up on the plot as I settle her into a comfy chair and then begin to read:

> *"Oh God," a voice behind Eliza said. When she turned, there was me, a scruffy-looking derelict.*

"That is Boyt," I remind Mum.

"Yes," Mum says. "I'm following."

> *Eliza saw my limp and felt a twinge of pity for me. I was pasty and bearded in the most unkempt way. She might have been afraid except that I looked as if I might begin to cry.*
> *"Cristiana," I said.*
> *"No. I am not Cristiana. I'm Eliza Goss."*
> *"Cristiana," I repeated. They were just the same.*
> *"Twins," Eliza said. "My dead sister and I."*

Mum gasps here. I have her riveted. I am twisting all the histories into one. Does she feel this? I look over to see if I have hurt her, if I have managed to scratch some small crazing in the glaze of her guarded self. But she gathers herself enough and nods for me to go on. And so, I do.

Eliza had arrived at the home of Moser Blakey days before, like a whirlwind, her half mourning costume looking festive in the early morning sun. She was more tightly wound than her sister ever was, and she was not above much – there were hardened men who hid if they saw her first.

She disclosed, with a certain pique, that it had taken her years of intermittent research to locate me.

And now here I was, thousands of miles later. She didn't dare breathe. "I hear that you killed her," she whispered at the floor. She told me that she should have been frightened of me but that not much did frighten her. She told me that she had a pistol and knew how to use it. Also, she could see that I could not run, now could I?

When I didn't answer, didn't budge from where I stood, she looked over at me and saw Charles grown tall, peeping out from behind me. She gasped and I turned.

He was the most beautiful boy she had ever seen, she said, and yes, she recalled that impossible halo of golden hair, his eyes so expressive. She said that she saw everyone she had ever loved in him – her brother-in-law Henry, her sister Cristiana, herself, her folks, her grandfolks, all those relations she had known. She saw all the aunties and uncles, the whole of history in his eyes.

"I've kept him safe as I could," I said, biting my inside cheek. I half turned to Charles, brow furrowed, and said, "It's your mother."

"Aunt," she corrected.

My skin rose up in goosebumps, a ghost settled along my body. She squinted at me. She must have been wondering if I was indeed fully mad and dangerous or merely so sad there was not much to me.

"Cristiana never did mention a sister." I had never asked Cristiana a single question; did not know her, had failed in that regard. "You are a ghost, then," I said. I wanted so badly to believe she was still alive. But a twin is not ever entirely identical. Think how different Eb and me were, how antithetical were Henry and Moser. Things swirled oddly in my mind. I heard my own voice falter. I did not like this twist. I wanted what I wanted. "I have been declared fit." My voice was shaky and I was

staring at my fingers where they were placed on my lap. They were filthy, my nails torn. I kept opening and closing my jaw like a horse gnawing at the bit. I was not well.

"Charlie," she finally said, and smiled at him.

His eyes opened a bit wider that she knew his name.

"I knew you as a baby when finally your mama was freed by her odious master. Your daddy was my brother by marriage."

She produced a daguerreotype of Cristiana from the year she married Muldon. "I bought her that wedding outfit," she said.

The boy moved not a hair's breadth but stared into the image as if at a memory. Charles looked back and forth between her and the image.

"You're my mother," he said.

"We are exact in every way except in temperament," Eliza said. She fussed with her gown. "Cristiana was an angry woman. I knew that first-hand. But our mother used to say that where Cristiana came out angry, I came out frothy."

I reached over and took the picture, peered into it like a vanity mirror, muttering under my breath Cristiana's name over and over. When I handed it back to Eliza, she gave it to Charles and said he might keep it and sent him out of the house and away to play.

She checked the window to see that he was out of hearing. And then she swallowed and said, "That trail of paper says you strangled her with your bare hands."

"I must have been in the throes of what some call Soldier's Heart."

"The war has traumatized so many." Eliza's mouth was twitching with resentment and she did not try to stop it.

"They say so."

I slid to the edge of my seat, grabbed the table and got myself upright. Holding the table edge, I hopped toward the grain cupboard and, gripping the counter for stability, fished into the grain, which I could see was mealy and full of moth spawn. I pulled the doll out from the grain by its leg. Eliza let out a pained yelp. She took the doll and cradled it like it was a baby. I could see it was her turn to cry. She was the opposite of circumspect, keening over this doll, sobbing her heart out it seemed to me at the time. I touched her shoulder and she shuddered and shook me away. She did not want my consolation.

She clawed at the doll's back and pulled out the wad of money tucked there in its spine. She let it cascade over the table. "Ten," she said. "A genocide," and I was the culprit. She began to recite a litany of names. Each one brought forth some awful agony from her, and in the end, though they signified less than nothing to me at the time, the names acted as a sort of wordy vessel, knitted together toward some unfathomable grief for which the name Henry Muldon seemed a sort of exclamatory utterance, such as Halleluiah or Amen.

It was a prayer.

A prayer of names accumulating some hieroglyphic meaning I could not decipher. I watched and listened in awe. Charles was peering in through the window now. He kept looking up balefully at me, some horrified accusation crossing his face.

My mum wakes from a feverish reverie and says, "How did you know?"

"Know what?" She looks so bewildered.

"The thing about twins," she says, and I tell her to hush up and let me finish.

I then looked and looked at Eliza while she ululated into her open palms. She repeated this list like a rosary decade. I seemed to slip out of my very personhood and float – it was that incantatory. While she chanted, I vowed that in the morning I would take the boy and go north. My inertia was helping no one, and at least when I moved, I felt halfway sane.

Eliza's words glided out of her like unholy poetics. They flowed over and around me if I sat still, and I was frightened of her. When she ceased keening, she spat, "That was ten souls wrapped up in that stolen money." She turned toward Charles, who had sidled back into the house. "Never did the Lord give and take. He just only takes and takes and takes."

Charles hissed, "Aunt Eliza, please don't use the Lord's name in vain." He did not condone swearing, a thing that lingered from Moser Blakey's brimstone years.

"Well, let me burn," she retorted, her eyes so wide Charles fell into them. "I will sooner burn, and you should know your own story." She spoke with a special fury she seemed to have been saving up her whole life. "This man," she said, gesturing at me. "This man here thieved and squandered ten good souls."

"*I found that money.*" *I protested that I had dug it out of the earth.* "*You can have it all,*" *I said to Eliza now.* "*And so you know, I never spent one dime of it.*"

"*It's too late,*" *she said.*

"*I don't want it, anyway,*" *I said.*

"*That money was supposed to get south to free them, do you understand? And you kept it.*"

This made no sense. "*Then why did he bury it?*"

"*I buried it. Henry Muldon was to bring it farther south. Cristiana was protected from this knowledge, unless something should happen to Henry. Do you see?*"

I was beginning to see that I was trapped in a puzzle.

She named them off again but now with her fingers: "*Matthew Goodly, Ira Goodly, Aaron Peirce, George Porter, Carolina Gospeak, Gloria Mann, Sybilline Grady, Martinus Fitzgerald, Maura Fitzgerald and little Ira Fitzgerald. Between them were generations of stories, a family tree and all of them gone.*"

Charles said, "*What's a family tree?*"

"*That is a lineage of one's family, one's forebears.*" *I patted his shoulder and grinned sadly at him.*

"*Incorrect,*" *said Eliza.* "*I will tell you, Charles. It is what you will never have. Every branch cut off like that,*" *and she gestured lopping off this and that limb with her hand.* "*These few I named were not special. They wanted freedom. They received something else. The first was flayed. The second and sixth throttled. Two of them were made servants and all the rest were lynch-hanged.*" *She turned to look directly at Charles.*

"*All these folks,*" *she said, and listed them again. She was shrill up to the sky.* "*All these folks were your kin, Charlie. And when this dust here settles, I will take you south, to whatever family there might be left.*"

"*Hush,*" *I said.*

"*Ten dead Muldon kin,*" *she seethed at me.* "*Their blood is on your soul.*"

"This is conjecture," my mum says.

"It's fiction based on research," I say.

"What really happened lies buried."

I look at her and wonder what she means. "Mum, let me finish."

She looks so strange nestled on the chair beside me. Like a child herself, lost and confused. I hope the rescue team arrives soon. I really think she needs a doctor.

I say, "Russell Boyt was in the throes of madness. He would not see reason. He thought that he and all men were a kind of vast unstoppable machine – the soldiers, the industrialists, the sutlers, all of them. And now his body had become more and more articulated and mechanical. Was that his doing?"

"I remember now," Mum yelps suddenly.

"Shush," I say, and I read how Boyt set out to prove that Cristiana was not dead and buried there:

> *"You are not real," I said to Eliza. Heading out toward the henhouse, I grabbed a shovel and kept walking. I could see they'd put up a stone cross there for her but I still didn't believe any of it. When I got to the tree, I prayed to God and to the Devil, and to anyone in between them – archangels, priests, the constabulary – and I began to dig. I heard her phantom calling and heard Charles yelling, but I would not look up. I dug with utmost fury, dug and dug. I would prove that she was not here.*

Mum says, "*I* dug and dug."

"No. Are you okay? It's Boyt who dug and dug. He would prove this one thing – and it behooved him to prove it to himself. They were calling him – Eliza and Charles – but it sounded so far-off he ignored it, told himself it was a bad dream anyway, and he would prove it by digging."

"I'm fine," she says, "but it is such a sad story."

And stupidly, I keep reading:

> *When I reached Cristiana's skeleton, I was exhausted. What I expected would feel glorious was instead perplexing. It was true what everyone said. It had been no dream at all. I had killed her. I had done that. Her bones clattered. I screamed up to God and the Heavens but there was no one there. The world was truly disenchanted. Cristiana's body was fully decayed. Still, what my brain said, even as I had begun to fully know the truth, was, "Who left this thing in here?"*
>
> *I turned around at half speed and believed I saw Cristiana standing on the front stoop watching me, lilac-clad like a plumaged parrot-bird,*

and Charles awkward and face-creased next to her. It was Eliza, of course. And I had no idea what to do.

I walked back up the hill toward the stoop and stopped short. "Go away," I yelled to this spectre. "Git." But she did not flee, and Charles just looked at me, sad and fearful, clutching or being clutched by Eliza's hand. I would lose him, too.

Eliza called out to me, "It'll be okay, Mr. Boyt. It will all sort out." Because she was clearly now beginning to fully understand the extent of my instability. I wanted to die. I would enact this ending. The one I deserved. She tried. I will give her that credit. She tried even as she began to see that the puzzle was so warped and convoluted, there was no possible way out of it. She was surprised at her pity for me, I think. She gestured at me with her chin and asked Charles if I had ever been like this before.

Charles nodded. "He'll rattle out soon enough."

"Is there a stratagem?"

"Keep out of the way."

"Then that is what we will do."

They turned together as if they had choreographed this and re-entered the house.

Outside, the day had become overcast. There was no motion in the thickening air. My whole body was corroding, the apparatus, the workings. I longed to go back to Washington, to the room I had at the asylum and the freedom that privacy unleashed to me there. I was filthy with digging. The rain had begun. I should go. But at the same time, I could barely move, the dirt at my feet holding me as if steel roots. Her jawbone, nestled in the dirt, seemed to yammer at me. Could this really be Cristiana? It must be. I lay down with her and waited and waited, and nothing happened. The world kept turning faster and faster, it seemed, and the moon and the sun came and went. It was some perspective if you thought about it, but I did not stop to think about it, and after a time I did not think at all.

"No no no," Mum is muttering. "It didn't happen like that."

"It's not as if you were there."

"Of course I was there, honey. I recall it so vividly. Wulf was such a sweet child. A halo of curly hair, indeed."

233

I turn to look at her. This has become very strange.

"This is what happened," Mum mutters. "Wulf lived for two years, ten and a half months."

"What?"

"He was never even sickly. He thrived. He was a little athlete and such a charmer."

"What are you saying?"

"He went in the foundation hole. Your twin. He waddled to the edge while no one saw him. Or that is what we think may have happened. He was never found. We thought it best to keep it quiet."

I blink and blink to keep my tears back. I am the twin bundle in that photograph. I show it to Mum. "That's me?" I say. "My twin?" How you could not know a thing that you always knew.

And she nods. "Yes."

"He drowned?" My heart is cracking open.

"Or swam away." She pulls in her lips and bites them. She is precisely like a small child when she says this. "You were both in the water. You flailed and swam to shore when we called. But he did not. You were both too young to be swimming. But your hands –"

"– were webbed," I finish.

"He was the smaller twin. His hands and feet were also webbed, but he went under. Dad jumped in. I remember your father turning and turning, diving over and over. He was frantic. His only son."

"He lived a while," I say, recalling that Dad said this. I turn to her. "I had a right to know."

"You were so sensitive. So needy. We didn't dare. We buried him and the story. And then your sisters were born. Things got better."

But did they? And I begin to see the way in which I am not whole. I begin to see all the ways a person like me might find to fit herself in. I begin to understand why I do not feel comfortable in my skin.

"He was a selkie," I say.

Mum looks baleful. I can see she doesn't want me to follow this line of thought.

"Where is it? Where is that skin? I need it."

"It's just folklore," she says. "It's me who bought that skin. A stupid compensation that I forgot about until you found it."

"If enough people believe a story, is it not true?" I say. "Where is it?"

She won't tell me. She doesn't want to lose me or doesn't want to revisit the whole of this secret. "Go back to your children, for the love of Pete."

"I used to see him."

"All in your fantasy."

But it wasn't just whimsy and childhood fantasy. What can't be real is real. There is no such thing as fiction. No category as such. The world seems to glow suddenly. I will myself to see him in the back forest. He is shimmering far off in that golden glow of light that must be imaginary, or that only happens when the sun glances off the cedars at sunrise, floating on an island of deadfall and greenery. There he is – tousle-haired, straw curls and curious eyes, worry-strained. My happiness at seeing him again is both irrational and excessive. To see my twin is something of a magical feat, I can tell you. If I have to choose between what is real and what brings joy, I choose joy.

"Tell me everything," I say.

"There's a box somewhere," she says, "with photographs, medical records and jottings about him. It's not much."

And suddenly, Dad is there at the doorway. "I hear them coming," he says. "The rescue team."

It is all chaos then – dressing Mum, grabbing the suitcase and lugging the typewriter and the porcelain doll down the stairs and through the foot of water now there. Just before the rescue team comes, I say to Dad that Mum told me about Wulf.

He looks worried but then smiles a sad smile. "It wasn't out of malice," he says.

"I know. But she says there's a box. Where is it?"

"I don't know," he says. "It could be anywhere."

And then the boat is idling at the side door and we are being pulled into it. The boatman is Gerry Kopechnic, the ancient farmer from down the concession. "Oh, hi," I say. I have known him all my life. He used to swing me from his huge clasped hands.

"Long time no see," he says.

"How long do you think?" A shiver goes all through me because I suddenly recall him there, at the water's edge. "You were there, weren't you?"

"That terrible day." He nods.

"I was three."

"He was just like you."

"Do you recall him?"

"I see him in you – lively and happy. You must have a good life." He has laugh lines all over his face.

And it's trite, I think, but it pleases me to imagine Wulf is here in the water, all around us. Dad helps Mum into the boat and tells us to wait a second. He is gone for a while, long enough for us all to begin to get a bit concerned. But when he returns, he is smiling. He tosses a green hardcase box into the boat.

"For you," he says to me. "The archive."

My mother blinks and blinks.

It's the Remington typewriter's original zippered case, the logo emblazoned on the top and, over it, their motto in gold leaf: *To save time is to lengthen life.*

ACKNOWLEDGEMENTS

THIS BOOK TOOK MANY PATHS before it felt like it had become itself, much like me in the writing of it. I am grateful first and foremost to my mother and father for agreeing to talk to me about my brother and for graciously allowing me to use several family photographs, and to Michael Cooper for being my proxy brother, always. Thank you to my sisters, Lorraine, Susan and Clare, for allowing me to use old photographs in which they are featured. Thanks to the Library of Congress Prints and Photographs Division, the New York Public Library Digital Collections and the National Archives in Washington for granting permissions for several archival images. Howard White and Harbour Publishing graciously allowed me to use the beautiful and arresting poem "The Dead Poet" by Al Purdy both as an epigraph and as the source for my title, Wait Softly Brother. I feel very lucky to be able to feature this poem in my work, which is set close to where Purdy lived. I am grateful to my dear friend and writing buddy Sarah Henstra the Great for bearing with me over almost ten years of revision and for her hawk-eyed proofreading. Thank you to Jay and Hazel at Book*hug for publishing a small extract of this book as a chapbook through HIJ (and for the delicious butterscotch pie, too), to Chrissy and Kyle at Spark Box Studio in Prince Edward County for bringing me there to read early stages of this, to the Corporation of Yaddo for giving me much-needed time and space to write a first draft of Wait Softly Brother, and to the Virginia Center for the Creative Arts (VCCA) for the perfect welcoming weeks I spent there researching and honing early chapters. I am also eternally grateful to Stephen O'Connor, Shani Mootoo, Brian Panhuyzen and Heather Birrell for reading the manuscript in various stages of formation and for being kind no matter what. Adam Sol gave me courage in our conversations about the American Civil War era. The dazzling Christy Ann Conlin connected me to her brilliant historian brother, Dan Conlin, who set me straight on all things train related in the late 1800s. Ken Woroner walked me through camera jargon and logic. I am over the moon in love with the fetching cover that Salamander Hill conjured for us. The library at the University of Toronto provided me with a massive Civil War archive, and I lingered there for many weeks. Thank you to the team at Wolsak & Wynn and Buckrider Books: Noelle Allen, Paul Vermeersch, Ashley Hisson, Tania Blokhuis, Jennifer Rawlinson and to my fine editor, Aeman Ansari, who helped me tame this wild thing a little. Thanks also to Andrew Wilmot who knows about commas and quite truly saved me from myself. Huge gratitude to Sue Domshy for my studio, for help with proofreading and just because. Finally, thank you to the Canada Council for the Arts for supporting this project under their Explore and Create Program.

IMAGE CREDITS

Image 1, page 10: The author's mother. Courtesy of Walsh family.

Image 2, page 20: Unidentified soldier in Confederate uniform with shotgun sitting next to dog, c. 1861–65, Ambrotype/Tintype filing series, Liljenquist Family collection, Library of Congress Prints and Photographs Division.

Image 3, page 26: Civil War–era stamp.

Image 4, page 44: Three children in front of backhoe. Courtesy of Walsh family.

Image 5, page 75: Child in water. Courtesy of Walsh family.

Image 6, page 110: The author's grandfather and great-grandparents. Courtesy of Walsh family.

Image 7, page 115: "Dubois D. Parmelee Artificial Leg," US patent 37637, February 10, 1863.

Image 8, page 127: "Hospital, Washington," c. 1861–71, New York Public Library Digital Collections, Manuscripts and Archives Division, New York Public Library.

Image 9, page 198: "Preserve Room, 1895," Records of St. Elizabeths Hospital, National Archives photo no. 418-G-252.

Image 10, page 199: The linen sorting room circa 1897, Records of St. Elizabeths Hospital, National Archives photo no. 418-P-562.

Image 11, page 200: Ruins. Courtesy of author.

Image 12, page 229: Unidentified African American woman, c. 1860–70, Ambrotype/Tintype filing series, Liljenquist Family collection, Library of Congress Prints and Photographs Division.

Kathryn Kuitenbrouwer is the bestselling author of the novels *All the Broken Things*, *Perfecting* and *The Nettle Spinner*. She is also the author of the story collection *Way Up*. Her work has appeared in *Granta*, *The Walrus*, *Maclean's*, *The Lifted Brow*, Significant Objects, *Storyville* and others. Kathryn teaches literature and creative writing at the University of Toronto.